TAINTED LEGACY

GHOST SHOP PARANORMAL MYSTERY/SUSPENSE SERIES

BOOK 3

HEATHER AMES

Well of Ideas Press

Tainted Legacy. Copyright 2023 by Heather Ames
All rights reserved.

This book or any portion thereof may not be reproduced or used in any manner whatsoever without the express written consent of the author except for use of brief quotations in a book review.

Published in the United States of America.

This book is a work of fiction. Names, characters, places and incidents are either productions of the author's imagination or are used fictitiously. Any resemblance to actual events, locales or persons, living or dead, is purely coincidental.

ISBN (paperback) 979-8-9888834-0-1
ISBN (e-book) 979-8-9888834-1-8

CHAPTER ONE

Sunny Weston's feet sank into a patch of mud as she and Ash Haines followed Vincente Valderos's long, lean, and black-clothed figure across the base of a steep slope filled with wildly overgrown grapevines no longer secured to their trellises. Three weeks before Halloween, the Taricani Family Vineyard in Dallas, Oregon looked forlorn and abandoned.

The rainy season had started, bringing with it a cold wind that circled around the lifeless vines, rattling dead leaves still clinging to unpruned canes. The dreary landscape felt otherworldly. Brown; neglected...lifeless.

Sunny glanced over at Ash, eyes downcast and muttering to himself as he sloshed through a large puddle. He was probably swearing under his breath and making Valderos the target of his vitriol. She'd like to call Valderos a few names, too. More than a few. But she and Ash had no choice but to follow their self-proclaimed leader if they wanted to avoid taking a step down toward The Toasty Zone, as Ash called it.

Sunny blamed herself not only for signing the contract that had tied her fate to the whims of Valderos, but for convincing Ash to sign, too. Their souls remained in jeopardy until they had solved a total of five cold case crimes in the Willamette Valley. Currently, this was the third, unless Valderos changed more of the contract's wording, which had become fluid during their last investigation. She wondered whether he would make them solve this new case in an even shorter period than the two weeks he had given them last time. They'd barely managed to meet that deadline.

Valderos, striding along as though he was on dry ground, paused to look back. "Faster," he urged. "We only have a limited time before dusk. If you think it is difficult to walk on this wet ground now, wait until you cannot see where you are putting your feet."

"Vinnie, if you'd told us where we were going, I'd have worn waders," Ash protested. "This ground's like a sponge. All the water drained down the hill. Why couldn't we have walked up top?"

"Patience, Mr. Haines, and do keep up." Valderos picked up his pace, lengthening the distance between himself and his two companions. A mist drifted in, blanketing everything. The vineyard disappeared into swirling whiteness.

Sunny concentrated on keeping both men in view. Pulling her feet out of the mud became harder with every step. She was dropping farther and farther behind, but didn't have the strength to catch up. She struggled forward, taking small comfort that Ash was slowing down, too, while Valderos sailed along as though his feet weren't even touching the ground.

Perhaps they weren't, she thought, stopping to catch her breath. She sucked in frigid, heavy air while she attempted to see Valderos's shoes below his long, woolen coat. A pungent smell of mothballs drifted back, wafting up her nose. Stifling a sneeze, she wished she hadn't been so eager to take those deep breaths. Telling herself the sooner they got to their destination, the sooner they could leave the vineyard, was becoming less and less a motivating factor. They'd still have to repeat the trek back to Ash's SUV, that time uphill, and on tired legs.

Raindrops spattered puddles. Their miserable hike had lasted far too long. Sunny agreed with Ash…they could have made faster progress at the top of the hill. Raindrops enlarged and fell at a rapid rate, beating back the fog. A line of bare-branched trees and straggly bushes came into view. She heard the sound of rushing water.

"Our destination is ahead," Valderos called over his shoulder.

"Thank goodness for small mercies," Ash told Sunny.

He'd stopped so she could catch up with him. When she did, he took her arm. They made faster progress, although she almost lost a boot to one particularly gummy area. After Ash hauled her out, he kept his arm around her waist. They plodded over to where Valderos stood, one foot tapping the ground without sinking into it. He looked like he'd taken a leisurely stroll over a well-manicured golf course. His putty-colored eyes with their slitted pupils surveyed his companions from beneath the brim of a black fedora. His malodorous wool coat didn't even appear damp, and the black dress shoe on that tapping foot had been buffed to a high shine, no doubt by Serrano, his long-suffering man-servant, butler, and chauffeur.

"About time," Valderos's narrowed gaze penetrated the gloom as though lit by an inner glow.

Sunny averted her eyes to watch a fast-moving creek bounce over rocks and gurgle around a small pool before heading off at a slower pace as it widened. It branched into two tributaries a few yards away, one blocked off by a makeshift dam of burlap bags, stuffed full and piled several feet high.

The dry tributary ducked beneath a barbed wire fence. On the other side, regimental lines of trees formed an extensive orchard. The Willamette Valley was also home to a burgeoning cider industry. Sunny wondered whether the orchard supported a cidery. Perhaps even a cider house. If so, that would have meant competition for the weekend wine tasters.

"Okay." Ash moved away to take a wide, sweeping view of their surroundings. "So, what are we doing here?"

"This is the precise spot where Giuseppe, patriarch of the Taricani family, was found dead two years ago." Valderos pointed a long, bony finger toward a boulder hanging over the gurgling pool. "According to reports, his head struck that rock, and he was discovered face-down in the water. He was deemed to fallen, hit his head, and drowned."

Valderos gestured toward the top of the hill. "A year later his son, Lorenzo, was crushed when a tree fell on him while he was relaxing outside the tasting room. I wish to know whether both those deaths were indeed accidental. I am planning to purchase this vineyard, but not if there was murder on the property. The vines produced tainted wine after Giuseppe's death. After Lorenzo died, they failed to produce at all." His uncomfortably mesmerizing gaze fixed on Sunny. "First impressions, Ms. Kingston?"

"You're up," Ash whispered. He gave Sunny a little push.

She didn't appreciate being put on the spot. "My powers aren't turned on and off by an internal switch," she said, making sure she didn't quite make eye contact with Valderos. She gave Ash her best reproving glare.

However, since she wanted to escape Valderos and the abandoned vineyard as fast as possible, she curbed her indignation and stalked across river rock to the boulder Valderos had indicated. It was flat, gray, unblemished, and completely smooth. "When exactly did the death happen?" she asked.

"I already told you…two years ago. Were you not listening?" Valderos tapped his foot again. His aura pulsed a deep orange. Never a good sign.

"I meant time of year," she hastened to clarify. "Spring, summer? Do you have the precise date?"

"That is of no consequence." Valderos made a sound somewhere between a snort and a snarl. But his aura stopped pulsing and lightened to a tone somewhere between peach and salmon. "Spirits linger when there is unrest. You know this, already."

Sunny breathed a sigh of relief. Angering Valderos frequently meant Ash suffered the consequences when he stepped up to shield her. She felt him moving behind her. "My powers aren't always reliable," she quickly reminded their leader. "Especially when I'm trying to control them. They like spontaneity."

"Spontaneity isn't useful in this situation," Valderos sneered, the unparalyzed side of his mouth curving upward to expose jagged teeth.

Sunny almost recoiled, then reminded herself Valderos needed her intact, which she wouldn't be if he took a bite out of her. She crouched down, placed her right hand on the rock and closed her eyes. Something cold touched her cheek. It felt like a frozen hand. Completely unnerved, she jumped up. "Don't do that," she told Valderos. "You're completely despicable."

His black eyebrows rose. His pupils had become mere pinpricks in the waning light. "Do what?" he asked in the velvety tone he used when he turned into his version of a snake-charmer.

Sunny had already steeled herself to ignore the silky threads that wafted over her first, then through her if she didn't resist. "You know very well, what," she countered. "You touched me. That's against the rules you agreed to."

Ash stepped in front of her, providing a shield against Valderos's magnetism.

"I did nothing of the sort." Valderos's torso lengthened until he was towering over Ash. He leaned forward. His narrowed gaze slithered past Ash's head. The putty-colored eyes fastened on Sunny.

She raised the protective shield she'd learned to erect against forces other than Valderos. Even if it was ineffective against him, she refused to cower before the demon. "Well, someone did," she said.

Even though she wasn't sure whether she believed Valderos's denial, she looked around. No mists swirled. No moving shadows lurked. The rain continued to fall. Although she didn't want a repeat contact with the invisible hand, she squatted down again, placed her own hand on the rock and lowered her head. Rainwater streamed from the hood of her raincoat to join the flow bounding into an enlarging whirlpool.

Strangely, the rock felt dry and slightly warm. Sunny closed her eyes and tried to clear her mind, but icy water cascading over her fingers proved too big a distraction for achieving contact with a spirit. She got back to her feet. The creek had widened. It partially covered the boulder.

Rain turned to hail. Icy pellets from loaded clouds passed rapidly across the darkening sky. A strong odor of loam pervaded the area. Probably the result of decomposing plant materials, Sunny thought.

"We should go." Ash's arm encircled her shoulders, and he gently moved her away from the creek.

Suddenly, she spotted movement on the other side of the water, behind a veil of ice pellets. "I need a moment," she told the men. When they didn't move, she added, "Alone."

"Very well." Valderos beckoned to Ash. "We will give Ms. Kingston the space she needs. I will show you the grapevines, Mr. Haines." He moved away, the hem of his coat undulating in rhythmical waves.

"I'm not leaving Sunny alone to go look at dead vegetation with you, Vinnie," Ash protested.

"The vines are dormant, Mr. Haines, not dead." Valderos stood waiting, arms folded.

"I'll be fine," Sunny assured Ash. "If I'm not, you'll hear me screaming."

"That's not very reassuring," he said, but he trudged away to join Valderos. Side by side, they tramped toward the trellises.

"You can come out, now." Sunny kept her voice only slightly above a whisper.

The shadow reappeared. Shifted around in an agitated fashion until it hovered opposite her, on the other side of the creek.

"I want to help you," Sunny said. "I can't do that until you communicate with me. Was that you touching me?"

The shadow bounced around, even more agitated. Sunny waited. Without the trances she was conditioned to expect, she wasn't at all sure whether she should try to approach the shadow, which would mean fording the swiftly-flowing creek, or wait. She kept her eyes open. She needed to know what she might be dealing with. The shadow wasn't anything she'd encountered before. Sliding her right hand into her pocket, she fingered a little pouch Armenta had given her. Her assistant, the seer. Sunny silently thanked her stars for Armenta's wise counsel, and wondered what herbal concoction the pouch held.

"Ms. Kingston!"

Valderos's sharp voice snapped her back to reality. The shadow vanished behind sheets of rain.

"What?" Completely annoyed, Sunny pivoted to face him, but it had become difficult to see anything, even his imposing black-clad figure. The day had darkened considerably. Squinting, she made out two dim outlines not far away.

"Well?" Valderos asked, sounding even more impatient than before.

"Well, nothing, because you broke my concentration." She shoved both hands into her pockets and walked over to the two men. "I saw a shadow, but when you interrupted me, it vanished."

Valderos took out his pocket watch and peered at it. "Which is what *I* have to do." He dropped the watch back under his coat. "I will expect a progress report tomorrow afternoon. I will come to the shop as soon as it closes."

He disappeared, as though he'd been a mirage.

CHAPTER TWO

"Damn." Ash did a 360-degree turn, as though he couldn't believe what he'd just witnessed. "Vinnie really *did* disappear, didn't he?"

"Unless he used a sleight of hand that has him hiding in the bushes across the creek, then yes, he did." Sunny hunkered down inside her coat. "I wish he could have teleported us out of here before he left."

"I agree, even though being teleported was unnerving. You wouldn't know about that, since you've never had the experience." Ash crooked one elbow and offered Sunny his arm. "Want to lean on me? Walking uphill will be tough, but it's gotta be better than slogging back through this mud." He lifted one foot. The earth made a sucking sound.

"Worth a try." She hoped she sounded more enthusiastic than she felt.

They linked arms and began the climb. Ash pulled a penlight out of a pocket in his raincoat and snapped it on. Its beam illuminated severely overgrown vines flanking a ribbon of grass. Long, tangled canes twisted around each other as well as climbing trellises that stretched up the hillside into semi-darkness.

"I hate Valderos," Sunny said. "He probably checked the weather forecast to make sure we'd get caught in a downpour."

"He probably arranged the downpour." Ash sounded resigned. "Remember how the weather changed the first time we visited his vineyard for that wine tasting?"

"His awful Pinot Noir? How could I forget?" Her foot sank into the mud. Ash dragged her out and moved his arm to her waist again.

They continued on in silence. Sunny eventually heard Ash's rasped panting over her own. "Let's take a short break," she suggested. "I need to catch my breath. This vineyard goes on forever."

"It does." Ash drew in deep breaths. "We have to be getting close to the top by now." He shone the beam around, but all it illuminated was seemingly endless trellises.

Hands on hips, Sunny drew in damp air laced with a heavy aroma of wet leaves and soggy soil. It made her long for the scents of sandalwood, lavender and sage that permeated her metaphysical shop.

"Come on, Sunny, let's get this over with," Ash encouraged. "It can't be much farther now."

The rain fell in a relentless torrent. The incline steepened. Sunny's legs went from complaining to outright cramping. She leaned more and more against Ash, grateful for his support.

Her throat burned. She suspected witchcraft was afoot, stretching the vineyard into infinity. Infinity with an ever-steeper and muddier footing. Her tired feet dragged, and she stumbled. Ash's grip tightened. "Gotta stop, again," she panted.

"Okay, but only for a moment. This vineyard didn't look like it belonged in the Cascades when we arrived, but sure feels like it does right now. I swear, I'm getting more of a workout than I did hiking up Mount St. Helen's." He grimaced. "Of course, that hike was several years ago, but still…"

Sunny nodded. "I agree. I think we may be experiencing an illusion. There *are* hills around Dallas, but this isn't the foothills of the Coast Range. This slope's so steep, how could it be cultivated? The equipment would roll right down into the creek."

Ash grimaced. "I wish we'd brought Armenta. She could have cast a spell against whatever Vinnie conjured up."

"I'm not so sure he's responsible." Sunny felt uneasy, like someone was watching them. "This doesn't feel like one of his tricks."

"Are you sensing something?" Ash asked in an undertone.

He was definitely becoming attuned to psychic vibes, Sunny thought. She nodded. "I'm not sure, but I think someone else is here."

"Someone or some*thing?*" Ash shone the penlight around.

Its beam caught something huge. They both jumped. Sunny clutched Ash's sleeve.

"It's okay. It's a building." He tried to laugh, but it was a shaky, uneven effort.

"Oh, thank goodness." Feeling foolish, but still experiencing an unsettling combination of goosebumps and hot flashes, Sunny joined him in nervous laughter. "That has to be the tasting room," she said. "There should be an outdoor patio, overlooking the vineyard. Maybe with chairs. I don't care if they're wet. I need to sit down for a few minutes. I'm wiped out."

"Come on then." Ash tugged her. "One more push, and we're almost out of here." That time, he took her hand and yanked her into an ungainly, stumbling jog.

By the time they reached the edge of what was indeed a large stone patio, the rain had tapered off. Behind the patio, a very large, very dark building crouched like an overgrown toad. Three sets of glass doors faced the vineyard and whatever view should have been visible on a clear day.

Sunny perched on a low retaining wall that had probably been erected to prevent patrons rolling down the steep hill after guzzling too much wine. She surveyed the empty expanse. "You'd think they could have left one grouping of chairs out here," she complained. "I thought they wanted to sell this place? Between the neglected vineyard, the mud, and this ugly building with nowhere to sit but a cold stone wall, I'm ready to tell Valderos he should cross this place off his list if he's looking to expand his wine business." She wrinkled her nose. "Why would he want to own yet another failing winery?"

Ash shrugged. "None of our business what he does with his money. He only wanted us here so you could tell him whether the deaths were accidental. Maybe he's afraid ghosts would scare his customers. Are you still getting vibes about someone else being here with us?"

"I'm not sure." She tried concentrating on the sensation of being watched, but something was off, and she couldn't focus.

She pushed herself to her feet. She shouldn't be so tired. She didn't consider herself out of shape. Something about the entire place was oppressive. Like a heavy, stifling weight hung over it. She wondered whether Ash felt it, too, but she didn't want to influence him by asking.

"Stay here," she told him. "I'm going to walk around. Touch the building. See if I get anything more than I did at the creek. I won't go far. You can sit and take a break."

Although Ash looked doubtful, he didn't say anything. He sat down heavily on top of the wall.

Sunny took her time crossing the patio. An impression came to her of random people basking in the sun on a summer day. Voices mingled. Laughter rang.

She walked up to the doors, selected the set in the center, and reached out for the discolored brass handle. Reflected light sprang from splintered sun rays as daylight receded behind the Coast Range and the rainstorm moved east. The handle developed a golden glow.

She clasped it and pulled. The door opened. Surprised, Sunny hesitated, knowing Ash would be worried if she stepped inside before he'd checked for safety. Had Valderos arrived earlier and unlocked the building? Had he forgotten to lock it back up when he left? Or was someone else inside, waiting for them. Someone, or, echoing Ash's question…some*thing?*

"Ash," she said. "Should I go in?"

"Don't." He walked rapidly across the patio to join her. "It could be a trap."

"Why would you say that?" she asked, suddenly wary. "Is there something you're not telling me?"

"Maybe vandals got in," he said. "The electricity's probably cut off. We don't know who or what may be inside, and we could get jumped." He wasn't making eye contact.

Sunny released the handle. The door whispered shut. She turned to face Ash. "I may be a reluctant psychic, but even a woman's intuition could tell you're withholding information. Come on…spill. Tell me the truth. The whole truth. I'm not going inside or leaving this property until you do."

Ash shrugged. "Fine. I don't see why I can't tell you everything now Vinnie left." He led her back to the wall. "Sit down. This'll take a minute if you don't keep interrupting, or a lot longer if you do. Remember, it's almost dark and we're going to have to walk through the building unless we can find our way around the outside."

"My lips are sealed." She made a zipping motion across her mouth with the tips of her thumb and index finger.

"I'm holding you to that." Ash ran a hand over his face. "Vinnie called just before I picked you up. There are rumors the tasting room's haunted by Lorenzo Taricani's ghost, and the vineyard by Giuseppe. After Lorenzo died, superstitious workers refused to continue tending the vineyard or keeping the building ready for visitors. Those rumors quickly circulated beyond the Taricani family and their employees. Vinnie made it sound like half the Dallas community knows about this place. The new owner doesn't want to sell cheap. Our friendly neighborhood demon doesn't want to overpay and then have another problem business on his hands."

Sunny couldn't help interrupting. "I can see why rumors would fly around…this place looks as well as feels like it could be haunted. I can also see why Valderos would be interested in driving a hard bargain."

Ash gave her a quick smile. "You're right. I would also say the atmosphere probably attracted Valderos as much as the possibility he could pay less than market price for this place." He waved the penlight around the deserted patio. Its beam bounced back from the darkened glass, startling them both.

"Don't do that." Sunny pushed down the flashlight with more force than she had intended.

"Ow, that hurt." Ash rubbed his arm.

"Sorry; I got startled." She shuddered. "I swore I saw a face inside the tasting room."

"That's all I need to hear. We're out of here." Ash pulled her to her feet and began pulling her toward the far the end of the patio.

Sunny dug in her heels. "Stop it. Now we're both acting like scared adolescents. Didn't you bring your gun?"

"Of course I did, but I'm not going to risk shooting a stupid teenager who got in through the open door, or a caretaker who came to close up after the visitors." He released her. "And if we're dealing with something supernatural, a firearm's useless. Did Armenta give you something to sprinkle on the threshold or an incantation you can recite to keep us safe?"

"She gave me a small sachet to keep in my pocket." Sunny took it out and held it up. "It's not big enough to cover the threshold."

"She gave me the same thing." Ash took out a similar small packet.

"Look, she read the cards this morning, and she told me they didn't show any major disturbances. The runes didn't, either. I did a reading, as well." She put the sachet back into her pocket.

"We're probably both letting our imaginations run overtime," Ash said. "It's a combination of the weather, the surroundings, and the backstory Vinnie gave." He jerked his head toward the vineyard and grimaced. "I'm going inside. You should wait out here. Do you want me to leave you my gun? You know how to use it."

"I may know how to use it, Ash, but do you seriously think I'd risk shooting you if I mistook you for an intruder?"

"We don't even know if there *is* an intruder. You may have had a vision."

"I suppose," she reluctantly agreed. "But I don't think so. Usually, I get some sort of warning."

"You do." He sighed. "Okay, so what do you want to do?"

"Take a moment to calm down," she said. "This isn't the first time we've had a scare. I'm sure it won't be the last."

"I'll buy that. Better than me rushing inside waving a gun while you wait out here to be attacked." He gave her what he hoped was a reassuring grin.

"Ash…" Suddenly, she saw the ridiculousness of her panic. *Their* panic, to tell the truth. She returned his smile. "I'm sorry I got flustered. Why don't you finish your story while we both take a time-out?"

"I'm cool," he said, but he didn't look it. He'd unbuttoned both his raincoat and his jacket. Sunny saw the butt of his gun sticking out of the shoulder holster

He was acting like the Portland detective he'd been for years. Sunny appreciated his readiness, although she agreed his gun would probably be ineffective against whatever she was sensing might be inside that building. But voicing her concerns would only bring more anxiety. "So…" Her voice sounded squeaky. She cleared her throat. "What else did Valderos tell you?"

Ash snapped off the penlight. "You really want to do this *now?*"

"Yes, please." She sat back on the wall and patted it. "Come on. Sit down. I'm not sensing anyone watching us right now." That wasn't entirely true, but she wasn't going to tell him.

"All right." Ash sat down a couple of feet away. He took a good look around before continuing his recounting of Valderos's story. "When the nephew, Bill Hixton inherited the winery instead of the direct heirs, he tried to sell it for event space. The only bite he got was a low-ball bid from the neighboring cidery. Evidently, there was an ongoing dispute over the property line and who owned rights to the creek. The Taricanis put up the fence, said they'd had the land surveyed, and the property line wasn't in the middle of the creek. They stopped the orchard using the water for irrigation. By then, the vines weren't producing, so having all that extra water was more of a dog in a manger situation than anything else. Vinnie wants you to determine if there really are spirits here before he starts negotiating. If you can confirm this place is haunted, he's convinced he'll get a better price. After the deal goes through, he wants us to solve any crimes and have you and Armenta appease or banish anything supernatural. Then he can actually make money on his investment."

"All that makes sense," Sunny said, "but why did he only tell *you* the full story?"

"He didn't want to taint your first impressions. I only agreed to withhold the information until we'd come for the first visit. Then you had that weird experience and Vinnie disappeared. I should have told you the entire story while we climbed up here. It might have made the trip go a little faster."

Sunny got to her feet. "I'm not happy about being kept out of the loop. That's unfair, expecting me to produce results without having vital background information. It could even be dangerous, for me *and* you. What if a crime *was* committed? Don't you think whoever did it would want to keep that secret? We're beginning to be recognized for what we do. We get requests from concerned, even distraught friends and family members who want us to consult on other cases."

Ash grimaced. "I realize that. But we're tied to Valderos until we solve two more cases. He's calling the shots."

"I'd like to shoot him," she said. "If I thought that would have any effect on him, I'd have borrowed your gun by now."

Ash gave her the disapproving look he usually reserved for his daughter, Katie on the rare occasions she misbehaved. "You're a pacifist. You wouldn't do it. But I agree it probably wouldn't have any effect on him, except he might get really angry. That wouldn't be good for either of us."

"I'm sure it wouldn't." She shuddered. "Even thinking about how he could retaliate gives me the jitters."

"Let's stop procrastinating and get this over with." Ash got up. "If there really *is* someone inside the building, and it's a spirit, you should try to communicate. If it's an intruder, I'll make sure that person's very sorry. I'm not in the mood for confrontations."

"Sounds like a plan to me." She yanked the door open. One overhead light flickered on inside the tasting room, swiftly followed by others. The entire room lit up.

"What the hell?" Ash strode across the patio to join her.

A tingle shot up Sunny's arm. She blocked the door open with her hip until Ash grasped the handle. Since he didn't comment, she thought the sensation must be reserved for her. She stepped over the threshold.

"What are you doing here?" asked a man's voice. Loud and rumbling, it echoed around the cavernous space.

Startled, Sunny jumped back, landing on Ash's feet. With an oath, he pulled her outside. The door slammed shut.

CHAPTER THREE

"What's the matter?" Ash grasped Sunny by her elbows and stared down at her shocked face "Are you hurt?"

"Not until you grabbed me." She winced.

When he released her, she rubbed her right elbow. He felt bad about hurting her, but in his book, she'd done something really stupid. "Sorry," he said, "but you should have let me go first."

"I know. I'm sorry I trod on your feet. Does that make us even?" She gave him a weak smile.

"Maybe." His toes still smarted. He returned her weak smile. "I should have bought steel-toed work boots. What happened in there?"

"Some guy called out. He asked what we're doing here."

"And that made you do an about-face? You're totally capable of confronting a spirit, but when a person asks you why you're walking into a building, you turn tail?"

"He startled me." She sounded indignant.

Ash sighed. "Sometimes, I wish I was back at the police bureau, with a male partner." He moved her aside; gently, he hoped. "Out of the way. I'm going in first."

Her eyebrows rose. "Since when did you become a chauvinist?"

"Never; I swear. Let's put a lid on this argument and get back to work." He grabbed the door handle.

"Fine. Lead the way." She stood back and lifted her chin, jerking her head toward the door.

"We'll talk more about defining our roles some other time." Ash opened the door, stepped inside. And held it open for her. Without commenting on whether she thought his chivalry was a little late, although she looked like she was probably thinking that, she blocked it with her hip and motioned him forward. Ash hoped she'd simmer down before the trip back to Salem. Three failed marriages had taught him he might be a crack negotiator in his professional life, but he sucked at interpersonal relationships. Keeping it professional with Sunny had kept theirs cordial until that moment.

Inside, a huge and very stooped old man waited at the back of what would have been a very large room if he wasn't in it.

"I asked what you're doing here." His voice boomed around the space and echoed from every corner.

"We had a meeting with Mr. Valderos, the gentleman interested in purchasing the vineyard," Ash explained as he walked slowly forward. He took a fast look at what the man held in his hands. Either a broom or a shotgun on his right side. His left hand was hidden by his rain gear.

"After dark? In a rainstorm?" The man lurched forward on legs resembling tree trunks. His feet, covered in dark brown boots, scuffed the floor.

His voice reminded Ash of the sound made by wood being planed against the grain…jarring enough to set his teeth on edge. He wondered whether Valderos had actually made any calls to set up an appointment to view the vineyard. Maybe that was the real reason they'd traipsed around in the mud, mostly out of sight at the bottom of the hill…to avoid being seen.

Their interrogator had to be either a caretaker or a security guard. Maybe both. Or a former bouncer from days of wine-tasting customers who had over-indulged. He could have tossed out any number of drunks without breaking a sweat.

Despite Ash's attempt to shield her, Sunny was peeking around his arm. Not for the first time, he thought working with civilians must be a punishment for prior wrongdoings. When he tried to discretely push her behind him, she resisted.

The giant was getting closer and enlarging every step of the way. His head missed a chandelier dangling from the vaulted ceiling by mere inches. His face wore more wrinkles than a dried grape. Ash was relieved to see he carried a broom in his right hand, instead of a shotgun, and a large flashlight in his left. His navy-blue rain gear swished with every step. Water dripped from his face as well as his clothing. His boots, despite being heavily covered with mud, unaccountably left no footprints on the highly-polished parquet floor.

"It was raining hard when we finished our visit." Ash made sure he kept his tone low and calm. "Mr. Valderos left before we did, taking the same route back to the parking lot. My partner and I thought it would be easier to climb the hill. Our mistake. It took a lot longer than we expected." He tried smiling at the guy, but all he got in return was a grunt. "The back door was unlocked," he added.

The man raised his flashlight, passing the beam across their faces. Ash quickly averted his eyes and hoped Sunny had, too. He heard the floor creak as their interrogator approached, boards protesting under the strain.

"There's a path around the side of the building," the man rasped, "but it's too overgrown for you to use."

"The rest of the property's in need of some TLC, too." Sunny stepped away from Ash. She smiled. "Are you the only one working here? If so, you have a very big job."

He watched the man's frown deepen as Sunny slowly walked toward him, and wondered if she ever really listened to his warnings. He was supposed to be her protector, but he couldn't be effective if she got within grabbing distance of the behemoth blocking the way through the building.

As though she heard his silent reproach, Sunny gave him a sideways glance that told him in no uncertain terms to back off. She'd told him before that she couldn't work if he was hovering nearby. Much as his instincts were to shield her, he bowed to her wishes. She must be getting signals that their interrogator might not be as human as he looked.

The man smelled like the vineyard they had just left: A strong odor of loam with an underlying aroma that reminded Ash of corked wine…dank, with undertones of wet cardboard or a moldy basement. Maybe even wet dog, he thought, after taking a deeper breath. Jake, his Australian Shepherd, carried a similar fragrance after romping around the back yard in the rain.

Sunny extended her right arm, her intention clearly to shake hands with Mr. Flashlight.

"I'm Sunny Kingston," she said. "This is my partner, Ash Haines."

The man ignored her gesture. He peered at them with frank suspicion. "You're realtors?" His eyes narrowed to slits reminiscent of Valderos's concentrated stare.

Sunny slowly lowered her hand. "We're not realtors. We're connected with Valderos Vineyards." When he failed to comment, she added, "In Oak Grove." She dug into a coat pocket and produced one of Valderos's cards, a wine bottle and glass clearly visible beside the embossed copperplate lettering.

The man leaned forward, which wasn't much of an effort, and peered at the card without touching it. "I heard something about selling when that impostor, Hixton was here a few days ago." The crags on his face deepened. "He cares nothing for this vineyard. He should *not* have inherited it." He shook his head so forcefully, his hood fell back, revealing a full head of long, black hair.

Suddenly, it was raining inside the tasting room. Droplets flew from the man's hair. Ash felt them pepper his face, and revulsion turned his stomach. The guy was not only wet, he was covered in clods of mud, which were taking off like projectiles. Ash ducked as several landed on top of the bar, while others splatted against the front of its wooden frame.

"Fall came early this year," the man continued, a gravel-like quality to his voice. He waved the broom toward the glass behind Sunny and Ash. "Hixton ordered the sour, moldy grapes get churned into the soil." He leaned closer to Sunny, his thick eyebrows quivering. "Sofia would have known better. *She* should be running the winery." He growled his disapproval. "Giuseppe used the old ways. He cared for the vines. Lorenzo poisoned them. Hixton's going to kill them." He upended the broom. The handle hit the floor with a resounding thud that reverberated beneath Ash's feet.

Ash steeled himself to remain calm. Sunny had been slowly backing up. She came close enough for him to grab the belt on her raincoat and steer her back to his side.

"So, who are you?" he asked the man, whose eyes were fixed on the darkness beyond the tasting room. "What's your role here?"

The dark eyes shifted, locking gazes with Ash. "I'm the caretaker."

Ash waited for a name to be added to the title. It wasn't. "We should go," he said, as his staring match with the caretaker lengthened. He broke eye contact first, switching his focus to Sunny. She looked a little uncertain, but not frightened, which was a good sign. "So, are you going to show us out?" he asked the caretaker.

"I'd rather send you back where you came from."

That sounded ominous. The caretaker was staring at Sunny, which Ash definitely didn't like. But since she still didn't appear alarmed, he felt slightly less worried about their immediate future.

"We don't like people tracking mud through the tasting room." The beam from the caretaker's flashlight swung around to spotlight Ash's muddy boots. "It shows they don't care about damaging the property."

Ash decided not to remark on all the mud still clinging to the caretaker, much less call attention to the clods that had landed on the bar. Instead, he shrugged. "It's Oregon. Rain and mud go together, like Pinot Noir and the Willamette Valley." He hoped he was using the best tone for elderly, mud-covered custodians.

The giant gave a brief nod. "That's true." He directed the flashlight's beam to an archway at the back of the tasting room. "The front door's through there." He gestured for them to walk ahead of him.

Ash refused to turn his back on the caretaker. The guy might hit either of them with his two props or his ham hock-sized fists. Trying not to appear like he was doing a crab-walk, Ash managed to keep Sunny slightly ahead of him, while his eyes remained glued to the caretaker. It wasn't easy, but they walked into what had to be the reception area. To the left, Ash saw a couch and a coffee table. To the right, a counter for visitors to check in or pick up wine orders.

Their host flipped a wall switch at that point, illuminating their surroundings. The décor was more French Provincial than Oregon Cabin. Lots of gilt accents and mirrors. A wall of glass sported a door topped by a green exit sign. Ash wondered why that hadn't been visible before. Emergency exit signs were usually on separate circuits and remained lit even when the rest of a building was in darkness.

"Keep moving," the caretaker instructed. "Straight ahead. No lights in the parking lot, but your vehicle's where you left it."

"I'll get the door, Sunny." Ash reached for the handle, but she brushed his hand aside.

"I'll get it." She gave him a quick, very direct look that said 'hands off.'

Ash waited until she was almost outside before he grasped the door. "I'm sure Mr. Valderos will be in touch," he told the caretaker.

He received another grunt in response. Or maybe a growl. He wasn't sure. But as soon as he stood outside with Sunny, he heard the door lock.

"There was a big argument in that tasting room," she said. "The archway vibrated when I touched it. So did the back and front doors."

"What about the caretaker?" Ash almost didn't want to hear what vibes she'd gotten from him.

"He had a strange aura. Mostly green, tinged with orange."

"So Vinny was right to be suspicious." Ash didn't make that a question. "You need to come back, don't you?" he asked, although he was already resigned to the fact before Sunny nodded.

"Definitely," she said.

He felt a faint vibration beneath his feet. He hoped Armenta had some really strong protection spells up her sleeve.

CHAPTER FOUR

Armenta Kaslov had stayed after the metaphysical shop closed and brewed tea in Sunny's apartment. Sunny thanked her, even though she suspected her assistant's thoughtfulness had more to do getting a blow-by-blow account of the winery outing than providing comfort to the cold and bedraggled.

After hanging wet coats on a rack in front of the space heater, Sunny and Ash related all the details while emptying a pot of green tea they were assured was not the swirling kind that produced brain fog. Her brow furrowed, Armenta removed a cozy from the second teapot. A pleasant aroma wafted up when she took off the lid to stir the contents.

Ash to a sniff. "That smells different from any of the other teas you've brewed. Are those herbs?"

Armenta nodded. "Linden, lemon balm, chamomile, orange, poppy, woodruff, hawthorn, hops, verbena and a pinch of centella." She gave a dry-leaf cackle. "One of my own blends. Would you like me to put a spoonful into a plastic bag, so you can have it analyzed?" She passed him a full cup.

"That won't be necessary, unless I hallucinate or pass out." Ash took a cautious sip. "Not bad."

Armenta placed a cup of the tea in front of Sunny. "It's a sad commentary on our relationship, Ash, that you still don't trust me not to spike your tea."

He studied her across the table. "You don't have a good track record. You've served that toad tea to unsuspecting visitors in the past. I know chamomile's good for relaxation, but you listed a lot of other ingredients." He placed the cup back on its saucer.

"All those herbs are for calming frazzled nerves." Armenta took off the lid of a tin she produced from beside her. "Have a cookie. Oatmeal raisin with almonds." She held it out toward Ash.

Ash took it and sniffed the contents of the tin, too. "They smell good." He offered them to Sunny.

She refused to be tempted. "I'm supposed to be calming down. I don't need a sugar spike."

"I used agave." Armenta took the tin away from Ash and presented it to Sunny. "These won't give you a sugar high."

"Then I'll have one." Sunny took a cookie and bit into it. "Thank you. It's delicious." She passed the tin back to Ash.

"Thanks for baking." He took two cookies.

Sunny wondered which of them had endured the most stress that day. Armenta looked tired, her long face moon-white with dark smudges under her eyes. Ash didn't look any fresher. He had mud stains on his suit, stubble on his chin, and a dullness in his brown eyes she hadn't seen before. Maybe all the trekking around the vineyard, followed by that unsettling interaction with the caretaker was responsible. Or maybe Ash was just tired of having so much of his retirement spent with a psychic and a fortune-teller. He had to be sick of being put into situations over which he had so little control.

"I will have to go back to the winery," she said, moving the cookie around on her napkin and wondering whether she should wait to eat it until after she'd had supper. "I didn't spend enough time beside the creek, and we only passed through the tasting room. What's the weather forecast for tomorrow?"

"More rain," Armenta said.

"Heavy showers or the continuous variety?" Ash had finished his tea and cookies. He crumpled up his napkin and laid it beside his empty cup.

"Continuous, by the sound of it. But you could ask Vincente for a localized dispensation of rainclouds," Armenta suggested. "I'm sure he could do that for you."

"I'm not asking him to perform any magic, however minor." Sunny abandoned her tea and sat back in her chair. She didn't like the new blend, and when she coupled it with the thought of Valderos executing any kind of spell, her stomach churned. Goodness knows what he'd conjure up.

"I'll second that." Ash toyed with the handle of his cup, which was decorated by tiny sprigs of lavender. "With him, a little magic can turn into a whole lot of hocus-pocus with inconsistent results. After we solve this case, we only have two more. I'm not jeopardizing that by asking him to interfere. He could tell us afterward the entire case doesn't count."

"That would be horrible." Sunny got up. The tea had dried out her mouth. She took three bottles of water from the refrigerator. "Let's go out there without telling Valderos, and I'll try to bring that spirt back so I can communicate with it. But what if I'm unsuccessful? Armenta, do you have any potions that would enhance my powers?"

"Hmm." Armenta tapped her gold front tooth with a black varnished nail. She got up and poured more tea into Ash's cup without him asking for a refill. "Here's another thought." She sat back down, picked up a teaspoon and waved it in Sunny and Ash's general direction. "The rain may have allowed the spirit to achieve a form. If so, then tomorrow's rain will be a blessing in disguise." She chuckled, the sound less than mirthful. "I suppose that's a pun. Blessing in disguise…reluctant manifestation…"

Sunny did see the connection, but found it lacked humor. She chose not to remark on Armenta's wordplay skills. "I guess that's possible. I only saw it when the rain got really heavy." She knew what she needed to do, but she also knew Ash wasn't going to like it. "I must go down to the bottom of the hill alone. If possible, I should make the trip while there's a downpour."

Ash had his cup halfway to his mouth. It crashed back onto its saucer. "You're not going anywhere on that property without me. Don't even think about it."

"I *have* to, Ash. Otherwise, we're not going to know what the spirit wants, or if it has any useful information for us." She watched his frown turn into a glower of disapproval. "But don't think you're getting off scot-free," she added. "You're going to have to keep that weirdo caretaker busy if he gets curious."

"The caretaker you said wasn't human." Ash vigorously rubbed his chin, producing a rasping sound. "How do you suggest I keep him occupied? Ask him to show me how he sweeps with that broom, or should I let him hit me over the head with his enormous flashlight?"

"If you put obstacles between me and my job, I may ask to borrow his flashlight and hit you over the head with it, myself." After a moment of silence, Sunny watched the corner of Ash's mouth twitch, and she breathed a sigh of relief. Either Armenta's relaxing tea blend was working, or the cookies had restored his sense of humor. "You can't always be in charge, Ash," she reminded him. "I have to be able to do my part."

"The last time you wanted to act alone, you ended up lost in a wood being used by a coven of witches to create black magic." His eyebrows drew toward each other.

Armenta cleared her throat. "Sunny, why do you think the caretaker isn't human?"

An image of him flashed into Sunny's mind. "Because he looked like a troll."

"How do you know what trolls look like?" Armenta's voice held laughter. "I don't remember you ever meeting any." When Sunny looked her way, the seer's eyes danced. "I can't say I've ever noticed any in the shop, either." Her mouth lifted into a grin. Her gold tooth glimmered.

"I only meant he *looked* like a troll." Sunny wasn't going to back down. "In books, they're really ugly, they smell bad, they have long noses, and no necks."

"He did meet all those criteria," Ash agreed. "I thought he smelled like the vineyard itself…composting plant matter and rotting grapes."

"Yuk, that describes his odor down to a T." Sunny wrinkled her nose.

"He sounds more like a goblin than a troll." Armenta ran her corded belt through her fingers. Bells tinkled. "But the way he smells doesn't fit any mythical beings I'm aware of."

"I want to know how he just happened to turn up in the tasting room." Ash planted his elbows on the table and steepled his fingers. "There were no other vehicles in the parking lot when we arrived, and both outbuildings were padlocked. Why would he be inside the main building? What could he possibly be sweeping, and why did he need that big flashlight? The power's on. He knew that…he turned on the lights."

"I wonder whether Valderos decided to go to the winery without calling anyone to ask permission." Sunny took another drink of her water as she thought. "Maybe that's why he insisted we go through a side gate and down the hill."

Ash shrugged. "I doubt Vinnie would care about being seen. He could mess with their minds. Make them think they were seeing things." He rubbed his chin again. "Maybe the caretaker lives on the property and doesn't have a cell phone. He certainly didn't look like someone who would know how to use Wi-Fi. He was more like the kind who still uses carrier pigeons to send messages."

"He *does* sound like he isn't human," Armenta agreed.

"You know, I never questioned how Valderos got to the winery in the first place," Sunny mused. "His limo wasn't in the parking lot. Serrano must have dropped him off before we got there. But why would he have gotten there early? He's always punctual, but I think he's too impatient to stand around waiting for anyone."

"He was even more impatient than usual, so maybe he *was* early." Ash frowned. "Or he gave us the wrong meeting time."

"Don't you think he would have said something about us being late, though?" Sunny slid her index finger around the rim of her cup. The thin china felt cool and reassuringly solid. Sometimes, she needed to ground herself when discussions headed into the realm of impossibilities. "He was snippy the whole time, but he didn't do anything to get us to the creek faster. He's teleported you before, Ash. Why didn't he do that to both of us?"

"Maybe he can only send one person at a time?" Armenta fussed with the numerous bracelets on her left wrist. They jangled like a dozen tiny, discordant voices.

"I don't think so." Sunny wished Armenta would stop bringing extraneous noises into the conversation. Her nerves were beginning to jangle worse than those bracelets. "Remember how he said dogs don't like him, so he sent Jake home and said Ash's neighbors were looking after him, the evening we all went to the mansion?"

Ash nodded. "That was a complex situation. The neighbors were away at a wedding. He had to get them to my house and at the same time, transport Jake from my Rover. He also altered the couple's memories. They said they'd gotten my message after arriving home and had gone over to let him out and feed him. All they remembered was enjoying the wedding. They were completely vague about how they traveled back to Salem. I didn't push for details. Moving us from the parking lot to the creek should have been easy for Vinnie."

"I never know what he's capable of," Sunny said. "I'm pleasantly surprised when I find he has limitations."

"I believe those limitations are diminishing," Armenta said.

A chill ran up Sunny's spine. "Why?"

"A subject for another time." Armenta drained her cup.

Sunny yawned and stretched. "I've had enough tea, and I'm tired from hiking around that muddy vineyard all afternoon. I'm sorry you had to mind the store with only Stella for back-up, Armenta. We were gone a lot longer than we expected."

"Don't worry about it." Armenta waved off Sunny's apologies. "Stella's making strides on all fronts except one. Having the new cash register really has improved our speed of service, except when she jams it up. I still haven't figured out how she manages to get the cash drawer stuck."

"Me, neither." Sunny rubbed her cheeks with both hands. It felt surprisingly good. "I try to keep her away from cashiering as much as possible. It's like she's got a bad mojo or something. But apart from Stella suddenly discovering her inner-bookkeeper, my only other wish would be that we had a way to display more new merchandise."

Ash leaned back in his chair. "You know the answer to that is taking over the space next door."

"I already told you that's too risky," Sunny reminded him. "I did the math. Expansion would send the store back into the red." She didn't want to waste any more time dreaming about how the space formerly occupied by the insurance office could be utilized to expand the metaphysical shop. Having all that extra square footage could potentially double the monthly sales. But she couldn't afford the lease.

Armenta stood up. "Time for me to go. I'll see you both in the morning." She picked up her big tote and left through the back door so quickly, her departure reminded Sunny of a whirlwind.

Ash turned in his chair to face her. "We all know the space won't stay vacant for long. Business in this part of town is picking up. Both Grant and Highland neighborhoods are continuing to grow in economic value. Do you really want to risk some other business going in there that won't be compatible with yours?"

"No, of course not You don't need to give me examples, if that's what you're planning." Sunny stopped slouching. Problems at the store always seemed to tighten her muscles. "There isn't the space for it to become a fast-food restaurant or yet another used car dealership, but a weed shop or even a tire shop could go in there. The warehouse behind it also became vacant last month."

Ash stood and stretched. "You're always complaining about moving merchandise around and having to utilize more and more shelving units as you try to cram everything in. You'd be able to set up more dedicated spaces than the gargoyle corner. You could have a costume shop for Halloween..."

"I know, I know." Sunny ran a hand through her hair. "I've been thinking along those lines since I heard the insurance company wasn't renewing the lease."

Ash started to clear the table.

"Leave that and go home," she told him. "It'll give me something to do while I'm thinking." She stood, too. "You want to go out the front?"

"No, I'll go out the back." Ash took his coat from the drying rack. "See you tomorrow morning?"

She nodded. "Are you going home to research the winery?"

"Yes, and learn about its former owners' unfortunate accidents." Ash put on his hat. "If Vinnie's involved us, then at least one of those accidents was more likely a murder."

"Probably," she agreed, trying not to look as dispirited as she felt.

"See you tomorrow." He gave her what she recognized as his encouraging smile, meant to assure her everything was going to be absolutely fine. She'd seen him use the same smile on Katie, when his daughter was upset over something. "Try to get some sleep." He sounded more like her father than her partner. He buttoned his coat.

"I don't think anything's going to keep me awake tonight." She stifled a yawn. "I'm going to bed early, for a change."

After locking the door, she opened the refrigerator, staring without enthusiasm into its bright-white depths. Did she really want leftover Chinese from two days ago? She thought there might be a can of corned beef hash lurking somewhere in the back of the pantry. She pushed aside cans of peas, beans, and green enchilada sauce to find she was correct.

"Why don't we talk while you warm up that hash?" Tina suggested.

CHAPTER FIVE

Ash dropped his keys into an ashtray on the table by the front door. A reminder of the days when he smoked, it was made of cut glass that sparkled whenever he turned on the overhead light. He left his shoes on a rack, jammed his feet into a comfortable pair of slippers and hung up his outerwear on the hall tree. The house felt warm, welcoming and familiar. A far cry from the apartment he'd occupied in Portland after he and Caroline broke up for good. Jake came running, tail wagging enthusiastically.

"Hi, bud." Ash gave the dog a good scratch before sending Jake outside for his constitutional. He got a seltzer out of the refrigerator and took a long drink before throwing the Australian Shepherd's favorite ball around the back yard for him and playing tug of war. After hiking around the vineyard most of the afternoon, he didn't feel like taking their usual long walk.

Returning inside, he ignited the gas fireplace. After noisily slurping water, Jake flopped onto his bed with a contented grunt. Ash knew his own needs included a long, hot shower and dinner. But instead, he popped open a beer he'd stowed at the back of the vegetable bin, turned on the TV and searched for something interesting to watch while resting his aching joints. The news was too depressing, reruns were of shows he'd already watched, and even the Travel Channel was showing a repeat.

Katie would be back that weekend, he reminded himself, glancing at the coloring book and watercolor paints on the coffee table. He decided showering could wait until he got ready for bed. He went back to the kitchen and opened the refrigerator. He had leftovers to reheat, followed by an evening of research into the Taricani family and their vineyard. Vinnie and his vineyards, both producing bad wine, Ash thought, sparing a wry chuckle as he scraped the remains of a burrito from a take-out container onto a plate and wondered whether he really wanted to eat it or order take-out.

He missed having Katie around all the time. Since she'd returned to living with her mother during the week, he'd not only stopped watching the cooking class they'd both participated in regularly, he'd quit making his own meals on a regular basis. He was falling back into very bad habits. If he didn't mend his ways, he'd regress to spending hours on the patio with a cigarette in one hand and a beer in the other. He refilled Jake's kibble, refreshed the water, and opened a can of the dog's favorite wet food, which he shook into a bowl. Jake awoke from his power nap when he heard the can open. His tail swinging in circles, he bounded into the kitchen. While his furry companion ate, Ash finished the beer, and because he felt guilty, chugged down the last of the seltzer.

He knew he needed a social life, but after so many years maintaining a distance from the general public while he was a police officer, forming new friendships had proved even more difficult than he'd expected. He'd established passing acquaintances with other parents at the stables where Katie took her riding lessons on Saturday mornings, and he waved at his neighbors, but didn't stop to chat.

He wasn't into online dating, book clubs or frequenting bars since he no longer smoked or drank more than an occasional beer. He decided being in his mid-forties and single wasn't turning out to be what he'd hoped, although it did have one big benefit: No daily fights with Caroline.

Maybe he should take Jake over to the big dog park on Minto Brown Island and try to strike up conversations with other dog owners. Maybe he'd even meet a nice woman with a compatible friend for Jake, he thought as the dog returned to his bed, gave a contented sigh, and closed his eyes.

Ash decided he was above reheating the decidedly less-than-appealing burrito and tossed it into the garbage. His cell rang while he was rolling up his sleeves in preparation for making an omelet out of the last two eggs, filled with the last slice of processed cheese he'd bought to put into sandwiches. The caller ID made him frown. What did Sunny want less than an hour after he'd left the shop? He hoped she hadn't been visited by the spirits of the dead Taricanis.

When he answered, she told him: "Tina put in an appearance." She sounded worried. "Do you have plans, or would you like to come over for dinner? We could work on our research together. I don't want to be alone here right now. I feel really spooked. The phantom cat's prowling up and down the back of the couch, and Watcher's flapping around the store. They're really agitated, and so am I."

The thought of Watcher the concrete gryphon zooming around the rafters at The House of Serenity was even more disturbing than eating a questionably-fresh burrito. "I was trying to convince myself an omelet with processed American cheese was a gourmet dinner," he told her. He opened the garbage can and tipped the sad meal into it. "You want me to pick up something from the store?"

"That would be great. I've got pasta. If you brought a jar of sauce and a bagged salad, we could have Italian." He heard her rummaging around. "Okay, I have salad dressing, grape tomatoes…and…yes, parmesan cheese." She sounded like the cheese was a victory of sorts.

"I'll pick up a baguette so we can have garlic bread, too," he said. "You need butter, garlic?"

"Not unless you can't handle a plant-based spread. I've got plenty of garlic." She gave a nervous laugh. "I always have garlic. You know…to keep the vampires away. Thanks, Ash. When should I get the pasta water going?"

"The groceries won't take long. I can be at your apartment in thirty minutes. And I'm fine with the fake butter. It's probably better for my health."

He promised to text her when he left the store, and they hung up to complete their assigned tasks.

Ash shrugged into his still-damp coat. His shoes were dry inside. He put on a different hat. But when he went to pick up his keys, they were no longer in the ashtray. Swearing, he went into the bedroom and retrieved his spare set.

"You'll pay for this, Valderos," he said before he closed and locked the front door behind him.

CHAPTER SIX

"That was a good meal." Ash laid his napkin beside his plate. "I'm a lot happier than I'd have been with what I had at home."

Sunny smiled. "Good company, and the dinner was easy to put together. I thought you were turning into a gourmet cook with those classes. What happened?"

"My motivation slipped when the custody arrangements returned to normal." Ash didn't want to elaborate further on his feelings of isolation and borderline depression over Katie's absence 5 days out of the week.

"It's an adjustment, I'm sure." Sunny leaned back in her chair. "What part of the research do you want me to tackle? Shall I make coffee first?"

"Coffee sounds like a really good idea. Trekking through that muddy vineyard wore me out. I haven't been to the gym regularly, either, since Katie went back to Caroline during the week. That daughter of mine always added gym visits to my calendar with alerts on my phone. Katie thinks she's the voice of my conscience." He began gathering up the dishes. "You make the coffee; I'll take care of these."

"Deal, but let me put up the left-overs first. You want to take some home? There's too much for me to eat in one meal, and I never feel enthusiastic about the same food by the third day."

"Okay." He watched her distribute the spaghetti into two plastic containers. "You should be going out evenings, not inviting me over for dinner. Getting out of the apartment might settle things down."

"I don't think me leaving would do anything but delay the inevitable."

Sunny had a wry smile. "I do go out sometimes." She sighed. "Unfortunately, I seem to be spending those evenings with Mark. I keep telling myself I know better, but that doesn't seem to work for me. I told myself I'd never see my ex again after my move to Salem. Now he's living here and working in local government. Makes me wonder about karma."

"I've learned to never say never." Ash piled the dishes into the sink. "Speaking of facing exs, I frequently have to see my ex-mother-in-law when I pick up Katie, and she never hides her disapproval. Maxine moved in temporarily to take care of Caroline during her recuperation. Then she rented out her house. As long as her property's leased, she'll keep giving me her death-ray glare every time she opens the door."

"Well, at least you know Katie's with her grandmother now when Caroline's off showing a home or putting in time at the office." Sunny filled the coffeemaker and spooned coffee into its basket. "I thought I was under an enchantment when I told Mark I'd have coffee with him one afternoon after work. That coffee date turned into a couple of drinks and then dinner. Not only once, but at least once a week. I asked Armenta to cast a spell to make Mark go away. She said my attraction to him wasn't the result of witchcraft. I wasn't convinced, so I took my life in my hands and called Valderos. He swore he wasn't responsible. I guess Armenta's right. My attraction to Mark never really went away. I just hid it and deluded myself."

"Sunny, you were attracted enough to Mark to marry him, and you didn't stop loving him because of your marital issues, from what you've said, or I've seen." Ash ran hot water over the dishes and squirted soap into the water. Bubbles surged, and a pleasant aroma of green apples floated up.

"You can look at people and see right through their armor." Sunny pushed a button on the coffeemaker. A moment later, water gurgled and the brewing process began. "Even more now Valderos enhanced your skills of observation. So, can you tell me if Mark's really mended his ways? His *wayward* ways." She leaned against the counter and ran a hand through her hair. "I'm keeping him at arm's length, but it isn't easy."

"There'll come a time when you're going to have to make the choice to either trust him or wear blinders where he's concerned." Ash scrubbed the dishes with unnecessary vigor. He kind of wished he was scrubbing Mark's face.

He didn't like the direction the conversation was taking. He and Sunny didn't have that kind of relationship. Theirs was professional, not personal. But when he saw the doubt on her face and the pain in her hazel eyes, he found it hard to stay detached. He had finished washing the few dishes, so he emptied the bowl and rinsed suds down the drain. He dried his hands on a kitchen towel and hung it to dry.

"I suppose." Sunny averted her gaze, like she suddenly felt as awkward as Ash did. "Cup or mug?" she asked. "Armenta left a tin of chocolate chip cookies. She must have known we were going to work together this evening."

Ash saw the tin sitting beside the TV, where Armenta usually left her bag. "Definitely a mug." He brought the tin to the table. "Do you still feel spooked?"

"A little. Not like before. Thanks for coming over." Sunny took two mugs out of the cabinet.

Ash hadn't wanted to broach the subject of Sunny's best friend's apparition before dinner. "What did Tina say?" he asked.

"It was more what she *didn't* say." Sunny carefully placed the mugs on the table, like she needed a moment of reflection. "She didn't say anything about Valderos or the vineyard. She wanted to bash Mark, followed by complaints about the direction the shop's taking. She tried to tell me how to run it. Honestly, Ash, she's like a thorn in my side. I'm beginning to wonder whether she's a figment not only of my imagination, but my alter-ego. Like an enlarged version of the little voice that whispers in your ear and tells you nothing you're doing is any good, and you're about to set yourself up for another heartache with the same man. All your short-comings in brilliant color."

"Maybe she's the angel on your shoulder," Ash said.

"Or maybe she's more like the devil's advocate in my apartment. This time, she really upset Watcher and the cat. Honestly, I need to find out where they both came from, and what they're doing here."

Vigorous flapping came from inside the shop.

"Cut it out," Sunny called. "I'm not talking about sending you away. I just want to know more about how you got here and why you stay."

"You think he really understands, don't you?" Ash took the lid off the cookie tin and offered it to Sunny. She shook her head. He selected one of the largest cookies and took a bite. Delicious, as usual.

"Watcher *does* understand. But he makes his own choices about whether or how he's going to respond."

The coffeemaker beeped. Sunny brought the carafe to the table and filled their mugs. She returned the carafe to its base to keep the coffee hot, fetched creamer from the refrigerator and sat down opposite Ash.

"Okay, let's put all this heavy chit-chat to one side," he recommended. "I brought my laptop." He took it out of its carrying case and laid it on the table.

"I'll get mine." Sunny quickly retrieved hers. "What do you want to start with first?"

"Why don't you research the family? Find out where they came from, how long they've been living in Oregon, and who's still here? I'll check out the winery. See what the news reported about the deaths. Valderos told us very little this time."

"Ash, do you think Valderos teleported himself between the vineyard and Oak Grove?" Sunny chewed her bottom lip, a habit that showed she was still agitated.

Ash tried to remember what happened after they drove into the winery's parking lot. He couldn't. He only remembered following Valderos through a lot of mud to the creek. "You know that disappearing memory trick he pulls on us in his house?"

"You think he's causing memory loss anywhere he wants, now." She looked across the table, her face draining of all color. "That's absolutely terrifying."

CHAPTER SEVEN

"Let's get on with the research," Ash suggested.

Sunny looked even more drained than when he'd arrived. He could have kicked himself for bringing up the supernatural side of her life…a frightening shadow-realm that hovered between reality and make-believe. Only make-believe was *real* in Sunny's world, he reminded himself, and increasingly, in his, too.

"Something concrete. I like the sound of that." She turned her attention to her laptop.

Ash did the same, chewing his way through three cookies while he browsed page after page of accounts in social media and various news outlets of a feud between the Taricani family and their neighbors, the Fortunas, who owned the Clear Creek Cider House and its orchard.

He read that Taricani family members were prone to in-fighting as well as having disputes with their neighbors. Lorenzo's son, Arturo, decided to become partners in a small organic winery on the other side of McMinnville instead of adopting his father's more progressive methods of viticulture. His sister, Sofia, despite a BS in viticulture and enology to go with her MBA, was passed over in favor of a nephew, William Hixton, who went by Bill and ran a used car lot in Salem.

Bill was the eldest son of Lorenzo's sister. The young man was an unsuccessful entrepreneur who knew nothing about the wine business. He continued Lorenzo's modernization, which should have improved the vineyard's production and refined its end product. Instead, the vines ceased to produce, and the wine from the previous year remained in the cellar. Hixton put the winery on the market, no doubt to cut his losses. Both Arturo and Sofia were vocally outraged, but unable to either persuade Bill to reconsider or expand his search for a bank willing to make a loan on a highly questionable investment.

Ash decided all the family drama was enough to stir up a hornet's nest of rivalry, jealousy, and a good half-dozen other emotions. He couldn't even imagine how Lorenzo's decision must have specifically impacted Sofia, who must have planned to take over the business.

According to the investigative reporting by a local journalist, after Giuseppe passed away, both the quality of the wines and the output of the winery deteriorated. Previously devoted wine club members informed the journalist that by the second year, the wine became undrinkable.

Hixton had tried negotiating water rights with the Fortunas. When negotiations stalled, they offered to purchase the vineyard, but leave Hixton with the huge tasting room, extensive lawn, and parking lot, to be used for events. Their bid was too low for Hixton to seriously consider. By then, the orchard was suffering the consequences of inadequate irrigation and the Fortunas had a cash-flow problem.

Sofia and Arturo re-entered the picture. Arturo's organic methods had resulted in fine boutique wines. The siblings wanted to purchase the entire property. They were going to farm organic grapes. Create new wines. Relaunch under a different name. It all sounded like an exciting return of the Taricanis, but their offer was only slightly better than that of the Fortunas.

Suddenly, an anonymous bidder made an offer that eclipsed the other two. Ash knew that bidder had to be Valderos, who no doubt had deep pockets to go with his supernatural powers,

But why would Valderos want to buy another failing winery, especially one with such a checkered past?

CHAPTER EIGHT

Sunny searched through the Taricani family's roots. They left Sicily in the 1950s to make their home in Northern California. Giuseppe took a job at a winery producing Cabernet Sauvignon and learned the business literally from the ground up. He advanced from field laborer to sommelier by working hard and very long hours. He made sure he brought his son, Lorenzo into the business the same way. Years later, Lorenzo reminisced about those early years without showing much gratitude. He'd hated working in the fields. His back hurt. His fingers became permanently stained by the grapes. Sun exposure had resulted in several procedures to remove cancerous lesions from his face.

But Giuseppe made full use of his knowledge when he formed a partnership with a friend from a neighboring vineyard. They moved up to Oregon's Willamette Valley to start their own vineyard at a time when every winery in that area was new and untested. Their first attempt failed. The partner sold his interest to Giuseppe for pennies on the dollar and returned to Napa. Giuseppe soldiered on with the Vitis vinifera vines. Slow to grow, and even slower to produce, he had to have patience as well as the funds to continue waiting. Almost bankrupt, he was finally able to bottle the fruits of his labor into a Pinot Noir that garnered honorable mention in several competitions. The Taricani vineyard prospered.

After Giuseppe's modest success, Lorenzo renewed his interest in the family business. His attempts at modernization caused friction with his father, who made no secret of the fact he believed the old ways were, and would continue to be, the best ways to cultivate, ferment, and otherwise produce wines carrying the Taricani name.

Then Giuseppe's accident occurred, and Lorenzo was able to make all the changes he'd unsuccessfully promoted. A large tasting room was built to attract wine-enthusiasts, replacing Giuseppe's practice of selling to wholesalers. Lorenzo changed Giuseppe's farming methods after hiring a new foreman who believed in crop accelerants, herbicides, and pesticides, replacing what Lorenzo termed 'archaic organic farming.'

The year he took over brought many changes, stressing the vines and depleting the financial reserves. Then the tree fell on him, killing him instantly. His children were devastated by his death. They were even more devastated by the terms of Lorenzo's will, leaving the business to their cousin. They made no attempt to disguise their dislike for Bill Hixton, who was only one-quarter Italian and had no prior experience or interest in the family business. He was already talking about trying other grapes because the market, in his opinion, was over-saturated with Pinot Noir.

Her eyes tired and her throat dry, Sunny took a break. She brought two bottles of spring water from the refrigerator and placed one in front of Ash, still caught up in his reading. She wondered what he had discovered. Her own research had revealed conflicts, jealousy, and what she thought was justifiable resentment from Lorenzo's children. She sat back down and watched Ash rub his chin, a habit that showed he was getting tired, too.

She wondered why she had chosen to call Ash and ask him to come for dinner instead of Mark. Was it because she still hadn't told Mark about her visions, Watcher, Tina, or the phantom cat? The ghostly feline had paraded into the apartment and settled down to sleep at the end of her bed while she was getting another cup of coffee. She wondered whether Ash had merely ignored the cat or hadn't seen it. He'd told her he'd seen it some other times, but he'd denied ever seeing Tina, and so had Armenta.

Sunny was done with researching the squabbling Taricani clan, but Ash didn't look like he was ready to call it a night. The thought that he could sit silently for even another 15 minutes made her antsy. Taking a surreptitious look at her tracker, she noted it was 10:45 PM. Time to give Ash a nudge, but the thought of him leaving her alone in the apartment wasn't appealing, even if Tina hadn't reappeared.

Since Ash was so engrossed, she took a moment to study him. She'd never been a fan of curly hair on men, but it suited Ash, especially with gray mixed into dark brown. His eyes, downcast at that moment, were also a warm shade of dark brown. His nose definitely leaned toward patrician. His lips were generous for a man, but not overly so. She began comparing his face with Mark's, then gave herself a mental reprimand as her eyes moved down to study Ash's chin, firm and covered with a dark haze. He had said on more than one occasion that growing a beard would be very easy for him. But he told her he always shaved, even on vacation.

Sunny asked herself why she considered Ash a friend and partner instead of anything even slightly romantic. Was it their age difference? Her psychic power? No chemistry? She thought about his protective hand in the small of her back, on her arm, or holding her hand in his when there was a scary, unsettling or potentially dangerous situation, and how comforting his touch felt.

Ash stirred. Looked up. Locked gazes with her. Sunny felt embarrassed he had caught her studying him, but he gave her a half-smile.

"Tired?" he asked. "Ready to call it quits?"

She nodded. "Definitely, but let's quickly review what we found before you go."

"You want to do that because you're afraid you'll forget some of it by the morning, or because you're putting off being left alone?" The half-smile looked rueful. "Do you need me to sleep on the couch?"

"No, of course not. You should sleep in your own bed." Suddenly and inexplicably uncomfortable discussing sleeping arrangements, she got up, swooped up the empty coffee mugs and took them to the sink with the carafe.

She ran water into the bowl. It splashed out, cold and fierce. She'd been so preoccupied with her disturbing thoughts, she'd turned on the wrong faucet. "Why don't we go back to the vineyard tomorrow? We can exchange information during the drive," she called as she turned off the cold and turned on the hot. She squirted dishwashing liquid into the bowl. It bubbled up like an erupting volcano.

"Is Stella working?" Ash asked.

Sunny cast a glance in his direction. He was putting his laptop into its carrying case. She thought he might be trying not to laugh at the soap bubble lava flow as he concentrated on carefully closing the zipper. "She is. All day. So we won't have to hurry back."

She thought she should have phrased that sentence a little better. She wondered whether Tina had really been Tina, or whether some gremlin had used her friend's apparition. Her thoughts were becoming scrambled. Was fatigue really the cause?

"Okay, then what time do you want me to pick you up?" Ash was putting on his coat.

"We should get permission before we drive out there," she said. She had washed and rinsed everything while she was completely distracted. Placing the carafe in the rack to dry, she turned to face him. "I can make the call, but to who? The attorney?"

"I'll do it." Ash put on his hat. "I'll call you as soon as I've talked to him. I'll make sure the caretaker has our names and knows we're coming. I'll tell the attorney we want to look inside all the buildings and see the vineyard in a better light. I checked the forecast. Scattered showers tomorrow. No more downpours. Either Armenta was mistaken, or she gave us bad intel."

"Thank you. That's a relief, knowing we won't be caught in another deluge."

"I'm not convinced that's a true forecast." Ash grinned. "Wear your raincoat and boots, and don't forget your umbrella."

"I will, and I'm going to make sure my boots are completely dry inside." An image of the strange caretaker popped into her head. Suddenly cold, inside and out, she wished she'd turned on the space heater.

Ash went over to the back door. "Make sure you lock up," he instructed.

"I will. No worries." She followed him.

"And tell that damned cat to get off the bed," he added before he stepped outside.

Sunny felt relieved she wasn't the only one who had seen it.

"Sleep well." Ash lingered a moment on the threshold. "If you get spooked again, call me. I'll pick you up. You can sleep at my place. You've done it before."

"I know, but I'm sure I'll be okay." Her fingers rested on the doorframe, inches from his. "Goodnight, Ash, and thanks again for coming over."

He stepped away, waved without looking back, and headed off down the alleyway.

Sunny closed, locked and bolted the door. The little apartment felt bigger and very empty without him.

"Move over, Mr. Kitty," she told the cat. "I'm taking off the comforter."

The cat vanished. Sunny felt even more alone. More than that, she felt lonely.

CHAPTER NINE

"So, I talked to the attorney this morning," Ash said as they travelled on Hwy 22 past the exit for Independence. "He didn't know anything about a caretaker, but he'll contact Hixton and make sure he instructs the guy to keep out of the way unless we ask for assistance. That'll get him out of your hair while you're doing what you do."

"I wish you wouldn't call my psychic skills 'doing what you do.'" Sunny gave him her most disapproving glare. "It sounds demeaning."

"Well, what would you like to call it?" Ash accelerated and passed several slower cars. The speed limit was evidently only a suggestion for him that morning.

"I have visions," Sunny said.

"Those aren't all you get." Ash passed another three cars.

They sped across a landscape of flat fields toward Hwy 99's overpass at the little community of Rickreall. A cluster of buildings to the left included a large dairy farm. Between the fertilizer used on crops and the waste pools from the dairy farm, Sunny wondered whether Ash's heavy use of the accelerator was to make the trip as pleasant as possible. Questions over the source of an obnoxious smell in the area had made the pages of the *Statesman Journal* in the past.

"I have a lot of other reactions, too," Sunny had to agree. "Sometimes I get vibes about something or someone who lived in a place. Yesterday, I had the impression of a large party with lots of laughter and loud conversations when we were inside the tasting room. I don't like experiencing those. They can be intrusive, like a tug on my arm or someone poking me with a finger and telling me I need to listen."

"I wouldn't like to feel any of that," Ash said. "I prefer to make my own deductions based on facts. What you do, and what you feel, those are way past anything I can relate to. I can only guess what they must feel like."

His rich voice sounded sympathetic. Sunny's slight irritation over what she felt was his belittling of her psychic abilities receded. "It isn't easy, and it isn't comfortable, opening my mind to be invaded," she told him. "I invite spirits into me. Mostly into my head, but sometimes they occupy my body, too." She grimaced. "I don't like it when that happens. I've been trying to have more control over what I receive and how I receive it. Armenta's helping me the best she can, but it isn't easy. In fact, it can be downright exhausting."

"I know it tires you. That's where I come in….giving you physical and moral support." Ash's voice was soft.

When Sunny looked over at him again, his concern was plainly written into the deepened lines on his face. "You *do* help me," she assured him, patting his arm. "I don't know what I'd do without you and Armenta. I hope I never have to find out, although I'll have to assume that Armenta will live to be at least a hundred and twenty."

"At the very least." Ash nodded. "And she's not the only one. I'd have to get really long in the tooth to stick around for you on an indefinite basis."

"Your fangs would only need to reach your chest." Sunny had to smile at the image that conjured up. "Armenta's would be scraping the ground."

"You think she's that old, huh?"

"I have her personnel file," Sunny said. "I'm not divulging her age to you, but according to her driver's license, she's not yet ready to claim Social Security, although she will be in less than a decade."

"I think she either altered that license or paid someone to forge it," Ash said. "Armenta looks like she's been around for many moons, especially when she's hanging out in that arbor with its poor lighting."

"I know…I'm surprised none of her clients have tripped and fallen while trying to find her in there, but she's absolutely refused to have more than the lamp you put in there and the lights I strung across the front of the canopy.

It's her domain, and she intends to keep it that way. She wouldn't even consider moving to a different part of the shop."

"Like you could find her a better location for that arbor?" Ash shook his head. "You're running out of room, Sunny. Face it." He accelerated again as he cruised into the left lane, in preparation for the turnoff to Dallas.

"You're speeding." Sunny clutched her seatbelt. "Are you in a hurry to get some place else after we're done out here?"

"No, but I'd like to be out of the vineyard before the rain starts. I had enough of the mud yesterday. I'd have liked to bring Jake…he'd enjoy a good off-leash run, but I'd need the Rover detailed afterward. Let's go to the creek first, while it's a little drier."

"Good thinking, but you should slow down. If you're pulled over for speeding, you'll get a ticket and we could miss out on the good weather."

"Yes, Mother." Ash scowled, but he did stick to the posted speed limits. By the time they arrived at the battered sign for the Taricani Winery and Tasting Room, clouds had gathered over the Coast Range. He made several frustrated grunts while they bounced over potholes and around tight corners on the narrow access road. "As bad as Vinnie's driveway in bad weather," he remarked. They drew into the forecourt of the tasting room. "And the parking lot's worse."

Sunny released her seat belt and opened her door to find water-filled potholes spread liberally throughout the lot. "You've got that right." She searched for the best place to land and jumped out, narrowly missing a puddle.

"Forget detailing…the Rover's going to need a new suspension if Vinnie keeps giving us cases in rural areas," Ash complained. "I'm sick of traipsing through fields. I never was a big fan of the countryside." He got out and after Sunny closed her door, he slammed his and locked the SUV.

Sunny left him surveying the outbuildings and zig-zagged her way across the obstacle course of puddles to a gate leading into the vineyard. "Doesn't look any more inviting today, does it?" She waited for Ash to jog up to her.

Ash glanced up at the sky. "No. In fact, it looks worst. Those clouds are moving in fast. Let's get this over as quickly as possible."

Sunny realized Ash was correct…the cloudbank she'd seen to the west had billowed to greater heights and size. It resembled a fast-approaching gray army. "You really think we can beat the rain if we hurry?"

"Probably not, if Vinnie has anything to do with it." Ash made a sound close to a growl. "I'm convinced he does."

"Me, too." She wished she could get her throat to make a similar sound. Menacing, fed up, and ready to do battle, all rolled into one. "I still remember the sudden switch in weather the first time we went to his tasting room."

"I wonder why he thinks this vineyard will improve his vintage?" Ash started down the slope ahead of her.

"I should go first," she protested.

He ignored her and jumped from one grassy hillock to another. "Those vines look dead to me," he told her. "After having the soil treated, Hixton'll need everything ploughed up before he can replant." Suddenly, Ash's foot slid out from under him. He almost fell. Windmilling both arms, he managed to regain his balance. "Damn." He looked at the ground and frowned. "I don't see any reason for me to slip. You've to the advantage, bringing up the rear. You'll have something soft to land on if you slip, too."

"Very funny." Sunny still wasn't sure Ash should be in the lead. The ground had shifted beneath her feet right before he almost landed on his back. But she kept her misgivings to herself. Maybe the soil was so wet from the rain, it had become unstable, or perhaps whatever farming methods Bill Hixton had signed off on had caused soil erosion.

She carefully followed, stepping into his tracks as much as possible. It took them 20 minutes to reach the bottom of the slope. Ash paused to wipe a hand across his brow. "I worked up a sweat."

Raindrops spattered Sunny's raincoat as well as diving into the puddles around her boots. She placed a restraining hand on Ash's arm. "I'd better go on alone."

His frown returned. "You know I don't like you doing that."

"I do, but yesterday, I think the shadow would have tried to communicate if you and Valderos hadn't been there. I think it's timid."

"Usually, I trust your intuition, but I'm not getting warm, fuzzy feelings in this vineyard. What if you need me, but I can't get there fast enough?" He sounded more than worried.

"It'll be okay, I promise." She left him looking as worried as he sounded. Mud sucked at her boots like it wanted to pull her into the ground.

By the time she reached the creek, rain was pounding the vineyard. "This really has to happen *now?*" she muttered to herself. "Sometimes, I really hate fall and winter in this region. Maybe even spring. Depending on how long the rainy season actually lasts." Recognizing her monologue for what it was...nervous prattling...Sunny closed her mouth and refused to engage further with the anxious thoughts bouncing around in her brain.

She approached the creek, which had swollen since the day before. It flowed fast across the rocks. Overhead, a crow cawed, startling her. It brought back troubling memories of their previous case...the Bricklighter farm and its wooded area. The flock of crows that had followed her around.

Sunny shook off those memories with more effort that she liked. If she continued to dwell on the horrors of the past, how could she cope with whatever might be in store for them in the future? Two more cases after their present one, she told herself. Two more. Unless Valderos made more changes to the contract.

She found the spot on which she had stood when she'd noticed the figure. She told herself she should have thought to ask Valderos for the exact date of Giuseppe's death. Or she could have asked Ash. She wondered whether the Taricani patriarch had frequently walked beside the creek, or whether he'd gone there to make sure the Fortunas hadn't removed the dam so water could flow into their orchard.

Trying to ignore the icy rain striking her face, she closed her eyes and opened her mind. Again, flashbacks of the Bricklighter farm flowed in. She opened her eyes and stared across the creek. The rain slowed, then stopped, like a sluice gate in the heavens had closed.

The crow cawed again. Sunny looked up and spotted a nest. A big black bird took off, flapping up into the leaden sky. It whirled around in a circle, evidently caught up by thermals that carried it off toward uncultivated fields beyond the Taricani fence-line.

Sunny turned her attention to the opposite bank of the creek. Something moved. Behind a tree trunk. She tried to stay as still as possible.

The caretaker stepped away from the tree. He held a bundle of wire in one hand. His heavily packed toolbelt clunked as he moved. "I thought you wanted to go into the tasting room," he shouted. "I left the patio door open."

"What are you doing here?" Ash's voice was sharp.

Sunny heard her partner approach, but kept her eyes trained on the huge, stooped figure standing at the very edge of the swollen creek, water lapping over the toes of his mud-caked boots.

"I'm repairing the fence." The old man held up the wire and shook it. "Deer came through last night. I caught them chewing on the vines." He peered at Sunny. "What were you expecting to see down here?" His bristly gray eyebrows drew toward each other. "Mr. Giuseppe's ghost?"

Sunny watched him chuckle, his long, straggly beard bobbing up and down. The sound coming from him was even less reassuring than his presence. Something between a rasp and a hiss. A cold draught found its way inside her raincoat, chilling her to the bone.

"There's nothing to see down here." The man grinned, revealing yellow, broken teeth. A tongue that looked longer and blacker than it should, snaked over his bottom lip. Sunny wanted to run, but she refused to show fear, despite her revulsion. She'd learned well from Armenta. Always confront the foe and appear invincible, even while you're trying to figure out how to stay alive and escape.

"You're right." Ash came up to Sunny and took her arm. "There's nothing to see down here. We'll go up to the tasting room and leave you to your work. Thanks for leaving the door open." He tugged her into motion. "Come on, let's go, already." He winked at the caretaker, like the guy was a co-conspirator. "Women. They always want to look at accident sites. For some reason, this one gets a thrill out of it."

Sunny dug her elbow into Ash's ribcage before allowing him to steer her away. As they began the climb, she glanced back. The caretaker was gone.

CHAPTER TEN

"I don't want to alarm you," Sunny said, as she trudged along ahead of Ash.

"Go ahead, alarm away." Ash's voice sounded like it took a lot of effort. "But let's take a short break while you do it." He stood several paces behind, hands on hips, chest heaving.

Sunny realized she must have been going really fast. She'd ignored her hammering heart, figuring it resulted more from anxiety than exertion. "The caretaker vanished," she said.

Ash turned to look downhill. "He could be hidden by the trees. Even the bushes. He said he was repairing the fence."

"I dunno. Could he really move that fast? He had all those tools weighing him down and the wire." She squinted. "Ash, he left the wire behind."

Ash shielded his eyes with his hand. "Yeah, he did. I see it beside the creek."

"If he was repairing the fence, he'd need that. Something's fishy about him. *Really* fishy."

Ash pulled his hat down as a strong breeze blew through the vineyard. "You believe we're dealing with more than Vinnie's tricks, don't you?"

One of the unpruned vine canes slapped Sunny's back. She almost slapped it back, but she didn't want to startle Ash even more. He already looked wary. She tried to maintain a neutral expression while increasing the distance between herself and the vine, which had multiple long canes twisted around its trunk and the trellis.

"You think he's manipulating everything again." Ash said. It wasn't a question.

"I do, but better him than Valentine making a repeat appearance." The very thought of the fake Valentine returning brought a chill to Sunny that had nothing whatsoever to do with cold weather. The woman was truly evil. She'd bewitched Vincente Valderos, convincing him she was his girlfriend. Even Valderos had wanted to love and be loved, Sunny thought with a shiver. Warily, she looked around.

Everything appeared normal. Benign.

No shifting reality. Birds chirping and flying over the vines.

But never landing on them.

An unwelcome thought stole into Sunny's mind. The way those vines were stretched across the trellises, they looked trapped. Imprisoned. Tortured. Like they wanted to escape, but were bound so tightly, they couldn't move.

She wondered who had been pruning the canes. Surely not the wizened caretaker? His bowed legs didn't look capable of supporting him down the hill. Yet there he'd stood, hailing her from the other side of the creek. How had he even gotten over there?

"Vinnie promised Valentine wouldn't be back, if his vow's worth anything," Ash said. "Come on, let's get back up top. We might as well go inside. I know…." He held up one hand when she began to object. "We could come back… but you've got enough coverage at the shop today for them to manage. Tomorrow, Belinda's in school. With Halloween only weeks away, the shop could get really busy."

"But what if that's what Valderos wanted?" Sunny protested. "For us to come back?" She wrung her hands, although the hopelessness of that gesture wasn't lost on her. "Or maybe he wants us to go inside the building? What if he's laid a trap?"

"Then Armenta will have to come and rescue both of us with spells and a generous dash of whatever she's got boiled up on the stove today." Ash ushered Sunny forward. "I'm not going to try out-guessing Vinnie's motives. He sent us here to solve our next case. We're going to do it, regardless how many obstacles that demon tries to put in the way. His offers to help are always back-handed."

"I know," Sunny agonized, "but Ash, we have to look out for ourselves."

She felt his hands firmly but gently enclose her waist as he propelled her up the hill.

"March," he instructed. "Less talking and more walking."

"Ash," she tried again, then gave up.

He was insistently propelling her forward, and if she didn't pick up her feet, she was going to land face-down in the mud. That was enough of an incentive. They covered the second half of the climb a lot faster.

Ash flopped down on the wall when they arrived at the patio. "Go try the door," he panted.

"What if I get sucked inside and it locks behind me?" She made a face at him, but his only response was to wave her forward.

She pulled the door open and breathed in stale air filled with aromas of wood, acidic wine and what well could be mold. Not exactly inviting, but definitely far from the fire and brimstone she had conjured up.

"Come on," she told Ash. "You were so eager, let's get on with the tour."

"What if I stand right inside the door while you walk around?" Ash got up slowly, apparently reluctant to leave his seat.

"I saw a couple of chairs inside the door before we got chased out last time. You can sit and rest."

Ash rolled his eyes. "We weren't chased, Sunny. But I will say that caretaker does a good job of deterring visitors."

"He does, and I've already seen too much of his grumpy self. He had to have been told we were coming, or he wouldn't have unlocked the tasting room. But why did he decide to lurk around the creek and ask if we were looking for Giuseppe's ghost?"

"Probably hoping to scare us off. Well, you, anyway." Ash joined her at the doorway.

"I was startled, not frightened." She stood back. "Why don't you go inside first?"

"I doubt I'm the one the spirits want to communicate with." Ash thumbed his nose at her, but he did step inside ahead of her.

Once Sunny's eyes adjusted to the gloom, she noted a lot of furniture piled against a rustic wall of wooden planks. A small stage in the far corner must have been constructed for visiting musicians. Stools ringed the crescent-shaped bar, which tapered to a point before an arch, above which was an illuminated exit sign.

"I'll see what's up front." Ash pointed toward the arch. "You're sure you'll be okay here alone?"

"I'm not getting any bad vibes." She wasn't sure what she was getting. Beneath her feet, the floor gently vibrated.

Ash walked away. Their muddy boots were leaving footprints on the hardwood floor. That would be certain to displease the caretaker. Willing extraneous thoughts from her mind, Sunny closed her eyes and opened her arms wide. Faint sounds of Ash's footsteps echoed around the cavernous space.

Sunny sensed a busy environment. Laughter, light banter. Clinking glasses. An occasional cork popping. Faint music. All normal sounds of a public place. She tried diving deeper into her subconscious. Superfluous sounds receded. A deep male voice dominated several others, but his words remained muffled, indistinguishable. Men and women at the back of the room murmured, low key. A deep discussion, perhaps, more than a disagreement? Sunny tried harder to fine-tune the words.

Her effort paid off. Very loud and very clear, a deep male voice told her to "Get out!"

Startled, she pulled back from her trance. An impression of shadows receded, but not before she made out several outlines. Who *were* those figures? Could they be the dead Taricanis or someone else? Maybe even Valderos, lurking in the shadows.

"Ash?" She heard the panic in her voice.

She listened for his footsteps, but heard only rain heavily beating against the windows behind her. She reluctantly turned to look through the panoramic display of glass at yet another squall moving across the vineyard.

Thinking Ash must be out of earshot, she followed his muddy footprints. Voices came to her, and they didn't belong to spirits. One was low and well-modulated…Ash's. The other belonged to a male with a higher pitch. They were approaching, and she didn't want to appear anxious, so she hurried over to stand in front of the bar.

"I'm sure you can understand how difficult this has been on all of us," said the other man. "The last thing I expected was to become heir to a vineyard, winery, or whatever you choose to call this place. I know zip about growing grapes, much less turning them into wine. And there's something going on with the stuff that's fermenting in the basement. Or aging. I don't know the difference between the two. Not really interested in finding out, either. Selling to Mr. Valderos would be a big relief, but I'm the only one who sees it that way. The rest of the family, well, they think I should bankrupt myself for the sake of the Taricani name. They tell me its indistinguishable from their legacy of great wines. Personally, I always thought the tannins in their Pinot Noir made it bitter. Undrinkable. But then, I'm no connoisseur. I prefer beer. The only way I could make this place pay for itself is to rip out those vines and plant apple trees. Bring more cider into the mix. This area's oversaturated with inferior wines. The Dundee Hills produce better wines, and their wineries are more popular. McMinnville's bigger than Dallas, and it has a lot more retail shops and restaurants."

The man strolled into the tasting room ahead of Ash. He saw Sunny and came to an abrupt stop. "Is this your partner, Mr. Haines?" Without waiting for confirmation, he strode over to Sunny, right hand extended. "Thank you so much for coming here today. Mr. Valderos sent the right people to represent him." He grabbed Sunny's hand and pumped it enthusiastically.

She didn't like it. In fact, she didn't like him. But was that because someone was whispering ever so quietly in her ear, telling her *not* to like him? Or was it because he reminded her of Mark, both in build and manner? Mark, who would stride up to strangers and show himself eager to meet them. It was a marketing technique he had successfully transitioned into working in local government. Word was, Mark was on a fast track to the governor's office.

She plastered a fake smile on her face. "Are you Mr. Hixton?"

"I am." Hixton grinned. "Call me Bill."

"Don't trust him," whispered the voice.

CHAPTER ELEVEN

Sunny decided that close-up, Bill Hixton's resemblance to Mark was slight. For one thing, his eyes were brown, while Mark's were blue. His hair, flopping boyishly over his forehead, was loaded with some kind of hair product that kept it anchored in place. The result resembled royal icing that had been piped into a wave that ended with a defined point.

His nose was bulbous at the tip, and when he smiled at her, she noticed a small chip at one corner of his left upper front tooth. Above his lips, a thin moustache fluttered, like a trapped winged insect. She pulled her hand out of his grip.

"So good to meet you both." Hixton stepped back a few paces so he could shift his attention from one visitor to the other. "I was told you were coming today. Mr. Valderos's attorney spoke with my attorney. You know how attorneys are…always communicating." His smile focused on Sunny.

"We understood we'd have the vineyard and tasting room to ourselves," Ash said. "We encountered the caretaker by the creek, and now you're here."

"To answer any questions you might have." Hixton's smile faded, to be replaced by nodding that continued unabated while he assured them, "As the winery's owner, I should be here to greet visitors."

"If you were selling a house, you wouldn't expect to remain in it while prospective buyers toured through." Ash's tone was dry and matter-of-fact. "If you felt uncomfortable leaving us unsupervised inside the building, why didn't you suggest having your attorney meet us here?"

Hixton flushed. "I didn't speak with him personally. His secretary emailed me. I thought you'd like me to be here. I wasn't able to meet with Mr. Valderos yesterday. I felt bad about that. It's a muddy mess down by the creek. There are a couple of ATVs in the maintenance shed, so you could have ridden down, not walked. I should have told Mr. Valderos, but he's not the easiest person to reach, let alone communicate with directly."

Sunny thought Valderos probably wanted to keep his distance as much as possible. His appearance wouldn't be reassuring to an anxious property owner. Sending the two members of his team who actually looked 'normal' allowed him keep his involvement low key while information was gathered.

"Why don't you show us the rest of the premises?" Ash asked Hixton.

"I'd be delighted." Hixton offered his arm to Sunny.

She ignored the arm. The whispering voice continued to hover nearby. "Lead the way," she told their host, whose moustache was fluttering like the insect had flown into a wind tunnel. "We'll follow."

"Very well." Hixton lowered his arm, disappointment plainly written on his face.

As they walked through the cavernous space of the tasting room, he explained how Lorenzo's renovations had vaulted the ceiling, enlarged the original tasting room, and added three sets of double doors without, in his opinion, a thought for how those changes would adversely affect heating and air-conditioning costs.

As he segued into an explanation of how all the barrels of wine aging away in the basement had been declared 'not ready' for bottling by more than one expert vintner, Sunny took Ash's arm. She successfully tuned out their talkative host and allowed her mind to drift. A constant hum of low voices accompanied them through the vestibule. The hum continued at an even lower volume while they toured several private rooms designed for small parties, followed by the office spaces. She was unable to detect any words.

At the end of a narrow passageway, they came to a door. Hixton pulled out a key and unlocked it. Sunny surfaced from her half-trance.

"The barrels are down there." He flipped a switch. Stark whiteness from fluorescent tubes illuminated a set of steep stairs. Dampness mingled with an odor closer to vinegar than wine. He tapped a wooden rail on the wall. "Hold on, and watch your step. I've almost fallen down here a few times. Sorry about the smell. Personally, I think those so-called experts were wrong about the wine needing more time to ferment, or whatever the process is. I think it may be rancid. If so, I'll have to get rid of it."

Several of the fluorescent tubes flickered.

Hixton gave a nervous laugh. "I hate basements. They're always filled with spiders."

Ash turned to Sunny. "Do you want me to go first or follow you?"

"I'll be right behind you." She already felt a wave of anger rising from the cellar. She wasn't sure whether it was directed at Hixton or all of them.

Ash slowly followed Hixton's halting descent. Sunny placed one hand on Ash's shoulder, the other on the wall, and stepped down. The stairway, made of what looked like whitewashed concrete, felt slick. Cold and damp air covered her like a heavy blanket. Impressions came to her of men hauling barrels and crates up and down the steps. Odors of old sweat and fermenting wine threatened to gag her. Underlying angry murmurs ebbed and flowed. She interpreted them as residual memories of everyday disagreements between people working in tight spaces underground.

Arriving in the cellar, Hixton flipped more switches on a large wall-panel. Lines of barrels came into view below a low ceiling. Crates stacked floor to ceiling. Bottles, some empty, many full, standing upright on the floor.

"I closed up the cellar after I found out the wine wasn't ready," Hixton said. "No point in wasting electricity, and it always stays cool down here, or so I've been told, even in summer."

"It should." Hands in pockets, Ash gazed around. "Basements or cellars usually do stay cool, and this one was probably built with wine storage in mind." He left Sunny standing at the bottom of the stairs and walked over to check out the rows of barrels. "How much wine is down here, do you think?"

Hixton shrugged. "A lot. But since nothing's ready for bottling, if Mr. Valderos is in a hurry to use this cellar as an adjunct to his own, he'd have to dump the wine and have all the barrels cleaned out…sterilized or whatever's needed. I've already sold all the bottles. They're supposed to be hauled out of here by a private recycling company in two weeks."

TAINTED LEGACY

"Why in the world would you do that?" Ash asked. "The buyer's going to have to factor in replacing them as well as everything else needed down here. That's a big additional expense."

Hixton shrugged. "Everything in the price is negotiable, Mr. Haines. With a soil treatment, a new vintner, and this cellar made usable again, the winery could be operating in, say, three years. Or the place could be turned into event space much faster. Weddings, anniversaries, reunions, that type of thing. The basement would be more useful if it became storage for tables, chairs, canopies, seasonal decorations…whatever events needed."

The lights flickered again. Somewhere deep in the cellar, something crashed to the floor. The rancid odor intensified.

Hixton gave another nervous laugh. "A barrel must have fallen. A little additional cleanup to be done." One of the fluorescents buzzed loudly before going dark. "And apparently, some electrical work, too." He edged back toward the stairs. "There's a bargain to be had, here. Mr. Valderos will have everything he needs for his expansion. My advice to him is to till under all those useless grapevines and lay sod. Develop the event angle. But I understand he's only interested in purchasing another winery."

"Yeah, that's what he told us, too." Ash tapped several of the barrels closest to him. "Are all these full?"

"I haven't checked, but I was told they are. Like I said, I don't like coming down here. I did have a winemaker give his opinion. He told me the wine's got some sort of bacteria. Even I could have figured that out from the smell. He said everything has to go and the place needs fumigating. Another couple of vintners had different opinions. One said the wine already bottled was drinkable. The other gave me a price for treating the bacteria. Too high, when I weighed that price against disposal of the wine and selling all the equipment."

"Those vines must have produced at some time, or all these barrels wouldn't be full. How long ago was that…one year? Two?"

"No idea." Hixton hopped from one foot to the other. "You'd have to ask my cousins…Arturo or Sophia. He owns a winery. She's the one who wanted to inherit this place. She studied someplace in Europe and is supposed to know how to run the business."

He walked up to Sunny. So close, he crowded her. It was evident he wanted to leave the cellar. Maybe because he'd decided he'd talked to Valderos's team members enough for one day. But she felt his reason had more to do with an undercurrent of animosity that had built to such a degree, it had become difficult for her to take a deep breath. If she didn't step aside, she thought Hixton might elbow her out of the way.

"Wine's a man's business" Hixton pronounced. "Giuseppe's words, echoed by Lorenzo when the will was read." He started up the stairs, climbing a lot faster than he'd descended. "Let's get out of here," he called. "This place gives me the creeps."

Ash raised his eyebrows. Sunny shrugged. She was as ready to leave the cellar as their host. She gripped the rail. It vibrated. Sunny ran up the stairs. She heard Ash's footsteps behind her.

Hixton closed and locked the door as soon as they were all out of the stairwell. He held out his hand first to Sunny, and after a brief handshake, to Ash. "Thanks for coming. Let me see you out." He strode ahead and opened the front door as they stepped into the reception area. "Mr. Valderos can contact me through my attorney if he's still interested in buying. If not, then I'm ready to put this place on the auction block." He ushered them outside

When Sunny looked back, Hixton was walking under the archway, presumably on his way to lock the back door. His car, a dark grey Lexus, was parked alongside Ash's Range Rover. Sunny wondered whether Hixton owned it or had borrowed it from his used car lot.

"What a waste of time." Ash unlocked the SUV "We didn't learn much we didn't know, except Hixton hates spiders and wants to sell his inheritance as soon as he can find a buyer."

"It wasn't a complete loss," Sunny told him. "The spirits here don't like the new owner. Neither does the wine."

CHAPTER TWELVE

Sunny's phone rang as Ash was about to ask her to clarify her comment about the wine not liking Bill Hixton.

"On our way," she told the caller before turning to Ash, who was wondering whether Hixton had gone back down to the wine cellar, because lights were blazing from glass block windows just above ground level.

"That was Armenta. They're swamped. I need to get back to the shop ASAP," Sunny said.

"It won't take long." Ash backed up and turned. He spotted the caretaker standing at the corner of the building. The old man watched them leave before continuing on his way. "You're right about that guy," he told Sunny after they were bumping and bouncing their way back down the uneven driveway. "He *is* downright disturbing."

"Who, Hixton?" She was brushing her hair.

"No, the caretaker. Didn't see him standing in the shadows?"

"I didn't. I guess I was still thinking about Armenta's call." Sunny pulled down the visor and grimaced at her reflection after they bounced from uneven gravel onto paved road. "I look like a goth."

"You look fine," Ash said.

He thought she always looked good, even when she wasn't wearing makeup. She had a flawless complexion and silky hair. So different from the women he'd always been attracted to. Especially Caroline, who always looked like she'd just come from back-to-back sessions with a makeup artist and hairstylist. Caroline spent hours on her appearance. Sunny could be ready to go in five minutes or less; an attribute he really appreciated about her.

"I need lipstick. I don't want to arrive looking like I belong in the Halloween display." She opened her shoulder bag. "Can you give me a minute before you turn onto the highway?"

"Don't you think you'd be good for business?" He grinned when she gave him a playful smack on the arm.

He thought about asking if she was expecting Mark to drop by, but decided against it. Bringing Sunny's ex into the conversation could potentially take all the pleasure from their lighthearted exchange. They deserved a break in the tension that always accompanied their work…their paranormal investigations. Ash mentally shook off the derisive thoughts that continued to plague him about how low he, a former Portland Police Bureau robbery detective, had sunk to become a member of such a weird team. Sunny broke into his painful internal monologue.

"I hate to ruin the moment," she said, "but I need to change the subject." She had found her lipstick and held it up, like she was about to conduct an orchestra. "What are your impressions of the Taricani Winery's new owner?"

"That he wanted to get us out the door as fast as possible. I don't think it was because he had another appointment…my take is he'd rather be anywhere but inside that building." Ash applied the brakes and coasted to a stop before taking a right onto Hwy 22. "Gussy-up fast," he told her. "There's a break in traffic."

Sunny gave both lips a quick swipe. "Go," she said, before checking the results. "I think I smudged it, but whatever."

Ash turned, accelerated, and headed back toward Salem. "You'll have time to check your looks in better lighting when we reach downtown," he said. "I never make all the lights."

"I suppose." Sunny closed her purse and pushed up the visor. "Hixton couldn't wait to get out of the wine cellar. The atmosphere down there was thick with animosity."

"Even *I* knew something was off. Nothing specific. You think he's an empath?"

"No; I didn't get an inkling that he had any kind of psychic gift. But all

TAINTED LEGACY

the energy of the spirits was focused on him. Even the most earthbound people get vibes if the concentration's strong enough."

"That explains why the air felt charged."

A cold draft crept across Ash's shoulders. An involuntary glance into the rearview mirror showed only empty back seats. Ash relaxed the tension in his shoulders and told himself he was an idiot for wondering whether they had gained a spectral passenger.

"That was even more disturbing than seeing the caretaker again," he remarked, uncomfortable with a sudden silence that had developed, broken only by the purr of the Rover's engine. He glanced at Sunny. She was looking out the window as they sped past the exit for Independence. Brightly-lit buildings began to populate both sides of the road as he drove past the outskirts of West Salem.

"He was so nervous, he couldn't stop talking," she said.

"Yeah, I had difficulty getting a word in, and I'm usually a skilled interrogator." Ash ran a hand over his chin and felt stubble beneath his fingers. "He didn't need to be there. He could've gotten the caretaker to show us around. If Vinnie didn't go through a realtor, I wonder how he even found out about the winery being for sale?"

Sunny abandoned her window-gazing to give him a long look. "Come on, Ash...you're talking about Valderos. He knows anything he wants to."

Ash shrugged. "I guess." He wasn't convinced Valderos hadn't heard about the vineyard from some other source than the supernatural. But could he see a demon joining the local chamber of commerce or participating in an association of local winery owners?

They both lapsed back into silence until Ash joined thick traffic streaming over the Center Street Bridge, which crossed the Willamette River in an easterly direction. He eased into the center lane, avoiding a long line of cars taking the off-ramp to Martin Luther King Parkway and the route to I-5. "Sometimes, I really envy Valderos's abilities," he said. "Then I remind myself he's a demon."

Sunny gave a murmur of disagreement. "A demon who has never hurt us, although he's threatened to."

"Speak for yourself. I've been frozen to the spot too many times to feel charitable."

"Armenta and I had that experience once. It wasn't fun, but I didn't feel any residual effects." Sunny rummaged around in her purse. "Mints?" She held up a box of Tic Tacs and shook it.

Ash held out his hand and she dropped several of the small mints into his palm. He sucked on them as they cruised through an ever-changing landscape of new construction that hoped to revitalize Salem's core with upscale apartments in addition to the retail, bars and restaurants that had sustained it in the past.

"We're not going to get into an argument over who felt what," he said, taking a left onto Broadway. "I know you're stressed. I can help out at the shop. I don't have any other plans apart from figuring out what to eat for dinner."

Sunny lightly squeezed his forearm. "Thanks, Ash. I never turn down your help, although I think I should be paying you."

"No, you shouldn't. You've got two part-timers on the books now. How's that working out for your bottom line?"

"We're making payroll, managing to order new merchandise, and keeping the lights on. I think that may be the best I can hope for, given the square footage of the shop."

"You need to take over the lease for the other part of the building," he said. "It's time to expand."

She clasped her purse against her chest, like she needed it as a shield. "I'm so afraid of getting in over my head. I've done the math. Expansion would allow me to offer a larger selection of merchandise and give me the space to bring in other diviners. Armenta likes her exclusivity, but there are other types of readings. I'd like to be able to offer those." Sunny shifted in her seat. "I don't want any charlatans. Armenta's gifts are real."

"She's still trying to read my tea leaves," Ash said. "I'd like to suggest we move away from loose teas to tea bags, but they don't have the flavor."

Sunny laughed. "I can imagine how upset Armenta would be if you brought in tea bags you'd purchased at a grocery store. She orders from a couple of suppliers. She won't even give me their names. Sometimes, she lets me reimburse her, but not very often."

"She won't tell you where she's getting the wolfsbane and other mind-altering concoctions?" Ash chuckled.

"Armenta would never serve you anything containing wolfsbane," Sunny told him. "As for hallucinogens, I'm not sure. I still don't know what's in that green tea...the one that swirls."

"I hope I never have to find out. I'd probably keel over on the spot."

The little parking lot outside The House of Serenity was full. Cars lined both sides of Norway. Ash turned off Capitol onto Jefferson and parked on the street, almost a block away from the shop.

"I've got a proposition for you," he told her as they walked back at a brisk pace. "I was planning to ask you over dinner, but since Vinnie's coming for an update, and you're worried about your future, I don't want to wait any longer, especially after you said you don't think you can afford to expand." He stopped her with a hand on her arm. "What about taking me on as a partner?"

Sunny's face was illuminated by a street lamp. She looked shocked.

Worried over her reaction, Ash plowed on. "Think about it," he urged. "I'll front the money for your expansion. You'd solve your space issues, and you know you'd be able to improve your sales figures. I'm not that hard to get along with. I already help out in the shop, and I'd like to continue doing that. I swear I wouldn't interfere, except we'd have to make financial decisions together, and if I really thought you were about to do something risky, we'd have to discuss it. I'd have a business manager draw up a contract. No surprises. No hidden clauses."

Sunny opened her mouth, but no sound came out.

"I'll keep out of Armenta's corner. She can stay right where she is," Ash assured her. "We'll work around her with the expansion. You can have your separate areas for new palmists, or whatever specialty you think would do well in the shop. You can hire Stella full-time. She needs the job. She's spread too thin working at that healthcare facility half the week and spending the rest at The House of Serenity. She's studying under Armenta, and she looks really tired. Belinda's going to be leaving after she graduates in the spring. You could hire another full-timer, or a part-timer if you trust me enough to work the rest of the hours."

Sunny found her voice, but it sounded distinctly shaky. "Ash…I really don't know what to say." She looked more than shocked. Astonished didn't really do justice to her expression, with her wide eyes and pale cheeks.

"You're not going to have to give me a decision right this minute," he said. "We'll talk more about it tomorrow. This is the first time I've ever heard Armenta ask you to come back because she can't manage by herself."

They hurried across the street toward the brightly-lit shop. "She's never said that," Sunny agreed. "They *must* be swamped. Look at all these cars." Then she looked through the front window. "Oh, no." She groaned. "Stella's at the register. That means Armenta has a client and can't supervise her. There were two openings on Armenta's schedule. She must have filled them before a rush started."

"I wonder customers haven't left their merchandise and walked out," Ash said. "Stella should have mastered that new register by now."

"What can I say?" Sunny broke into a jog. "Stella panics when the line builds up, but she's great manning the floor."

"Maybe I'll take back that comment about her becoming a full-time employee." Ash opened the door and waved her inside ahead of him.

Sunny gave him a brief smile. "You're right…let's talk more about this tomorrow." She hurried over to join Stella behind the counter.

Ash walked the aisles, helping shoppers retrieve items from higher shelves. He brought several orders out of the storeroom for regular customers, who then joined the line for the register. At least that line was growing smaller as Sunny deftly rang up purchases. Stella kept a smile frozen to her face. She thanked customers for their patience and wrapped their merchandise in her haphazard way. The line dwindled to five people within 10 minutes. The majority of shoppers left with several bags in hand. The Halloween area looked like a swarm of locusts had attacked it.

Ash entered the gargoyle corner at 5:50 PM and spotted Watcher on the highest shelf. He wondered whether the gryphon had left his usual spot on the counter because he couldn't handle any more of Stella's ineptitude, or her stress.

He still had trouble talking to Watcher, even after seeing how animated the concrete statue could become. Watcher defied the laws of gravity, physics, and a normal person's belief in what was real. Hearing rustling above, Ash involuntarily ducked. He straightened up to find Watcher had coasted down to a lower shelf and was staring him right in the face.

"So, you're a mind-reader, too?" he asked, before he could stop himself.

Watcher spread his wings, stretched a leg, and gave a soft caw.

"And I'm talking to you as well, now." Ash ran both hands through his hair, which he was relieved to find wasn't sticking straight up.

Watcher took off, wheeling soundlessly above the gargoyle corner before weaving his way through the exposed support beams to hover over the counter. As the last two shoppers moved up to Sunny and Stella, he landed close to the door and folded his wings neatly across his back. Ash watched, enthralled by the huge beast's graceful flight. No one else in the shop even noticed.

It was 5:56 PM. Ash hurried out of the gargoyle corner. Sunny followed the last customer to the front door. Stella grabbed her purse and coat from a hook inside the apartment, said goodbye and followed the customer outside. Sunny locked the door and turned the sign from Open to Closed as the two remaining cars left the parking lot. Ash turned off the neon sign in the window and all the shop lights except those above the center aisle.

"Armenta's brewing tea," Sunny told him. "Let's join her."

The front door flew open, and Vincente Valderos strode into the shop. It was precisely 6:00 PM.

CHAPTER THIRTEEN

"Good evening, Vincente," Armenta called from the back of the shop. She held the apartment door open. "I've brewed the tea."

"Good evening, Ms. Kaslov." Valderos removed his gloves, then his hat. He handed them to Sunny, like she was his valet. Unbuttoning his coat, he strode through the store. "Come, Ms. Kingston and Mr. Haines. There is much to discuss."

Sunny looked at Ash. He motioned her to go first. Wafting from Valderos's coat, the odor of mothballs mixed with a strong smell of dampness and a hint of something even more unpleasant. Sunny was reminded instantly of a cemetery. She'd visited Tina's grave the week before. Squatting down to place fresh flowers in the vase, she'd smelled something uncomfortably close to Valderos's coat, or was it Valderos, himself?

Water dripped from his coat and left a trail of droplets. She couldn't understand why his coat had become completely soaked during the short walk from his limo.

"My vehicle had a slight accident." Valderos removed his coat.

He handed it off to Sunny. It was so heavy, she almost dropped it. Ash grabbed it before it fell to the floor.

"I had to transport myself," Valderos said. "My teleportation skills, as you call them, are not up to par. I materialized in the middle of a busy intersection and was almost hit by a delivery truck. I became very wet." He sounded affronted. "A woman tried to give me money to buy a sandwich."

"It's the coat," Ash said. He dragged a chair in front of the space heater and hung Valderos's coat over it.

"What is wrong with my coat? It is of excellent quality. Burberry. Cashmere. Custom-made."

"When, back in the 1920's?" Ash asked.

"When, is not important." Valderos made a disturbing sound Sunny thought might be either a growl or a snort of disgust.

"You should really keep it in cold storage at a furrier's when you're not using it." Ash wrinkled his nose. "Mothballs went out of fashion years ago."

"Moths do not know that." Valderos sat down at the table as though he was settling onto a bench in front of a concert grand piano.

Sunny could almost envision him lifting the tailcoat. Then two other images floated into her mind: a forked tail and a trident. It took a lot of effort to force them aside.

"Ms. Kaslov, what flavors of tea have you brewed this evening?" Valderos asked.

"A yerba mate for you, Vincente, a lemongrass ginger for Sunny, and Oolong." She smiled at Ash when he joined them at the table. "I made the Oolong for you, Ash, in case you don't like these new blends."

Valderos leaned toward the steam rising from three teapots and visibly drew all three streams into his long, thin nose. "Delightful," he pronounced.

Sunny had often wondered whether Valderos breathed before she'd observed him blowing his nose when he'd caught a cold. But she'd never seen anyone inhale hot steam with such a forceful intake of air. Armenta had taken a seat on the pillow-topped packing crate. Sunny listened to a whisper in her mind that told her to take no chances. She left the other seat next to Valderos for Ash and sat across from their demon leader.

They stayed silent while the various teas were poured. Ash opted for the Oolong, presented to him in a cup decorated by anemones. Armenta joined Valderos in drinking yerba mate. Sunny cradled her lemongrass ginger between both hands, relishing the warmth filtering through the china. Her cup was covered with forget-me-nots. A large open tin of cookies occupied the center of the table.

"To accompany these herbal blended teas, I made honey, orange, ginger and cardamom cookies today," Armenta said.

Valderos flicked his index finger. The onyx ring with the white skull glinted. The cookie tin rose several inches from the table. "Ms. Kingston?" The tin sailed to her.

He was using magic more and more, Sunny told herself. Had he become too impatient with doing things the mortal way, or had he become more powerful? She took 2 cookies. They smelled so delicious, she actually wanted three. Another cookie wafted over to her napkin before the tin hovered in front of Ash. He waved it away.

"Would you prefer chocolate chip cookies?" Armenta asked.

"Are they in your bag?" Ash asked.

She nodded.

"Then, yes. Thank you." He got up and fetched the tin.

Sunny bit into her cookie. It was beyond scrumptious. Armenta had never baked such an exotic combination. Sunny wondered whether Ash didn't like the sound of the ingredients, or he refused to touch anything affected by Valderos's magic. She watched Valderos lift his cup and take a sip. The saucer had delicate single pink wild roses. The Eglantine rose, or Sweet Briar. She remembered Armenta telling her that particular rose was the favorite flower of demons. Her stomach knotted, and she put down her cookie. When had Armenta bought new cups, and why would she have purchased one specially decorated for Valderos?

Beside Armenta's thistle-decorated cup and saucer sat a pink box. She opened the lid and took out a donut. "Thank you, Vincente," she said. "You are most kind."

Valderos waved away the compliment. "I passed the shop on my walk." When he said "my walk" his orange aura pulsed with red overtones.

He was definitely upset, Sunny thought. His remark about having to walk from downtown showed as well as told that his powers were either still off, or had perhaps been permanently impaired by his unfortunate relationship with Valentine, his lover during Sunny and Ash's previous case. She pushed aside memories of walking in on Valderos entwined with Valentine. Months later, those recollections remained the stuff of nightmares. Unwelcome images of tentacles floated around in her mind…

"Ms. Kingston!"

Valderos's commanding voice snapped Sunny back to reality. "Yes," she said. "I'm listening."

"Now, yes. Before, you were not." His eyes blazed.

Sunny fought the impulse to recoil. She reminded herself never to show weakness. Never to let him get the upper hand. She was convinced it would always end badly for mortals.

"You have my full attention," she told him and gratefully watched the red tones vanish from his aura.

"Then you will recount your impressions of the vineyard and tasting room," Valderos said. "And do not leave anything out. I am not in the mood for window-dressing."

CHAPTER FOURTEEN

Sunny took a big sip of her tea. Scalding hot, it burned her tongue. Could the heat from Valderos's glare have affected the water's temperature? Although her first impulse was to spit tea all over the table, she swallowed and tried to ignore the burning sensation gliding down her throat. Ash looked concerned. He got up and handed her a small wad of paper napkins on his way to way to the refrigerator. When he returned, he handed her a bottle of water.

She drank deeply, the cold water easing the pain in her scorched throat. "Is that caretaker human?" she asked, dabbing her mouth with the napkins.

"What caretaker?" Valderos's dark eyebrows rose. "There is no caretaker. There is no need. All buildings are locked."

"He was definitely there," Ash confirmed. "We encountered him in the tasting room after you left. Yesterday, he was carrying a big roll of barbed wire and told us he was mending a fence after deer broke through. But then he disappeared and left the wire behind."

"Where was this?" Valderos paused, his cup halfway to his mouth. His pupils had become narrow slits.

"Beside the creek. We went back down there yesterday. Sunny wanted to see if she could connect with Giuseppe's spirit when she wasn't being interrupted."

"I never interrupt." Valderos's tone had lowered. So had the lights.

"Ash meant that I wanted to be alone," Sunny quickly clarified.

The lights brightened. Relieved, she stopped Ash from continuing the story by tapping his thigh under the table. He looked surprised, but didn't interrupt when she plowed on.

"I thought I saw a shadow the day before," she told Valderos. "I saw it behind the rain when we were all there together, but it wasn't substantial enough to communicate, or was too fearful. I thought maybe yesterday's rain and seeing me alone might make it manifest in a more substantial form. I believe it was hovering on the opposite bank of the creek, but then that caretaker came out of the bushes, and it vanished."

"Hmm." Valderos put down his cup. "I will speak with the owner about this."

"I'll do it," Ash said. "We met him, yesterday, too. I'd like to talk more with him. He rushed us out before we got to see much of the wine cellar."

"That was the most interesting part of our little tour, too." Sunny had finished her water. She went to the refrigerator and took out another bottle. Her throat felt raw; so did her tongue.

"Does the owner even want to sell the property?" Armenta asked. "He seems less than cooperative and obviously doesn't know how to deal with his staff." She turned to Sunny. "Were you able to get anything useful?"

Sunny shrugged. "Voices. Lots of them. Partying on the patio and in the tasting room. But only murmuring indistinctly."

"That wasn't the most enlightening part of your experiences," Ash said. "What you said when we left…"

Sunny pinched his thigh that time. She spoke into the void. "…was that we have to go back, and Hixton and his caretaker need to make themselves scarce next time."

Valderos looked suspicious. His dark brows had met in the middle, creating a long slash across his pale forehead. His eyes remained black slits. She tried to block any infiltration of her innermost thoughts. She hated his mind-reading and silently told him to get out of her head. When one of his eyebrows quivered momentarily, she knew he'd gotten the message.

"We definitely need to go back," Ash concurred. "I'll give Hixton a pass for being at the winery yesterday. He was probably curious about the prospective buyer. But the caretaker confronted us like we were trespassers. He's got to back off."

"I specifically asked that you were not to be disturbed in any way. Hixton's attorney agreed to this." Valderos drummed his fingers on the table. "I want to know the name of the caretaker."

"That makes two of us." Ash leaned back and folded his arms across his chest. "He wouldn't tell us. Something weird is going on at that vineyard. I'll do more research on Hixton. He has no prior convictions or history of risky behavior. He's the eldest son of Lorenzo's sister, Lucia. Wasn't expecting to inherit anything. I couldn't find any information that he'd ever visited his uncle or the winery. He says he knows zip about the wine business. No wonder he wants to sell."

"Why would he need to know about zippers?" Valderos levitated the teapot decorated with lilies of the valley. "More tea, Ms. Kaslov?"

"Thank you, Vincente." She smiled sweetly at him as the teapot glided over to refill her cup. "Do have another cookie."

"I will. Perhaps two." He gave her a long look.

Sunny thought it was disturbingly long. Armenta held his gaze. She didn't appear disturbed by his slitted pupils. Sunny cleared her scratchy throat. "Ash wasn't talking about zippers," she told Valderos. "It's an expression. It means nada, zilch."

"He knows nothing," Ash said, when Valderos turned his attention from Armenta to stare at Sunny.

"Ah. Another of those strange terms you humans are so fond of using." Valderos grimaced. "I have never kept up with these unnecessary words or phrases."

"I bet you've heard a ton of them through the ages," Ash said. "Probably back to Roman times…or earlier."

Valderos really did snort that time. "How old do you think I am?"

"Pretty damned old," Ash responded. He took another chocolate chip cookie and bit into it.

"And you are pretty damned rude." Valderos's aura was glowing red, again.

"Now, now, gentlemen." Armenta waved her napkin. "Please call a truce. We need a game plan for tomorrow. It's Friday, one of our busiest days. Sunny, you're not thinking of leaving again, are you?"

"I'm not." Sunny turned to Ash. "Are you going to use the day for more research?"

"No, I'll come here." He rubbed his chin. "The shipment arrives early in the morning. It's a big one, so I'll be kept busy trying to fit everything into the storeroom."

"Thanks for taking care of that for us." Sunny felt guilty about pinching him. "I'll try to send Stella back to help you."

"The shop. The storeroom. Everything comes before my needs." Valderos didn't sound at all pleased. "Remember the terms of the contract."

"I know I speak for Sunny as well when I say we *never* forget the contract," Ash told him. "However, us mortals have to work for a living, and Sunny can't do everything herself. She and Armenta work long hours. I'm splitting my day between the case and helping them out so we can get back to the winery as soon as *humanly* possible."

The corner of Valderos's mouth drew up into a sneer.

"I can go back to the winery on Saturday," Ash said. "I'll call Hixton tomorrow morning and arrange a meeting, so I can pump him for more information."

"*I* will call and arrange for your visit," Valderos insisted. "I will also speak with the attorney." Valderos sounded like neither man would be happy afterward. He drank down his tea, wrapped three of the orange cardamom cookies up in his paper napkin, and stood. "I must start my journey back."

"How? On foot?" Ash got up, too. "I'll drive you."

"Most kind." Valderos bowed before putting on his coat. His hat flew silently from one of the pegs on the wall and settled itself on his head. His gloves slipped into a pocket.

"Sunny, I'll call when I get home." Ash took his coat from a peg and put on his hat. "To let you know I made it back from Oak Grove."

"Really, Mr. Haines, do you believe I would make you vanish after you performed a favor for me?" Valderos tucked his cookies into a coat pocket, took out his gloves and pulled them on.

"Vinnie, I can believe anything where you're concerned." Ash opened the back door. A torrential downpour had overflowed the gutters. A stream of water shot down to a storm drain. "Can you make the rain stop?" he asked.

"Mr. Haines, your belief in my powers is truly gratifying, but I assure you I have no ability to dry out the entire Salem area. If I did, do you think I would have been wet when I arrived here?"

"No, but maybe you can't teleport and affect the weather at the same time." Ash jiggled the keys in his pocket. "Say goodbye to the ladies, Vinnie."

Valderos bowed to Sunny and Armenta. "Good evening. I will plan to meet with you, Ms. Kingston, as well as Mr. Haines, at the winery on Sunday morning. Mr. Haines, you will report the results of your meeting with Mr. Hixton."

"Armenta will make sure we have all the protection we need for both trips," Ash assured Valderos before they headed outside

"I am sure she will." Valderos paused briefly to tip his hat to Armenta.

The door closed by itself. The Kit-Cat Klock on the wall let out a loud meow. Sunny jumped. Armenta spilled her tea.

"This will be a difficult case," Armenta said.

"That's a prediction I'm not betting against." Sunny brought over a teacloth and dropped it onto the seeping liquid.

The spilled tea continued to roll across the tablecloth as though it was determined to reach Armenta. She pointed a bony finger toward the fast-moving liquid. "That's far enough."

The tea immediately stopped rolling.

CHAPTER FIFTEEN

After assuring Armenta she didn't need to stay and help clean up after the tea party, Sunny closed and locked the door behind the seer. It had been a long, strange day, she thought, relishing her alone-time. Even stranger than usual, although the usual was never, well, *normal.* She piled all the dishes in the sink and closed the lids on the cookies before she gave into temptation. The tea-stained cloth went into the bathtub to soak in cold water and a generous amount of soap.

How she wished for a washer and dryer. The hamper was already full, and she couldn't get to the laundromat until Monday, her only day off. She had used Ash's laundry room on occasion, but knew he wouldn't want her and her washing underfoot on one of his two weekends a month with Katie. They both cherished their time together. Sunny respected that, and always tried to give them the space they needed.

Unfortunately, Valderos and his dictates frequently interfered with any plans. She'd had to refuse an invitation from Mark to join him at an early Halloween get-together with his coworkers Saturday evening. She still wasn't sure she'd really wanted to go. Their dinners had been cordial, friendly, and ended with a quick kiss from Mark that she made sure landed on her cheek. Accompanying him to a party sounded more like an actual date. Sunny wasn't at all sure she was ready for that kind of commitment.

Deciding she wasn't ready to mull over solutions to her on-again, off-again relationship with her ex, she shifted her focus back to the winery investigation. If they were going back to Dallas on Sunday, surely Ash wouldn't take Katie?

Sunny wondered whether he'd drop his daughter off at her mother's home earlier than usual or bring Katie to the shop.

Katie loved to help out at The House of Serenity. She worked the register better than Stella, and her wrapping skills were superior to either of the part-timers. Somehow, her small fingers could deftly fold and tape any size object. Armenta always kept a good eye on their little friend, and when she wasn't in the shop, Katie read, painted, or watched nature programs on TV. She'd even made sandwich lunches for all of them on occasion. Ash said his daughter was very capable. Sunny agreed. Katie was definitely an old soul in a small person's body.

Sunny turned off the bathroom light, pulled the comforter to the foot of her bed and folded back the covers. As she fussed around, folding the afghan and returning it to the back of the couch, then tidying up research books she'd left scattered across the coffee table and the surrounding floor, she honed in on why she felt both distracted and fearful.

What *really* worried her, she had to admit, wasn't when she was going to fit doing her washing into her schedule or what Ash planned to do with Katie while they were at the winery. It was Ash volunteering to take Valderos. He didn't like or trust Valderos, which meant he wouldn't usually go out of his way to help him. Why hadn't Valderos rented a car or used a ride service instead of teleporting? He had credit cards. He'd used one to purchase the medicine buddha the first time he came into the shop.

Sunny wondered, for maybe the thousandth time, what would have happened if Valderos hadn't come into their lives. One thing she knew…Katie was safe because of him. He might be a demon, but if he was, then he was a completely atypical demon, because he had proved to be capable of doing good deeds.

She ran water into the sink and squirted dish soap. A little too much dish soap. Bubbles frothed up so fast and so high, they spilled over the edge of the bowl, crawled up the wall behind the sink, and traveled along the draining board before launching themselves at her feet.

She jumped back, amazed at the sheer volume of bubbles frothing up. She hurriedly turned off the water and emptied the bowl, hearing china clinking against china and hoping nothing chipped. The bubbles subsided. She rinsed everything and carefully stacked the dishes on the draining board.

Was Ash at that very moment pumping Valderos for information? If so, on what? The winery? The reason his limo had been in a so-called "small accident?" Or something else?

And was Valderos answering truthfully, or weaving some horrible spell over Ash while he was alone and without anything more to protect him than an amulet? What if he had forgotten to wear it?

"You should have washed those dishes more carefully," Tina admonished.

Sunny's heart leapt, but she stifled a cry of surprise before it left her throat. She tried to appear casual and unhurried as she turned her back to the sink. Tina was seated on the couch. "I wish you wouldn't do that," she told the apparition. "Can't you find a better way to announce yourself?"

"I'm a spirit; I can't knock on doors." Tina's aura pulsed orange.

Usually, she sat at the end of the bed, frequently with the phantom cat on her lap. Sunny didn't see the cat anywhere. "I suppose you can't." She took a seat at the table.

Tina's aura stopped pulsating. Instead, it swirled around her in an even more disturbing manner. It also turned a shade closer to yellow ochre. Sunny had never liked that color.

"Your attention is drifting all over the place this evening," Tina remarked. "You should be deciding how to manage that caretaker."

"Stay out of my mind," Sunny warned. "If you don't, I'm going to douse you with holy water."

"You don't have any. You're not a church-goer." Nonetheless, Tina's image dissolved and reappeared on the bed, farther away from Sunny.

"I can get some," Sunny threatened. "I'm sure this isn't a social call, so what are you really doing here?"

"You are right. It does take too much energy to materialize for idle chit-chat." Tina suddenly sounded more like Valderos than herself.

Sunny's protective instincts went into hyperdrive while she tried to remain outwardly calm. First the clock had meowed. Now Tina was using formal speech patterns and, despite Sunny warning her unwanted guest not to do so, mind reading. She wondered, not for the first time, whether Valderos was responsible for Tina's manifestations. Certainly, that could account for her deceased friend's behavior.

"You're getting mixed up in something bad, again," Tina warned. She sounded more like herself that time.

Sunny was not only tired, but beyond frustrated with Tina's unwanted appearances and veiled threats. "You always pop in to give me warnings, but you never give me any solutions. What good are your visits, Tina? All they do is verify what I already know." She threw up her hands. Tina recoiled, as though she expected Sunny to launch something at her.

Sunny reminded herself she wouldn't learn anything useful if she lost her temper. She made a mental note to ask Armenta what, other than holy water, could be used to make Tina disappear. "If Valderos is involved, then nothing about the case he's given us is going to be easy," she said, striving for a kinder tone. "I always have my guard up. So does Ash."

"Valderos believes his powers are growing stronger, but each time he summons evil, it backfires," Tina said. Her aura had morphed into a pale yellow, reminiscent of the sun shining on a cool, bright fall day.

Sunny felt encouraged. She could actually be speaking with Tina, who might be less influenced by the dark side if she wasn't being fed negative energy. "Of course he summons evil…*he's* evil. What do you mean by backfiring?"

"You know the answer to that, already. Don't underestimate him. Labels don't fit well on him."

"I hate it when you get preachy," Sunny told the apparition.

Tina vanished.

"Well, that was a complete waste of time." Sunny shouted. Maybe loud noises could penetrate the veil between the living and the dead.

Tina's favorite photo of her childhood home fell off the wall.

"Now you're just showing off," Sunny said.

She left the picture where it landed and put on her coat. "You're in charge, Watcher," she called into the shop before bolting the door between it and the apartment. Flapping assured her he'd heard.

Mexican food, she thought as she climbed into her Forester. Spicy and comforting. She drove downtown and found a parking space in front of her favorite restaurant. Tacos. Refried Beans. A heap of white rice. While she waited for her food, she'd have chips, salsa, and a margarita on the rocks, with salt.

She'd had enough magic for one day.

CHAPTER SIXTEEN

"I appreciate the ride, Mr. Haines," Valderos said as the lights of West Salem faded behind Ash's Range Rover.

"What happened to your limo?" Ash asked. "Is Serrano okay?"

"Serrano is well, thank you. My vehicle was hit by another while he was on an errand. It will require repair. Serrano is resting. The accident happened shortly before he was to return for me at the Taricani winery. There was no time to arrange alternate transportation."

"You could have asked me to give you a ride." Ash wondered whether demons had car insurance and decided to find out. "You do know that under your policy, you should be eligible for a rental car until yours gets fixed, don't you?"

"I do realize that, Mr. Haines. I have had car insurance for a long time." Valderos gave his unsettling version of a hollow chuckle. "Even those of us who are less than human need to obey traffic laws."

Valderos was more receptive to sharing details about himself than he'd ever been before. "Why do you opt for being driven around in that limo if you can pop in and out of people's lives any time you like?" Ash asked.

Valderos didn't answer immediately, like he needed to consider his response. "I have only used teleportation lately, and in a very limited manner," he said. "It took me an extended time to reach my home after I left the vineyard. I surprised a farmer by manifesting in his field, and a woman tending her garden was most upset when I trampled the last of her tomatoes. She chased me with a rake while I was trying to regain my strength."

TAINTED LEGACY

"I'd have liked to see that." Ash wanted to laugh, but he confined himself to a tight smile, because Valderos looked and sounded too serious for outright levity.

"I'm sure you would." Valderos turned his head toward Ash.

Ash made the mistake of taking a fast look at his passenger. Valderos's eyes blazed back at him. Temporarily blinded, he struggled to keep the Rover on the road. Blinking furiously and trying hard not to panic, he tried to brake, but the pedal wouldn't operate. The heat subsided, and his vision began to clear. The turn-off for Oak Grove swam into view. The turn-signal activated, the Range Rover braked, and beneath his hands, the wheel began a controlled turn.

Ash hurried to apologize. "Sorry, Valderos. I shouldn't make light of your situation. I'm sure you've found it very disturbing not to have your full powers at your disposal." It was a shot in the dark, but he felt control of the SUV return to him. Ash willed his galloping heart to slow, and wiped sweat from his palms onto his thighs, one hand at a time.

"I appreciate your understanding of my predicament." Valderos sounded surprised. "I was extremely disturbed to find myself standing in the middle of the intersection between Commercial and Center Streets this evening. Drivers were confused at first, then became agitated. Honking horns, shouting obscenities from windows. Most unseemly."

Although Valderos sounded outwardly calm, Ash detected a note of quiet fury. "That must have been unsettling," he said, choosing his words carefully.

"Unsettling, indeed," Valderos snarled.

The hairs on Ash's arms rippled to attention. He tightened his grip on the wheel and wondered what sort of madness had possessed him to suggest driving Valderos home. On deserted country roads. In the dark.

"Mr. Haines, I sense your anxiety. Let me assure you; I have no intention of turning into a monster and attacking you." Valderos sounded like he might be trying to laugh. Either that, or he was suffering through an acute asthmatic episode.

Ash knew better than to ask. "I think you see and sense a lot more than we all feel comfortable with, he said." He could certainly attest to being uncomfortable at that moment.

"That is true." Valderos folded his hands on his lap. "Why do we not complete the rest of this journey in silence? I am not one for idle chatter, Mr. Haines, so pumping me for information will get you nowhere."

"I was only planning to ask you a few general questions." Ash tried to sound casual. "They'll cut the time I'd have to spend researching answers you could give me in a few sentences."

Valderos didn't respond. Ash wondered if he was going to be ignored or tossed out on the highway. Even if Valderos had never learned to drive, he had definitely controlled the SUV when they turned off Highway 22.

"If you are direct, and I feel your questions are pertinent, I will respond."

Ash was surprised by Valderos's answer as well as relieved. "Good." He didn't want to sit sweating in silence.

Valderos snickered.

"You're reading my mind," Ash said.

"You are an easy subject. Your emotions flow closer to the surface than you are aware."

Ash decided to ignore Valderos's attempt to undermine his confidence in his interrogation skills. Demons were said to destroy the faith of humans in their own strengths, both internal and external.

"What made you decide to put in a bid for the Dallas vineyard?" he asked. "Did you put out feelers, or ask your attorney to be on the lookout for prime property? And if you did, why not a winery closer to the Dundee Hills? That area's renowned for its volcanic soil and longer growing season. Dallas and the surrounding area only recently became a designated AVA…American Viticultural Area. The smallest. It's short on wineries that cater to weekend tasters, and vintners in Dallas sell more grapes to bottlers elsewhere."

"Precisely why I became interested, Mr. Haines. I already have an inviting tasting room and foot traffic. But visitors do not return. My wine is inferior. The Van Duzer corridor has good soil and cool winds from the ocean. The Mount Pisgah viticultural area is relatively new, and becoming much sought-after. The unproductive Taricani vines must be removed. The soil will then be treated and new vines planted. My magic can shorten the time taken for new vines to mature. I envision the existing outbuildings at the Taricani

Vineyard being used for fermentation and bottling, and the extensive cellar for aging and storage. Wines will be sold at both tasting rooms."

"So your magic extends to accelerating growth, but not to modifying soil?" Ash was genuinely interested.

"My magic is complicated." Valderos didn't elaborate.

"So, how did you hear about the Taricani vineyard?" Ash asked.

"I put out feelers, as you phrased it. I initially spoke with the new owner last week. He is a very motivated seller. Too motivated. I knew he must be hiding something. Either it was problems with the winery or the family history. Perhaps both."

"Thanks for the info. See, sharing wasn't so hard, was it?"

"If you are done, then no, it was not. If you are going to continue questioning me, then you have a problem."

"Because you're done talking?"

"Precisely."

Ash heard the underlying threat in the last word. As a former detective, his instinct was to push. The subject was tired of answering, which could bring revelations from a normal person. But Valderos was far from normal.

Ash told himself to be patient. There would be other chances to learn more. He'd had enough prior experiences with the demon not to risk getting frozen while driving.

Valderos would no doubt survive the impact after they ran off the road. Ash didn't feel he wanted to test the limits of his own mortality.

CHAPTER SEVENTEEN

"I didn't learn much," Ash told Sunny the following morning as he opened boxes of new merchandise to be set out in the shop. "Talking to Valderos isn't easy. I got the impression he was withholding information he may have thought unimportant, even embarrassing."

"I'm relieved you're here," Sunny said. "I wasn't looking forward to driving out to Oak Grove with Armenta to confront him if you disappeared. What could we even threaten him with? Armenta's spells are strong, but I'm sure they'd be like a temporary nuisance for him. He'd probably retaliate by turning both of us into stone, or worse."

"I get it." Ash held up a box cutter. "But you can't come with me everywhere, like you're my personal bodyguard. Anyway, I'm supposed to be protecting you, not the other way around."

"I'm the one with the gifts," Sunny pointed out. "I might have gotten a premonition before he zapped you off to a remote Amazon jungle filled with poisonous everything and hungry jaguars."

They both stood silently for a moment. Sunny wondered whether she had touched a nerve, until Ash laughed.

"Seriously?" He shook his head. "You've got a vivid imagination. More vivid than mine. I only visualize him sending us to a desert island, where sharks circle close to shore and the only water source is protected by a giant cobra."

"Stop it." She had to laugh, then, too.

"Okay." He sliced through the tape on another large box. "Have you had

TAINTED LEGACY

any premonitions about my offer?" He kept his attention on the box as he opened the lid. "More Halloween costumes? Where are you planning om putting them? There's no room left."

Sunny carefully placed a delicate figurine into the center of the faerie display. She'd hoped Ash would give her a few days to mull over his remedy for her expansion debacle.

"Why do you want to do this?" she asked. "You told me you planned to spend as much time with Katie as possible." She hated herself for reminding him of the primary reason for that plan. His youngest daughter's murder must always linger at the back of his mind, affecting so much of his life going forward.

"Katie and I got to spend a lot of time together this summer while Caro was recuperating," he said. "Katie's now in 4th grade. In a year and a half, she'll be in middle school. She's already having sleepovers at friends' homes. She plays soccer. She asked Maxine to take her to practice instead of the shopping trips she hated. Turns out, Maxine loves soccer. She volunteered to take Katie and her friends to all the games." He smiled. "Katie told Maxine she'd really like those trips to the outlet malls with Amy to be her grandmother's special memories. She'd like to make soccer games *their* special memories."

Sunny watched him open the last box, close the box cutter, and lay it on the table in front of the gargoyle corner. He kept his face averted the entire time. She had no doubt he needed to compose himself and swallowed a lump in her own throat. She'd never met Amy, but through Ash and Katie, she'd come to know a little about the child who had been so outgoing and vibrant. So different from introspective and astute Katie.

"Katie's definitely wise beyond her years." Sunny heard the emotion in her voice and hoped Ash heard it, too. "She gets her wisdom from her father."

"Thank you." He cleared his throat. "Sorry. I'm not trying to influence your decision. I don't need something to occupy me because I'm at a loose end. I'm pleased my daughter's recovering from her sister's death and enjoying life again. I want to do that, too. Partnering with you in this business would be interesting, and I firmly believe financially rewarding for us both." He gave Sunny a weak smile.

She returned it with a wobbly one of her own. She didn't want to make a snap decision affected by emotion. What if he lost his investment because she made a bad financial decision? But he'd told her they would both have to agree to any major changes she wanted to make in the future.

"If we do this, then there has to be a legal contract," she said. "I don't want any surprises, especially unpleasant ones. We've got enough of those because of that other contract I talked you into signing." When he started to interrupt, she threw up her hands. "Don't try to disagree with me. Valderos's contract's my fault. You were emotionally vulnerable, and my own decision affected you. End of story."

"Which one of us is responsible for us both signing that damned document is going to remain debatable," he said. "That's a discussion for another day. Getting back to me partnering you in this business," he waved one arm around to encompass the entire shop, "of course we'll need to have a contract drawn up. Both of us should be protected, in case something happens to one of us." He grimaced. *Especially* if something happens. We both know these cases we're working on for Valderos are dangerous."

"Yes." Sunny locked gazes with him.

Ash's dark eyes held a mixture of doubt and anticipation. "You're going to say yes, aren't you?"

"Probably," she said. "But I've got reservations. The dynamics around this building and the separate warehouse are strange. Originally inherited by two brothers from their parents, the eldest sold his interest in this shop to Tina. But the younger brother still owns the smaller side, plus the warehouse. When I took over from Tina, he offered me a two-year lease. The monthly rent would be larger than the mortgage payment on this side. If I wanted the warehouse, which I would need if I took over the other space, then I'd have to pay rent for that as well. And he asked for large, separate deposits for the office space *and* the warehouse."

"Have you thought about offering to buy him out?" Ash asked. "I agree the situation right now is far from ideal. You've got no control over what goes in next door, and your storage room isn't big enough for your current needs, let alone an expansion."

Sunny shook her head. Ash had no prior experience with retail businesses, and it showed. "I'm just climbing out of the red with the space I have. I couldn't qualify for another mortgage. And, as you already know, I'd have to hire another part-timer to cover that much space. I might need a second cash register. Utilities would be much higher. I'd have to buy more shelving..." She grimaced. "The list goes on and on."

"Which is why you need a partner. You have the potential business. The shop's crowded most days, especially on Fridays and weekends. Belinda and Stella are barely managing the floor, which leaves you alone at the register, where you're also wrapping purchases. Your customers are remarkably patient people, but there's a limit to how long anyone will stand in line. You could expand to online sales, but you'd need additional staff to wrap, pack and ship. If you're worried about having me underfoot, I could be a silent partner, although I wouldn't like it. I enjoy coming here. You've got great clientele, the merchandise is intriguing, and Armenta bakes the best cookies in town. Giving you first refusal, I could try to purchase the other side, plus the warehouse. Maybe that younger brother's one of those neanderthal types who prefer to talk business with another guy."

Sunny worried her bottom lip, a habit she was trying unsuccessfully to break. Mark had told her she had to control the urge if she wanted to be successful in negotiations. She wondered if she'd involuntarily shown her weakness to that brother.

"I'll give you his card." She went behind the counter, retrieved a thick business card binder, and flipped through it until she came to one card on a page. "This is it." She pulled it out and handed it to Ash.

"Arnold Seabower," he read. "Entrepreneur." He looked up at Sunny. "Does this guy own more than one property? Did you check him out?"

"I did, and no, he doesn't." Sunny wrinkled her nose. Arnold Seabower had left a sour impression. "He walked into the shop not long after I reopened it. Told me about the lease being up on the other side and him doubting the insurance company would renew. He smelled like he hadn't bathed in a week, and he had long, dirty nails."

"He doesn't sound like someone willing to negotiate." Ash was filling a large galvanized tub with smudge sticks.

"Definitely not. Kind of like Valderos."

"You can reason with Vinnie some of the time." Ash broke down the empty smudge sticks box and opened another. "Witches capes," he said. "Do you have enough out, or you want me to add these to the rack?"

"If you can jam them in, great. That'll cut down on boxes in the storeroom. We should be able to sell almost all the Halloween merchandise." She shooed Watcher down the counter so she could open a smaller box sitting next to the register. It held amulets. "When do you want to call him?"

Watcher flapped his wings, folded them neatly on his back, and settled down for a nap.

Ash checked his watch. "After the store opens. I'll make a coffee run. Armenta, Stella, and Belinda are all on the schedule."

"We're should be really busy today." Sunny pulled out trays, refilled them with amulets, and broke that box down, throwing it onto a pile in front of the counter. "The capes will go fast. Ditto the witches' hats and children's costumes. That box you left in the middle of the floor has to be emptied into the Halloween corner, as well. Lots of duplicate costumes to the ones already on display. You can leave them in their plastic bags and pile them up under the table. We'll pull them out as needed. I don't want the box to go back into the storeroom. I'm worried it'll get overlooked, then I'll have to put everything on sale in November."

"What if I pick up some Halloween decals for the front window while I'm out?" Ash suggested. "Maybe they'll bring in more customers who want costumes."

"That's a good idea, but don't spend more than thirty dollars. I'm on a strict budget."

"I'll see what I can find at the party store." Ash rubbed his hands together. "I used to love Halloween as a kid. Katie says she's going to be a witch this year. She doesn't care if it's cliché. And she wants striped stockings. She said to tell you that you need to hold your nose and order them, if you haven't already."

"So much for being a dignified shop," Sunny said. "Not what I envisioned."

"And you with a marketing degree." Ash tsk-tsk'd. "You should know better. Halloween is crass, tasteless and a lot of fun. Get with the program. Wear a costume. Embrace the look."

"I'm not dressing up as a witch," Sunny protested. She felt a little embarrassed. "I bought something else."

"What?" Ash asked.

"It's a secret." She wagged a finger. "No amount of wheedling will even buy you a clue."

"Well, I'm not keeping any secrets. I'm dressing up as a pirate. Katie already made me buy the entire rig. I have a plastic sword, boots, you name it. She wants me to sew a toy parrot to one shoulder of my coat and get an ear pierced. I told her I'd find the parrot online and order it, but I refuse to get a piercing."

"Stand up for your rights." Sunny had to laugh. She could never imagine Ash with a pierced ear, even if it was only for one day. "Are you two going trick-or-treating?"

"Maxine and Caroline are taking her. There's a big party at her school, then a small private party at a friend's to get a meal into the girls before they go knocking on doors and consuming a boat-load of candy. The host family's barbequing. All parents are bringing a dish that doesn't include dessert."

"That's a clever plan for the get-together after school, but don't you think all the kids will have eaten a pound of candy before they even get to the barbeque?"

"Probably, but parents will feel better if they try to get some nutrition into the kids, and they'll get a meal before walking their trick-or-treaters around the neighborhood."

Sunny noted Ash hadn't included himself in any of the festivities. Nor had he mentioned other years he'd participated. "Have you ever taken Katie out yourself?" she asked.

Ash confirmed her suspicions. "No, but this year, for the first time, I'm going to the school's party. Katie insisted. That's why I have to be in costume."

Sunny heard the wistful tone in his voice. Ash must have been working every Halloween, or perhaps Caroline and Maxine had excluded him from the festivities, unless the event coincided with his weekend custody. She felt a surge of pity for him, but then she reminded herself she had no idea how contentious his relationship with Caroline had been during their marriage.

"Nice," she said, unable to think of anything more fitting.

"I know what you're thinking," Ash said. "I don't need any special powers for that." He started piling broken-down boxes onto the hand truck. "Caroline never had showings that conflicted with trick or treat hours. Too dangerous for the kids, and most parents don't want people traipsing through their homes while the doorbell's ringing every five minutes. I was usually busy at work, too. What better time to commit a crime than when crowds are out dressed in crazy costumes and not paying attention to anything but keeping kids safe and having a good time?"

"I never thought about that." Sunny added more boxes to the pile. "I wonder how crazy things will get in here before Halloween's over? Armenta already had to break up a tussle when two mothers wanted the same candy corn costume. We only had one left. It was hideous but really popular."

Ash laughed. "You had women scrapping in the aisles. Sorry I missed that."

"It didn't get physical, so don't go fantasizing about them rolling around the floor."

"Never crossed my mind." He grinned.

"Yeah, and I still believe in Santa Claus." She placed the last box on top of the pile and Ash secured the boxes with bungy cords. "No, the raised voices stopped as soon as Armenta got involved. She convinced them another shipment would arrive in time for Halloween. One of the mothers came to her senses and ordered the costume. I gave her a ten-percent discount."

"Spoken like a successful storeowner. Kudos to both you and Armenta for negotiating your way out of a situation. I wish more people would find better ways to resolve disputes." He started wheeling the hand truck through the store. "I'll take care of these. Belinda's at the door. I'll let her in, so she can empty that last box of costumes. I'll let you tell her she has to pile them under the table. It's got a lot of stuff under there already." He passed close to Watcher.

Watcher woke up from his nap, glared at Ash, then took off, gliding up to the rafters before descending noiselessly to land next to the register.

"I wish he wouldn't do that in front of me," Ash said. "You hear that, Watcher?"

Watcher sounded like a bird trying to laugh. It was an eerie sound. Sunny tapped one of his talons. "Shh," she berated him. The corner of his beak quirked. "And don't smirk, either."

"I'm going to get some advice on the situation with that brother," Ash said. He was at the front door. Belinda, on the other side of the glass, waved at him, and he waved back. "It's probably more easily resolved than you think," he said. Then he turned to face Sunny. "Is that the only hurdle to me becoming your partner in the shop as well as the crime-solving?"

Sunny took a deep breath. "I told you I have reservations. What if we have a falling out? What if you decide you want to spend more time with Katie and Caroline's amenable to that? What if my circumstances change, or yours do? What if one of us remarries? You could have more kids…"

Ash held up one finger to Belinda and mouthed something. She nodded and stepped away from the door. Ash came back to the counter.

"First of all, I don't want any more children," he said. "I've had four, already. I've also had three failed marriages. I'm nowhere near ready to try for a fourth. From what you've told me, you're not looking for more than casual dating." Ash gave Sunny one of those direct looks that made her feel she must be guilty of something, "You're not even over Mark. You've had dinner with him several times since he moved here."

"I know. Don't remind me." Sunny wished she'd gone back to the apartment to bring out the cash drawer. "I don't know what's wrong with me…I was so relieved I'd never have to see him again when I moved here from Portland." Suddenly tired, she leaned her forearms on the counter. "How do you do it? How do you manage to be civil but distant with Caroline? What about the mother, or was it mothers, of those other children?"

"My first marriage was short. No children. We were too young, and we realized what a big mistake we'd made in less than three months. The second marriage lasted five years. She ran off with another guy. Dumped our kids on her parents. I realized she'd done the right thing…they were better off with their grandparents than with me. There are two of them…a boy and a girl. We barely ever speak, but I did put them through college." He grimaced. "That's enough sharing for today, and Belinda's cooling her heels in the parking lot. I don't like talking about myself, but if I want you to trust me with your financial wellbeing, then I should share some details that could make a difference. Maybe you'll think I'm unreliable, but I assure you, Caroline made me learn my lesson."

"Perhaps you haven't been a good husband in the past, but you've more than proved yourself as a partner for me," she said. "I've already trusted you with my life on more than one occasion."

"I dunno, Sunny." He gave her a quick smile. "I might be more of a liability. Especially where Valderos is concerned. I'm the one he picks on when he wants to prove a point or show he's in complete control."

"It's probably a guy thing," Sunny speculated.

"You keep telling yourself that." Ash walked away. "I'd better get that door open before Belinda quits."

"Thanks for sharing." Sunny felt the need to run her hand down Watcher's concrete back. His feathers rippled in response, and for a moment, she envisioned him as a proud beast of flesh and blood.

"Don't hold it against me," Ash said.

"I won't."

"I'm really hoping you mean that." He unlocked the door. "Good morning, Belinda," he said as she walked in.

Belinda smiled. "Good morning, Ash."

Although Belinda didn't comment on the length of time she'd spent waiting outside in the cold, Sunny knew the young woman must have questions. She plastered on a fake smile. "Good morning," she said, trying for a light and airy tone. "I've got a job for you after you put up your coat and purse. Ash is going to make a coffee run in time for our break."

"I'll get right to work, then." Belinda walked briskly through the shop to stow away her coat and purse.

Sunny followed. She still had to count the drawer and get it into the cash register before they opened. She wasn't sure what to think about Ash's last remark, but she didn't have the time to dwell on it, and she certainly didn't feel comfortable asking him what he'd meant.

A couple of times during the busy workday, she caught him studying her. The first time, she gave him a quick smile while she wrapped a customer's charm bracelet. The second time, he was distracted by another customer asking him a question. Sunny noticed Armenta intently watching from the arbor. The entire shop had strange undercurrents. Sunny wondered whether Valderos was responsible, or some other force they had brought back from the winery.

CHAPTER EIGHTEEN

Ash parked in the empty lot in front of the Taricani Vineyards tasting room at 9:50 AM. Arrangements had been made for a 10:00 AM meeting with Hixton.

The path around the side of the building had been cleaned up, with Douglas firs cut back to reveal a trellis covered in a trailing vine Ash suspected might be wisteria. He spotted the caretaker tucking random pieces back into the trellis and completely ignoring the Range Rover's arrival.

Maybe the guy was wearing ear buds, Ash thought, although he doubted the caretaker was the type to even know what those were. He killed the engine and sat watching for a couple of minutes. The caretaker continued along the trellis until he became hidden from view around the corner of the building.

Ash had wanted to look in the sheds. Both doors of the larger shed stood wide open. A wheelbarrow was propped against the door to the smaller one. If they only held farm machinery, garden tools, and the two ATVs Hixton had mentioned, then his curiosity would be satisfied. He got out of the Rover and quietly closed the door. If Hixton suddenly arrived, he would say Valderos had asked him to check out the sheds and their contents.

As he walked along, he looked through all the windows at the front of the main building. Apart from desks and chairs in the offices, he saw no other furniture, leading him to wonder if Bill Hixton had begun selling off assets to meet expenses. Operating expenses might be reduced while the winery and vineyard were closed, but a full wine cellar needed to be climate-controlled, emergency lighting had to be maintained, and the caretaker needed to be paid.

He thought of Sunny's strange comment about the wine not liking Hixton. With all the work to be done in The House of Serenity, he'd forgotten to ask her to clarify what she'd meant by that.

The smaller shed held the ATVs and a workbench with tools. He found two tractors inside the larger shed, one relatively new, the other definitely not. Walking around inside, he also saw a large riding mower, three more wheelbarrows and various other implements that must be needed to care for the vines and harvest the grapes.

"You looking for something in particular?" asked a grating voice.

Ash turned slowly. The caretaker stood in the doorway, a pair of shears in one hand and a full bucket of clippings in the other. "Nice to see you again," he said. "Mr. Valderos was wondering about equipment for the vineyard. Do you know if all these items are included in the sale?"

The caretaker's expression didn't change, but he laid the shears and bucket on top of a workbench. "I tend the vines," he said. "I tend the grounds."

"I'm sure you do." Ash didn't like the caretaker blocking his exit.

"Owner's not here," the caretaker said.

"I was supposed to meet him here at ten o'clock." Ash took a look at his watch: 10:15 AM. "He must be running late. Would it be possible for you to open the front door of the winery for me?"

The caretaker grunted, shrugged, and then, as Ash was about to ask if $20 would make his decision easier, set off for the main building.

Hurrying after him, Ash caught a whiff of something acutely musty, followed by odors of wet cardboard and wet dog. He remembered one unfortunate wine tasting when the Pinot Noir had been tainted by bacteria that rendered it undrinkable. He lagged behind while he tried to remember the name of it. Brett, he thought. Shortened from a longer name. The smell faded as the distance between him and the caretaker lengthened. Had he been tampering with the barrels in the cellar and spilled some on his clothes? Was Brett the issue with the wine?

The old man detached a bunch of keys from his belt. One of them ground in the lock on the winery's front door. Without a word, he walked off in the direction of the trellis. Ash decided against demanding to know the man's name. He'd wait until he was ready to leave.

He pushed the door open and stepped inside. No security lights, which he found odd. Hixton must definitely be trying to cut back on expenses, but neither the mortgage company nor the insurance company were going to like the new owner's frugality. Ash used his penlight to guide him past the front desk and into an even darker hallway. He flipped a light switch without any results. Had the electricity been cut off? He picked up his pace. The end of the passageway was even darker. His penlight flickered.

He put out one hand. It touched nothing but air. Although he remembered the passageway being completely empty, his foot struck something. He tripped and pitched forward. One flailing hand connected with a door handle. The door began to swing. Realizing he must be in front of the cellar stairs, he tucked and rolled away to the left.

His heart hammering, Ash flipped onto his back and stared up into darkness. He'd dropped his penlight. He fought off the fight or flight adrenaline rush by taking out his phone and turning on its flashlight. That flickered, too. What was it with that part of the building? Faulty electricity causing power surges? But that wouldn't affect a cell phone. Mindful that he could have injured himself, he took a quick health check before cautiously sitting up.

Deciding he hadn't broken anything, he got to his feet. Cold, damp and highly malodorous air told him he was very close to the cellar stairs even before he shone the flashlight in that direction. With one shoulder firmly wedged against the wall next to the open doorway, he looked around for his penlight.

He got shoved. Hard. Mid-back. That time, Ash was prepared. He spun around. Grabbed a handful of material and heard a ripping sound. His attacker ran away, footsteps echoing through the space in the same manner as Ash's voice had only moments before.

CHAPTER NINETEEN

Keeping vigilant, Ash made his way back to the entrance, his nostrils filled with a familiar rancid odor. He wondered whether the cellar smelled or the odor emanated from the wine itself. He decided to consult a knowledgeable vintner. He also admitted he wanted Sunny to accompany him into the cellar. Her skills might be a lot more effective than his own at combatting whoever or more likely, whatever was lurking in that building.

He wondered who had turned off the power, and who had tried to shove him down the cellar stairs. The caretaker was the likeliest candidate, but Ash doubted the old man had the strength he'd felt in that shove. If he hadn't been prepared for trouble, he'd probably be lying at the bottom of the cellar stairs, possibly injured. Heck, the cellar might be so well-constructed, it could block a cell signal if he tried to call for help. But if his assailant was Hixton, why would the winery owner want to injure someone he knew was associated with a potential buyer?

Halfway to the front door, Ash stopped. He needed to retrace his steps. See if the material he'd ripped off had fallen to the floor. Before that, he should locate the junction box and try to restore power. Even better, he'd find the caretaker and get *him* to turn it on. Make the old guy earn his keep and stay out of harm's way.

The decision he'd made to go alone had proved to be a mistake. The first rule of policing...make sure someone knows where you are...he'd got covered, but what he hadn't realized he needed was someone guarding his back. Striding through the tasting room, he unlocked the same door they'd used before and stepped out onto the patio. The door locked behind him. Now he really had to find the caretaker.

He went over to the trellised walkway, which was tidied up and empty. Ash took the path around the building to the parking lot. His Range Rover remained alone, exactly where he'd left it. He'd become spooked, and didn't like it. He snapped off the flashlight. His battery was at 20%. Time to recharge, but he wasn't going to leave his phone in the Rover while he went to see if the caretaker had gone into one of the sheds.

A brisk westerly wind whistled past, rattling dry leaves on the bushes at the front of the building, and gusting through the Douglas firs. Ash gratefully breathed in fresh air. The entire building had smelled dank with the cellar door open. He walked briskly down to the sheds. All doors were not only closed but padlocked. The old man must have gone home. Maybe because he needed to change his ripped shirt, Ash thought. He went back to the Rover, made sure he was the only one in there, and locked the doors before charging his phone.

He felt like he was being watched. Where the hell was Hixton?

A text came in from Valderos. *There is no caretaker.*

CHAPTER TWENTY

Ash turned off the engine. Who was this person who called himself the caretaker? Why did he have a big bunch of keys that apparently opened every door?

He got out, locked the Rover, and returned to the back patio, where he surveyed the vineyard. Long grass shimmered and swayed in the wind like a body of green water. Unpruned canes waved as though attempting to attached themselves to the trellises. From his vantage point, Ash could see all the way down to the creek. No one walked between the rows of vines. The backs of the storage sheds held only rainwater collection barrels and rusted farm equipment. The creek flowed silently from that distance.

"What are you doing, Mr. Haines?" Valderos asked.

Startled, Ash jumped. His heart racing, he turned to find Vincente Valderos standing at the other end of the patio, his cloak flapping like a giant black wingspan. Ash blinked. When he looked again, the patio appeared to be empty.

"What the *hell?*" Ash had no doubt he was hallucinating. Or having a vision. A very unpleasant one.

"Again with the Hell word, Mr. Haines."

Valderos's voice came from behind his back. Ash whirled around so fast, his head spun. His heart pounded so hard, his chest hurt. "Are you trying to give me a heart attack?" he asked. Making sure he kept Valderos in view, he sat on the wall. "What are you doing here?"

"I rescheduled the meeting with Mr. Hixton." Valderos peered at Ash. "I seldom see you startled. It does not look good on you."

"A lot of things don't," Ash responded. "You gave me the second scare I've had in the last fifteen minutes. Someone tried to push me into the cellar."

"Hmm." Valderos sat beside him. "That is indeed strange. Did you see the person responsible? The caretaker you and Ms. Kingston reported seeing, perhaps?"

"I don't know. All the lights were off, and I dropped my penlight, so I couldn't see anything. It was too dark in the hallway."

"I was unaware the power had been turned off." Valderos sounded more concerned about that than Ash's safety.

Ash decided against pointing that out. "Me, neither. Hixton didn't say anything about turning off utilities when we met him before."

"I will ask him as soon as he arrives." Valderos stood back up. "Would you like to accompany me, or are you too frightened? Do you need to go home and take medication for your heart?"

"I don't take any medications," Ash assured him. "I'm perfectly healthy. Sorry to disappoint you. Yeah, I'll stay. I want to hear what kind of spin Hixton puts on what he tells you. I also want him to clarify who's taking care of this place. I'm not imagining things. Sunny and I have both had brief conversations with the old guy who calls himself the caretaker, although he's not much on giving useful information. He's over six feet, although he's stooped over, so he appears shorter. Weighs maybe two-thirty. And smells." He wrinkled his nose at the thought of the caretaker's odor.

"That's enough." Valderos held up one hand "I do not need further details."

Ash wasn't done. "Sunny said he looks like a troll."

"Ms. Kingston has had experience with trolls?" Valderos's eyebrows rose.

"No, of course not. She said she'd read about them, and the caretaker fit the description."

"I am tall, too, but I am not a troll." Valderos's eyebrows quivered in their raised position.

Ash thought the mobility of those eyebrows might not be a good thing. "What time is Hixton coming?"

"Now." Valderos pointed toward the back door of the tasting room. "Shall we go in? The door is unlocked."

"It locked behind me when I walked outside," Ash said.

Valderos either wasn't listening or had performed another parlor trick. He strode over to the door and stood beside it. Evidently, Ash had also become a doorman.

Annoyed, he pulled the handle. The door opened and warm air wafted out. Another surprise. The interior had been cold the entire time he was inside. "After you." He bowed as Valderos passed by, then gave the demon's back an uncharitable hand gesture. The hem of Valderos's cloak snapped sharply, inches from Ash's face.

"Mr. Hixton." Valderos strode toward the winery owner, standing in the middle of the archway beyond the reception area. Behind his back, he wagged the index finger with the onyx ring at Ash. "Kind of you to meet us today," he told Hixton. "You've met Mr. Haines, I understand."

"Yes." Hixton didn't offer his hand to either of them. "You wanted to tour the buildings?"

"Mr. Haines would like to visit all of them." Valderos looked down his long nose at Hixton. "For myself, I wish to partake of the wine you have in storage."

"It's not ready." Hixton sounded extremely uncomfortable. "I had another vintner come in yesterday. He told me the fermentation process was over, but the wine has to age." He avoided eye contact with Valderos. "It's from the previous year's harvest. There were no grapes this year, so there won't be any more wine until you've replanted."

"If I have to remove those vines and replant, there won't be more wine for two or three years." Valderos sounded very displeased.

Ash was glad to be a silent observer. He didn't need to study Valderos to know how uncomfortable Hixton must feel, but he did want to see how the winery owner reacted.

Hixton was looking everywhere but at Valderos, and his complexion had faded to a pallor Ash had only seen on corpses. Sweat glistened from the wavering moustache.

"Well, Mr. Hixton? What do you say to that?" Valderos demanded.

"It sounds like you're trying to get a rock-bottom price out of me." Hixton drew himself up. His shoulders quivered. "I know what this property's worth. The land alone…"

"The land that will not produce a harvest," Valderos cut in.

"That's because we're in need of not only new management but an entire new team, both inside the winery and outside in the vineyard." Hixton moved away from Valderos and focused his attention on Ash. "I imagine Mr. Valderos will want you to hire staff. I can give you folders for all the workers employed here in the past. They were all unreliable. I wouldn't want you inadvertently hiring any of them."

Ash wasn't sure how he felt about being mistaken for Vinnie's manager, but he didn't correct Hixton's misconception.

"Did the vintner feel something was done to the wine during the fermentation process?" Valderos asked. "Mr. Haines told me there is an unpleasant smell in the cellar. When was the last time Taricani wine was sold?"

"Three years ago," Hixton said. "Before Giuseppe's unfortunate accident. The grapes that year had some sort of fungus, my cousins told me. They all had to be disposed of. Burned, I believe. The following year, there were leaves but few grapes. The wine from that harvest is in barrels. This year, even the leaves fell off the vines." He laughed, his inappropriate mirth echoing around the tasting room, which had good acoustics. "My recommendation to you, Mr. Valderos, is to plow under all those vines and start from scratch. While you're waiting for the new vines to produce, this building, and the patio, will make excellent venues for events. Weddings, anniversaries," he pointed to the far corner, "even karaoke. Lorenzo used the stage to display the wine. Another big marketing mistake, but easily rectified."

Something heavy fell behind the bar. The crash reverberated. Ash started. He watched even the faintest color drain from Hixton's cheeks.

"Hmm." Valderos strode past the winery owner. "Interesting."

Ash followed him. Hixton brought up the rear, as though he needed protection. Valderos's aura must be affecting even him.

Three barstools had fallen. Interestingly, Ash noted, all three had sustained damage. One was missing half a chrome leg. The second had cracked right through the seat. The third had completely fallen apart.

"The furniture will not be included in this sale," Valderos said. "I am not paying for substandard fittings. I will send experts to evaluate all your wine-making equipment. If that is also faulty, you will have it removed at your own expense."

"I assure you, everything should be intact. I don't understand what happened here. The barstools weren't supposed to be on top of the bar. They were all in front of it last time I was here." Hixton scratched his chin and looked genuinely perplexed. He turned his attention to Ash. "Where did you see that man who told you he's the caretaker? It looks like he may be trying to sabotage the sale."

"By throwing barstools around?" Ash couldn't picture the old man hefting anything larger than any of the objects he'd been carrying.

"Let us not waste my valuable time on conjecture," Valderos said. "Let us go to the wine, Mr. Hixton. Are you accompanying us, Mr. Haines?"

"In a few minutes," Ash said. "I want to finish looking around this floor, first."

"Searching for the caretaker?" Hixton gave a nervous giggle.

Ash wondered whether Hixton had observed other strange happenings at the winery, or he'd become inebriated by testing the wine in a desperate hope it had become drinkable. But if he'd been on the premises a while, why hadn't he introduced himself?

As though suddenly anxious to leave the tasting room, Hixton trotted off in the direction of the cellar. Valderos followed him so closely, he practically stepped on Hixton's heels.

As their footsteps receded, Ash waited. Nothing else moved. No other sounds interrupted the silence.

He wondered how Sunny communed with restless spirits while he received nothing but the brunt of their displeasure. Unless he found evidence that the self-described caretaker was actually human and a trespasser, he'd need to keep his guard up the entire time he was at the winery. With a last look at the broken barstools, he trailed after Hixton and Valderos.

He decided he'd prefer being pushed by human hands than spectral. He knew enough about the spirit world to understand that anything from the ethereal plane capable of making physical contact with humans was a force to be very, very wary of 100 percent of the time.

CHAPTER TWENTY-ONE

"So, you don't want me to spend two minutes without you at that winery, but you almost got thrown into the cellar while you were there alone?" Sunny couldn't believe Ash had such a double-standard. She took the box he handed her, ripped it open with a box-cutter and placed it on the pile next to the already-loaded hand truck. There wasn't much room left in the storeroom either for boxes or merchandise.

Ash came down the ladder. "I know, believe me. It was one of the worst decisions I've made since we started paranormal investigations." He grabbed the truck's handle and began pulling the load out of the storeroom.

Sunny stopped him with a hand on his arm. "I've been thinking about your offer," she said. "Can we talk about it for a few minutes?"

"Okay." Wiping his arm across his brow, Ash perched on a bar stool with a cracked vinyl seat.

Sunny opted for a packing crate that wasn't directly opposite him. Ash always had the advantage in staring contests…an art he must have perfected as a detective. "You've made me an incredible offer," she began.

"Let's skip the pleasantries," Ash said. "The shop opens in thirty minutes. I have to toss all these boxes into the dumpster."

"I'm getting to it." Although everything she needed to tell him had sounded well-organized and defensible when she'd run through her spiel in the privacy of her apartment, her presentation got jumbled up in her head. "That brother's never going to come to an agreement with either of us," she began.

"I've talked to him, already," Ash said.

"You're interrupting," Sunny scolded. "This isn't an interrogation room, and I'm no suspect."

"Okay, okay." He held up his hands. "Sorry. Force of habit. Small room. Poor lighting…"

"Stop it." She had to smile.

"Go ahead." He returned her smile with a one of his own. "I can take it."

"There's Armenta to consider," Sunny said.

She felt a little less tense, and her thoughts were unscrambling. He was good, she thought. He'd probably won many arguments in his time. But not all of them. Ash had his flaws as a partner, at least in marriage. Perhaps he felt more uncertain about her accepting his offer than his poker face revealed.

"Tina left me a letter," she continued. "I found it in a drawer when I was packing up the last of her clothes. I hadn't been able to tackle that job until a couple of months ago. Sending her favorite outfits to a women's shelter was the right thing to do, but apart from the ugly lamp in the living room and the rest of her second-hand furniture, I don't have much of hers except her costume jewelry, which doesn't suit me."

Ash tapped his watch.

"I'm digressing; I know. But this is hard, Ash." She bit her lip. Living her best friend's dream was still emotional. "Anyway, Tina told me she'd offered Armenta a partnership, but Armenta was happy with things the way they were. The shop was in the red most months. If I was Armenta, I wouldn't have wanted to invest in this shop, either. She opted to keep their arrangement unchanged. Armenta billed her clients separately from any purchases they made in the shop, and Tina didn't charge rent for the arbor's space because Armenta's fortune-telling brought in a lot of business. Unfortunately, it was a lot of *small* business at the time."

Ash leaned one arm on the loaded hand truck. "That arrangement kind of made sense, I guess, but depending on the number of clients and Tina's overheads…" he trailed off.

"I know. I felt I had to continue the arrangement when I first took ownership of the shop." Sunny felt uncomfortable voicing her concerns to

Ash. She'd been unable to voice them to Armenta. "But now the shop's actually making money, and Armenta raised her rates. Her calendar's so full, clients have to call 24 hours in advance to cancel and reschedule. She has a waiting list. Her business is operating more like a doctor's office than a fortune teller's nook. I feel like I should be reviewing that agreement." Sunny stopped to draw breath.

"And before you could broach that difficult subject, I suggested becoming a third wheel in this already-complicated little scenario." Ash grunted. "Maybe everything's not as complicated as you think."

"I can't see why not."

"Because for one thing, I made the brother an offer he couldn't refuse." Ash swung one foot back and forth in a leisurely way. "Not for leasing. An outright sale."

"What?" Sunny was glad to be sitting. She felt light-headed. "You already bought the other part of the building *and* the warehouse?"

"I did." Ash grinned. "All I'd like from you is an agreement to our partnership. Then I can get the contractor in, the wall between the shop and the insurance office comes down, and all your stock-items move into the warehouse. To me, it makes sense to turn this storeroom into a small employee break-room with lockers and a bathroom. Install a small refrigerator, microwave, coffeemaker and sink. You'll be able to keep your apartment private."

Sunny needed to take deep several deep breaths. So many possibilities flashed through her mind. The witch corner enlarged, the delicate faerie display moved to a safer location, the gargoyles out of that dark corner, although Watcher might object. She reeled in her thoughts. There were other issues to resolve. "But what about Armenta?"

"Armenta's still uninterested in owning part of the shop," Ash said. "I already talked to her at length. I wanted to have all my ducks in a row before I spoke to you, again. She wants to stay right where she is. She said the spirits are happy there, and so is she. She'll continue to handle her own scheduling unless she has to leave unexpectedly for one of those sudden visits to the shaman. Then she'll need coverage from you or the staff to notify her clients and reschedule their readings. She's very amenable to a rent increase and a formal written agreement. I told her to discuss terms with you."

"Ash, I don't know what to say. I'm overwhelmed." So much of the baggage on Sunny's shoulders felt like it was about to slip off.

"So, how do you feel now about having me as a partner?" Ash's grin widened.

"Astonished. Grateful." Tears welled up. She couldn't finish her thoughts.

She wanted to hug him, but she thought that was probably not the way to start out a second partnership with Ash. They were already sharing a battle for their souls. Partnering in the metaphysical shop would tie their financial well-being together as well. That was a lot to digest. A lot for any mortal to handle. But the alternative was untenable. Ridiculous. Short-sighted. She thrust out her hand. "I accept," she said. "Let's shake on it. We'll need a formal contract drawn up."

"I'll get right on it."

His large hand closed around hers. Sunny swore his strength flowed into her. Warming. Calming. The fears dropped away with the baggage. The heavy burden of Tina's dream grew wings and flew away.

"The shop's going to have a bright future," Ash assured her. "You'll have everything you need to make it run smoothly without constantly worrying about the financial side."

He was still holding her hand, and Sunny didn't want him to let go.

Stella popped her head around the door. "Oh, sorry." She looked from one of them to the other. "Am I interrupting?"

The spell broken, Ash's hand left Sunny's. "We were having a business meeting," she told Stella. "What's up?"

"You have a visitor," Stella said. "Mr. Kingston was standing outside the front door, so I let him in. I hope that's okay. We're supposed to open in five minutes."

"Mark? This early?" Sunny frowned. "I hope nothing's wrong."

"He said he wants to invite you to lunch," Stella said.

Sunny hastily got to her feet. "I'll deal with Mr. Kingston," she told Stella. "You need to help Mr. Haines put out this merchandise."

As she hurried out, she cast a quick look over her shoulder. She noticed two things: A shadow passed across Ash's face as he watched her leave, and Stella's eyes brightened as she rushed toward him.

CHAPTER TWENTY-TWO

Suddenly, Sunny felt a twinge of uncertainty. Was Ash interested only in growing The House of Serenity and sharing in the profits, or did he have something more personal in mind?

If he wanted to be a hands-on partner, she'd see him every day, and he'd already expressed his opinion that she shouldn't have allowed Mark back into her life. Was that because, as he'd said, she couldn't trust her ex-husband to have changed his ways, or was it because Ash was developing feelings for her that went beyond friendship? She wasn't sure how she felt about either of those options.

Mark was lounging against the counter. He gave her one of his winning, boyish smiles. Even though she returned the smile, Sunny wasn't sure she was happy to see him. It was already turning out to be a strange day, and that was before she spotted Watcher sidling along the counter toward her ex-husband.

She wondered what the gryphon had in mind. Whatever it was, she doubted Mark would be a happy recipient. She broke into a trot, hoping he wouldn't think it was because she was so excited to see him.

"What a nice surprise," she said, awkwardly flinging herself between Watcher and Mark. Watcher's talons almost landed on her arm, stretched across the counter as a barrier.

Mark did a double-take. He straightened up and stared long and hard at Watcher. "Where did *he* come from?"

"Oh, you know, we're always moving merchandise around." Sunny gave Mark her sweetest smile. If she'd thought batting her eyelashes would have helped, she'd have done it. "Stella said you wondered if I'd be free for lunch?"

"Oh, yes." Mark reluctantly dragged his attention away from the gargoyle. "What's a good time? My day's flexible, for a change."

"I could go at eleven," she said. "I was so busy, I skipped breakfast, so I'll be pretty hungry by then."

"Eleven it is." Mark gave her a quick peck on the cheek. "See you then." He gave Watcher another long look before leaving.

Sunny watched Mark get into his red convertible Mazda Miata and leave the parking lot before turning her attention to the concrete statue. "Don't you ever do that again, to him or anyone else," she said.

Watcher squawked and took off. He flew into the gargoyle corner.

They opened promptly at nine, and the shop filled with customers from the little tour bus that came twice a week. Sunny got busy ringing up purchases for Stella to bag. Ash worked the shop floor to assist customers and field questions. They weren't able to finish putting out the merchandise from the storeroom before Mark returned.

Sunny had to delay her departure for thirty minutes while they cleared a long line at the register. She wondered whether she'd agreed to the lunch date to prove to herself that she had a life separate from the shop or because she was trying to make sure Ash knew it.

She wasn't at all sure what she was going to tell Mark when renovations started. He'd wonder whether she'd held back information about her finances during their divorce. He had certainly known that Tina's shop wasn't profitable. Sunny had wanted to give her best friend a loan, but neither Mark nor Tina was on board with that suggestion.

As Mark drove down High Street into downtown, Sunny pondered over how long the shop would have to stay closed while the wall was demolished. Would they be able to function in the colder months with only a makeshift barrier between the former insurance office and the metaphysical shop?

She hoped Mark wouldn't want to discuss Watcher's sudden migration from his usual perch beside the cash register while they were waiting for their food at the restaurant. With those talons and his curved beak, she was sure the gryphon could have ripped half Mark's face off. Had Watcher instigated his completely unexpected sneak attack, or had Ash put that thought into the gryphon's head?

No, Sunny told herself, that was too much of a stretch. Mark wasn't expected that morning, and Ash didn't communicate with Watcher, despite seeing the magical gryphon fly on more than one occasion. He'd even seen Watcher zoom down to destroy an entire copse of trees. Yet he remained reluctant to speak with one of their team's most useful members.

Why had Watcher stalked Mark? she asked herself. She knew Valderos couldn't be responsible for Watcher's aggressive behavior. Watcher would never listen to anything Valderos proposed.

Abruptly leaving her distracted thoughts when Mark swerved to avoid another vehicle changing lanes, she saw they were crossing the Marion Street Bridge spanning the Willamette River in a westerly direction. The Miata was in the far-left lane, taking Highway 22, not the far-right lane, leading to West Salem.

"Where are we going?" she asked. "I can't take a long lunch. We're too busy."

Mark's face fell. "I was going to take you to a Thai restaurant in Independence, followed by a walk by the river. I made a reservation."

Sunny wondered what he was thinking? He knew the shop's hours. "That sounds lovely." She tried to keep the edge out of her voice. "But it's out of the question. I don't know what I was thinking earlier this morning. I should have called and asked you for a raincheck."

"It's okay." His hand covered hers as she nervously twisted the strap of her shoulder bag. He gave her fingers a gentle squeeze before turning his attention to switching lanes and taking the off-ramp for West Salem. "We'll go back. I saw a small Mexican restaurant off Fairgrounds, not far from the shop."

"The food's good there," she told him. "Authentic. And they're pretty fast."

"Sounds like a winner. But you'll have to give me another date in the evening to make up for this." His hand found hers again after he had negotiated the somewhat complicated U-Turn onto the Center Street Bridge, and then stopped for a red light before traveling through downtown.

Sunny took a deep breath. That lunch, followed by a walk, had sounded like a real date, not a casual meal. She wasn't ready to progress to the next level of dating, if that was truly what Mark wanted. "I'm going to be really busy for the next few months," she said. "Ash is partnering with me in the business. We're expanding into the other half of the building and taking over the big warehouse."

Mark shot her a quizzical look before the light changed and he turned his attention back to the traffic. "Are you sure you want to do that? I know he's a good friend, and he's been helping you out, but do you really want to give him a financial interest in your business? I could loan you the money."

"That's not an option," she said. "I'm sorry, but remaining friends with you isn't the easiest. I wouldn't want to add owing you money to the mix."

"That's a bit harsh, Sunny, even though I know I probably deserve the dig at my character." Mark took his hand away as they drove north on Broadway. "I'm really trying to mend my fences with you. I want that second chance. I've told you how I feel. How I want the opportunity to show you I can be the best boyfriend…the best partner."

After they had passed the Broadway movie theatre on the left and a line of traffic waited for the light ahead to turn green, he stopped the car, applied the hand brake and leaned over, pulling her toward him. He kissed her lightly at first, then deeper. He held her head imprisoned. She couldn't pull away. Cars honked behind them. Sunny placed both hands against his chest and pushed hard. Mark broke the kiss. He ignored the frenzied honking and stared at her. He looked perplexed.

"What do you want from me?" he asked. "You're friendly, but you didn't kiss me back."

She felt used. Empty. "You still don't understand, do you?"

"Understand what?" Mark's blue eyes narrowed. He frowned, took off the brake, put the car into gear and accelerated, closing the gap between the Miata and the traffic ahead. He pulled into the far-right lane and turned onto Hood Street.

"We're divorced, Mark. For good reason. You cheated on me."

"That, again? How many times can I tell you I'm sorry? How many times do I need to tell you I've changed?"

TAINTED LEGACY

A woman pushing a stroller stood at the curb in front of a pedestrian crossing. Mark stopped the car and applied the hand brake again. He grabbed Sunny by her upper arms and gently shook her. Although he wasn't hurting her, she didn't like the physicality of it. More honking sounded from behind. The woman and the stroller had reached the other side of the road and were walking down a side street.

"I've changed, too," Sunny told Mark. "Our lives aren't joined anymore. I'm making a new one for myself, and I don't want you in it. Let me go."

His hands immediately fell from her arms. He looked stunned. She unfastened her seatbelt, opened the door, and almost fell out of the low car. More honking accompanied her exit. The driver of an SUV two cars behind Mark's yelled out of his window.

"Don't be silly," Mark shouted above the honking. "Get back in the car. I'll take you to the shop."

"Goodbye." She closed the door, mouthed 'Sorry' to the irate drivers behind, and walked away.

Mark followed her slowly in the Miata until Fairgrounds Road veered off to the left and Hood Street continued past the VFW building into the neighborhood of homes where Ash lived. Mark called to her out the window one more time, but she ignored him.

With a great deal of relief, she watched the red car accelerate into the sharp left curve and leave her behind, a conger line of vehicles following her ex's vehicle. She knew the occupants of all those other vehicles were staring at her, but she didn't care. She and Mark were truly over…finished…done, she told herself. When he'd laid his hands on her, she remembered how often he'd seemed to be on the verge of carrying their arguments into something more than verbal confrontations, and how she'd wondered whether one time in the future, he would. She never wanted to feel that uncertainty again

The day was cold but sunny. She continued on Hood Street, crossed Summer with a feeling of relief when she didn't see Mark's Miata heading toward her, and maintained a fast pace all the way back to the shop. By that time, it had reopened after lunch.

Armenta said nothing, but her bright eyes followed Sunny to the counter, where she took over from Belinda, who left for her babysitting job. Stella manned the floor. She told Sunny that Ash had taken off, too, saying he had business to take care of, but they had managed to get all the merchandise from the remaining boxes put out during a slightly extended lunchbreak.

Sunny hoped Ash hadn't left because he was upset with her. She told herself that if he was, then they'd have to make sure lines were drawn between their private and professional lives before she signed a contract that would make him so much a part of her business.

Mid-afternoon, a welcome lull came to the shop. Armenta, without any appointments for another hour, announced she was going to make tea. Five minutes later, she told Stella she was taking Sunny for a break and to call the shop's landline on her cell phone if she couldn't manage alone. After issuing the edict, Armenta pulled Sunny into the apartment.

"Sit," she directed. "Eat." She placed a ham and cheese sandwich in front of Sunny. "I heard you skipped breakfast, and I know you didn't eat lunch." She poured two cups of a fragrant brew. "White tea, lemon balm and honey." A full cup covered with a delicate design of lilies of the valley landed next to the sandwich plate.

Sunny thanked her before biting into the sandwich.

"It's over with Mark." Armenta said.

Sunny nodded, her mouth full.

"Good." Armenta dipped a ginger snap cookie into her tea. "Ash told me you'd accepted his offer. You made two very good decisions today." Her numerous bracelets tinkled.

A shaft of sunlight pierced a chink in the cover Ash had placed over the skylight above Sunny's bed. It landed on the table, illuminating an array of runes. Sunny swiftly gathered them up and stuffed them into their velvet pouch.

"If you used Tina's runes to divine my future without Mark, then the reading's skewed," she told Armenta. "Tina never liked him."

"I never use runes." Armenta placed her cup onto its saucer. Her china had sunflowers. "The girls know better than to touch any of our divination tools, and Ash would never go near them."

"Then either Tina manifested or Valderos was here." Sunny looked around the apartment. "For once, I hope it was Tina. The thought of that...that demon invading my home without my permission..."

"I don't sense Vincente's presence," Armenta said. She picked her cup back up and took a sip of her tea. "Did you even look at the reading before you put the runes back in the bag?"

"No. It would have been a false reading." Sunny looked at the black velvet bag lying beside her plate. "I keep them in the drawer of my bedside table when I'm not using them to teach a class. Tina's always complaining about not being able to manipulate anything, so it's very doubtful she's the culprit."

A soft caw came from the coffee table.

Watcher stood in the middle of it, perched on top of something that looked like a pamphlet.

"Are you responsible?" Sunny asked him.

The gryphon shook his head, ruffled his feathers, then knocked his beak against the paper under his talons.

Sunny walked over to see what he'd brought.

It was a rendition of the Taricani Vineyard and Winery, showing an apple orchard in place of the grapevines and an even larger patio outside the tasting room. On the lawn, a couple stood under a delicate arch covered with white flowers and greenery. The girl wore a flowing white wedding dress, her veil artistically flowing behind her. The groom wore a tuxedo. The sun shone down on the happy couple from a cloudless blue sky.

Watcher took off, wheeling his way into the shop. The door closed behind him. Sunny took the rendition back to the dining table. Armenta moved everything aside so she could spread out the pamphlet.

Attached to it was a note that read: *Plans for the new Fortuna Event Center.*

"I wonder where Watcher got this?" Sunny wondered aloud. Had Ash left it? If so, why hadn't he told her? "Are you really sure you don't feel Valderos's presence?" she asked Armenta.

"I'm sure." Armenta dipped another ginger snap into her tea. "I think Watcher took a reconnaissance trip. The question is...where?"

CHAPTER TWENTY-THREE

Sunday afternoon was quieter than usual at The House of Serenity. Stella asked if she could leave early. She had dinner plans with her family and could help her mother in the kitchen. She owned up to not being a very good cook, but she'd become eager to learn from her mother now she'd been in a relationship with her boyfriend for six months. She thought she should be able make more than a simple breakfast of packaged waffles and whatever fruit was in season or dinner from the freezer cases at Trader Joe's. Sunny wasn't about to sentence Stella's beau to a potential lifetime of microwaved meals. She told Stella to make sure she got hands-on instruction and waved her out the front door.

"Ready to go back to the winery tomorrow?" Ash asked. He was rearranging the crystal faeries display.

Sunny had never stopped marveling how Ash, with his big hands, could create such artistic displays throughout the store. She'd given him free rein, and been rewarded ten-fold. Customers had bought far more from that display since Ash had taken over responsibility for showcasing the wafer-thin glass figurines.

The shop's clientele had also bought a lot of merchandise Sunny never planned to reorder… black and white votive candles that smelled like unwashed armpits, keyrings with bright orange plastic pentagrams, and evil eyes swimming around in little snow globes. Instead of cluttering the counter in small tin buckets designed to encourage impulse purchases while customers waited in line, Ash put all of them into a half-barrel that had small plastic bags hanging on both sides. Bags could be filled for the bargain price of $2. To Sunny's surprise, the barrel was almost empty

Over the summer, she had delegated additional responsibilities to her staff as well as Ash. She still had more than enough to keep her occupied, both while the shop was open and after-hours, but she didn't feel so overwhelmed. She had been able to expand her rune readings and classes from one afternoon a week to two. Stella and Belinda were put in charge of dusting and sweeping. Belinda managed the register when she came in for her 4-hour shifts two days a week. Stella was a great asset to the store as long as she kept away from the register. Sunny reminded herself that Armenta was correct…people had their strengths and weaknesses. Her own weaknesses had included Mark until she'd had that pivotal moment in his car.

She'd finally admitted in the middle of a restless night that the memories of his infidelity and her own shattered dreams of marriage were still too raw to forgive and forget. She'd seen how he had expected her to drop everything for a two-hour lunch in the middle of the shop's busiest day, and how he'd been so sure she'd respond to his aggressive kiss by becoming putty in his arms.

"Sunny, are you daydreaming?" Ash's voice broke into her musings. "I asked if you're ready to go back to the winery tomorrow, since it's your day off?"

He'd brought Katie with him that afternoon. The little girl had grown considerably taller over the summer, and her resemblance to Ash, both in features and disposition, had deepened. After customers dwindled and Stella left, Katie and Armenta had gone into the apartment to paint. Katie had graduated from crayons to watercolors and from pencil sketches to charcoal. Caroline paid for art lessons after school two days a week.

"I'm available." Sunny shook off her wandering thoughts. "What time? Are you taking Katie back to Caroline this evening, or dropping her off at school, tomorrow?"

"Dropping her at school." Ash placed the last faerie in the display. "What with a sleepover Friday night and a birthday party at a friend's in Lincoln City yesterday, I haven't seen much of her this weekend. I only picked her up this morning. But she wanted to come to the shop right after breakfast, which allowed me to do some rearranging. Stella and I had pushed new merchandise in wherever we could find space. I've been able to tidy up." He walked over to the counter. "I need to get back to the gym. My back's letting me know I've been lax." He arched his back and grunted.

"You didn't hurt yourself lifting all those boxes, did you?" Sunny hoped he wasn't doing too much. He always said he was fine, but she'd caught him wincing a couple of times that day while stooping to place items on the lowest shelves.

"No, I hurt myself by neglecting the healthy diet and not exercising regularly." Ash grimaced. "Time to get back to basics. I'll drop Katie off and go to the gym at eight-thirty tomorrow. Back home and showered by ten. I can grab a quick breakfast and pick you up at ten-fifteen. Will that work? I'll ask Vinnie to get the buildings unlocked. Two hours out there, then I'll spring for a quick lunch at a Thai restaurant in Independence that has good food. I'll have you back here by three at the latest."

That had to be the same Thai restaurant where Mark had made a reservation. Sunny had a case of déjà vu, or was it a premonition? She didn't want to risk walking in with Ash to see Mark sitting at a table. Maybe he ate there regularly. Maybe he'd say something about her refusing to eat lunch there with him, because she preferred to eat with her partner. Maybe he'd even hint something more was going on between her and Ash, and that was the reason she'd rebuffed him. Unlikely? Yes. But possible.

"How about stopping for a drink at the cider house across the creek after we get done at the vineyard? We might be able to eat lunch there, too, and ask a few questions. Wouldn't you like to know how those folks feel about their offer to buy the winery being countered by Valderos?"

"You can't guarantee the owner or owners will be at the cidery tomorrow, if we just drop in," Ash said. "The cider house might be closed. Mondays are popular days off for more than retail. I should call and see if they'll be available and willing to talk to us."

"Okay. But if the cider house is only open for drinks, we shouldn't plan on more than one glass on empty stomachs," she said. "The ciders around

TAINTED LEGACY

here can pack as much of a punch as a beer."

He grimaced. "I'm on the wagon, again. Kind of. It's only got three wheels. One glass, okay, but no more."

"You're not drinking and driving, either," she said. "If I have to drink a flight to get information out of them, you'll have to drop me here afterward instead of taking me to lunch, so I can sleep it off. I'm such a lightweight, these days."

Ash shrugged. "It's only cider. But I agree it can have a kick."

Sunny checked her tracker. "Fifteen minutes left. Why don't you take Katie home and have an early dinner? I'm going to close out the register and send Armenta home, too. This has been a really slow day." She looked at the Halloween display. "I hope this doesn't become a trend. I don't want to deep-discount all that stuff. I think I over-ordered."

"It'll get busier," Ash predicted. "Maybe you should think up an ad campaign. Isn't that what you're good at?"

"Supposed to be." She frowned, looking around the store. "I'll have to be more inventive. More creative." Suddenly, she visualized a witch on a broomstick suspended from the ceiling. But she didn't have a mannequin, and she wasn't about to spend money buying one. She told Ash about her idea.

"I found an old dress form in one corner of the storeroom," he said. "It's on a stand. It was hidden behind a bunch of old tablecloths. I was going to ask if you wanted all that thrown out."

"How do you know about the correct term for a dress form?" Sunny asked.

"My first wife worked in a dress shop for a while."

"Ah." Sunny nodded.

She didn't try to get him to open up about that marriage. Ash didn't enjoy talking about his past. Any information she'd gotten out of him had been like she imagined pulling out wisdom teeth with pliers would be. Really painful.

"That form would definitely be useful." She took a black dress off a hanger. It had a shark bite hem, the hemline higher in the front and longer at the back. Both hem and neckline were decorated with sparkly black beads. She took a shawl from another hanger. Bright red, it had a long, black fringe.

119

"I'll get the dress form." Ash went back to the storeroom.

Sunny selected a long string of black beads from the costume jewelry. When Ash returned, they dressed the form. He was able to take it off its stand without breaking the pole, after which he taped one of the birch twig brooms to the improvised mannequin. Sunny made a hole in the neck of a foam wig head, and they anchored it to the form with a stout cardboard tube that had once held a large roll of wrapping paper.

The foam head already displayed a full wig with long, black tresses. Sunny added a pointed hat, tied its satin strings under the foam head's chin, and Ash brought in the ladder. They were able to suspend the witch from the rafters after he flung a thick black electrical cord over one of them. He'd found a box of old cords in the storeroom. He was about to wrap another cord around the waist of the dress form, but Sunny gave him one of her belts, which he used instead.

She contemplated their creation. "I'm afraid the belt could slip off. If our witch fell on a customer, even if the customer wasn't hurt, I could get sued."

"That belt's not going anywhere," Ash assured her. "It's cinched up so tight, if that torso tried to breathe, it wouldn't be able to." He climbed down from the ladder and stood back. "It looks good." He chuckled. "The dress is draping over the tape, and you can't really tell she doesn't have any legs. Do you want a couple more opinions?" He jerked his head in the direction of the apartment.

"Excellent idea." Sunny went back and popped her head around the door. Armenta and Katie were seated at the dining table. They had packed up the paints and were both eating cookies. Katie had a glass of milk. A teapot sat in the middle of the table, steam curling from the spout. Three sets of flowered cups and saucers were grouped together, waiting to be filled with tea.

When Armenta saw Sunny, she gestured toward the pot. "Almost finished steeping. I thought we'd have tea before Katie and Ash go home."

"I like the sound of that, but first, we want your opinions." Sunny explained what she and Ash had rigged up in the Halloween display.

"Ooh." Katie scrambled off her chair. "I can't wait to see it." She ran through the apartment and into the shop. Presently, Sunny heard a squeal of delight. "Well, one of you is impressed," she told Armenta as they followed Katie at a more sedate pace.

Armenta viewed the new display from all angles before declaring, "I like it."

Sunny closed out the register. Armenta turned off all but the center aisle's row of lights and locked the front door. After a quick cup of Chamomile tea, Armenta, Ash, and Katie left by the back door. Sunny locked that, too, kicked off her shoes, took off her makeup and changed into sweats.

After an easy dinner of bagged salad and canned salmon, she almost fell asleep watching TV. Jerking awake when her head bobbed, she decided to get into bed. Maybe she'd read a few pages of the new book she'd bought, if she stayed awake that long.

For the first time in a while, she'd picked up a Romance. She wasn't sure whether she'd needed lighter fare than the book on botanical medicine she'd been reading, or whether Mark had been more influential than she'd expected.

Before settling down for the night, she always made one final round of the shop, making sure the alarm was set and double-checking all the doors. Sometimes it seemed to be an unnecessary ritual, but she always kept to her routine. Anything to help her sleep better.

Months after she'd moved into Tina's apartment, and with the skylight above her bed covered, she still slept fitfully. Her next step was to buy a new bed, because replacing all the pillows hadn't resolved middle-of-the-night wakefulness. She also wanted to know where Watcher was spending the night.

When she walked into the darkened shop, something rustled. "Is that you, Watcher," she asked. "Or is it you, Cat?" She looked around. "I should find a better name for you, my ghostly feline friend. I'll start right now. Let's see…Blackie, Sooty, or Midnight?" She strolled down the center aisle and checked the front door, which was locked and bolted. "Smoky's another good choice." She made sure the storeroom was secure.

She looked for Watcher. He wasn't on the counter. She flipped on the light in the gargoyle counter. He wasn't there, either. She hadn't noticed him inside the apartment, and hoped he hadn't decided to take a trip over to Ash's home. He'd only done that once, when there had been a good reason for him to leave the shop. Otherwise, his only other sorties had been to fly her out of Valderos's mansion when she had made a stupid decision to confront their demon team leader, and when the gryphon arrived at the farm in Independence, after they'd discovered the remains of that poor young woman, the real Valentine Bricklighter. Sunny felt the hairs on her arms stand to attention as her mind turned to the malevolent being that had masqueraded as Valentine. So powerful, so evil, she had even mesmerized Vincente Valderos.

Something rustled again, that time in a different location. Sunny tried to pinpoint the noise. She told herself the rustling had to be coming from mice. Although she had no personal fear of rodents, she didn't want to risk a customer seeing one. Some people thought it necessary to scream when they saw small, furry creatures. She didn't want to set traps or call an exterminator. Neither option sounded at all appealing. She wondered whether the phantom cat could scare mice away. Perhaps…if they were phantom mice.

She heard flapping. "Watcher?"

Something flew at her. She ducked, but not quickly enough. Gauzy material passed across her face.

"Watcher, that's not funny." She raised her voice. "Stop that. What are you carrying around?"

The door to her apartment slammed shut.

Sunny's heartrate accelerated. She definitely wasn't alone in the shop. She heard scraping from inside the apartment, like something trying to get out. A screech told her it must be Watcher. But doors had never stopped him before. She headed for the light panel. She needed to see what else was flying around the shop.

A cold draft blew across the back of her neck. The unknown creature's flightpath was lower that time.

"Stop that!" she shouted. She hoped she'd used a commanding tone. "This is my shop, and I'm not putting up with your fooling around, Tina." She reached the panel and flipped every switch.

Light flooded the interior of the shop. Turning her back to the wall, she realized it wasn't Tina flying around, and it certainly wasn't the phantom cat, either.

It was the witch she and Ash had suspended from the ceiling, and it was flying at her full tilt.

CHAPTER TWENTY-FOUR

Sunny's first instinct was to panic and run. Her second was to hide under the table in the gargoyle corner. As she ducked for the third time, however, she told herself to get a grip. Apart from being at risk for getting knocked in the head by a broom, what could the jury-rigged flying witch actually do to her?

She picked up another broom from the Halloween display. As the figure came at her again, she drew the broom handle over her shoulder and crouched into the stance she'd used during her days on the ad agency's softball team. Her first swing brought down the head, leaving a grisly figure riding haphazardly around the store. Sunny struck the dress form again, but the witch continued to spiral around, lower that time. Worried it could take out half her merchandise, she decided to try a different tactic and hoped the door to her apartment had only closed, not locked.

Thankfully, the door opened when she pushed it. Watcher flew out, creating a draft that blew Sunny's hair back from her shoulders. The gryphon headed straight for the mannequin, his talons fully extended. He seized it and brought it to the floor, where it flapped helplessly against his weight. The phantom cat sidled past Sunny at chest level, its feet far from the floor. It made its way over to Watcher and his helpless prey, pounced on the broom and started pulling out birch twigs with teeth and claws.

Sunny picked up a pair of scissors from the counter and cut the jute twine holding the twigs in place. They fell away and the mannequin stopped jerking. Sunny and the cat stood back. Watcher raised a talon. Nothing moved. He stepped onto the floor, but kept one eye trained on his quarry.

"Thanks, you two," Sunny told her posse. "What in the world set this thing off?" She looked at the Halloween display. None of the other items appeared ready to take off. It had to be the dress form that was bewitched.

"Can you fly that thing out to the dumpster?" she asked Watcher.

He gave a soft caw.

"Let me open the storeroom door," she said.

But Watcher had already seized the witch. He flew at the front door, which opened wide. Outside, he took a sharp right, heading for the dumpster next to the warehouse.

A sharp clang announced the lid had opened. Another clang ensured it had been closed. Watcher soared back into the shop and landed on the counter. The cat sidled off to the gargoyle corner, that time at ground level.

Sunny locked the front door, then called Armenta.

"I'll come immediately," Armenta promised. "I've been prepared for something like this since Vincente first arrived."

"You think he's responsible, too, don't you." Sunny didn't mean her remark to be a question.

"I don't think he's *directly* responsible," Armenta hedged. "After I've completed the necessary rituals, I expect tea. I already have a bag packed. You can set up a bed for me on the couch. I'm spending the night."

"Does that mean you'll have to move in?" Sunny asked. "If so, you can have my bed. I'll stay at Ash's house. He's got a very comfortable couch, too, or I can sleep in Katie's room. After what just happened, I'll be happy to stay elsewhere."

"Just what those forces would like." Armenta sounded like she was ready to spit nails. "This is *your* shop. *Your* home. Make sure the spirits know you're not going to be forced out by any of their tricks."

"Easy for you to say," Sunny complained. "You didn't get sideswiped by a flying dress form."

"I don't expect you to put up with any more of that. You're in charge." Armenta's stern tone allowed no arguments. "You make sure you tell those irksome spirits, so they behave until I get there. You can control more than you believe you can, Sunny. Like your visions, a lot of what goes on around you is within your power to protect yourself and others."

Sunny heard something moving in the shop. She hoped it was Watcher. Even the cat. "Do you think you could stop lecturing and get over here?"

"At once," Armenta assured her. "In the meantime, mark my words: Be strong." She hung up.

Sunny wondered if pepper spray would deter anything else flying around the shop. She doubted even a taser would have any effect. But she grabbed her broom before venturing out of the apartment again, and she blocked the apartment's door open with the brick that had been left behind when someone had thrown it through the front door not long after she took over the shop. Sunny felt the gesture was symbolic.

She patrolled the aisles and found nothing out of place. Watcher was dozing on the counter, head down, like flying the witch out to the dumpster had been a heavy task. Perhaps it had been, Sunny thought, remembering the force she'd had to use to knock the figure's head off.

She found the wig stand, hair still attached, lying on the floor in the gargoyle corner. She left it there. She wasn't going to touch anything associated with the enchantment until Armenta had worked her protective magic. Although she knew Ash would be upset she hadn't called him as well as Armenta, Sunny told herself this was metaphysical business. Ash's enhanced detection skills wouldn't solve anything related to the incident.

She wondered exactly where he'd found that dress form in the storeroom, because she didn't remember a pile of tablecloths anywhere. That meant someone had been inside the storeroom without her knowledge. If they'd been able to place something as large as a dress form in there, what else could they have secreted?

She'd have to check under every piece of furniture in her apartment and take a full inventory of all merchandise. She made up a sign and put it in the front window. It said: 'Closed for inventory. Will Reopen in 3 Days.'

That should give them enough time to reorganize and regroup, she thought, watching Armenta's car draw up outside. She'd put the kettle on while Armenta worked. While she waited for the water to boil, she'd use a flashlight to check under her bed and couch, then inside the closet and pantry.

Even the kitchen cupboards. Something relatively small might have been left. It was going to be a very tiring night.

Armenta would probably prefer green tea. Her own needs included caffeine. She settled on gunpowder tea for them both. A good compromise with a decided kick. She'd like to kick the spirits in their ectoplasmic pants, she thought, glancing around as she heard rustling somewhere deep inside the shop.

She opened the door for Armenta. "I'm going to make the tea."

"Good. Then I'll get started out here." Armenta handed Sunny her big purse and a small overnight bag. She rubbed her bony hands together. "I can smell and sense the disharmony."

Watcher flapped his wings energetically, but stayed on the counter.

"I know, dear," Armenta assured him. "I'm going to work on the problem."

A yowl came from the gargoyle corner. Armenta's gray-flecked eyebrows rose. "And who is that?"

"The phantom cat," Sunny said. "He helped shred the witch's broom."

"That's very good," Armenta said in a slightly raised voice. "Now, both of you can be assured I won't bind either of you. I'll start by cleansing the perimeter and work my way back. Sunny, you're to keep the door to the apartment closed and locked until I tell you it's safe to open."

"But how safe will I be in the apartment? Whatever's in the shop might drift back there while we're talking."

"Your apartment is safe, already," Armenta's bracelets jingled softly. "I perform regular rituals, and there are talismans placed."

"None of them stop Tina." Sunny felt they should.

"Tina's magic was always equal to any task," Armenta said. "You'll have to learn to live with her."

"Oh, great. That's so helpful and reassuring." Sunny's agitation grew, knowing Armenta's powers had their limits.

"Some issues, you'll have to deal with yourself." Armenta went over to her arbor. "Tea, dear," she said. "Lots of tea."

"Coming right up." With a sigh that did nothing to dispel her frustration, Sunny took Armenta's bags into the apartment.

Tina was sitting on the end of her bed.

"Not now," Sunny told her friend's spirit. "Definitely, not now."

Tina vanished.

CHAPTER TWENTY-FIVE

"Why didn't you call me?" Ash asked on the way to the winery the following day. He glanced disapprovingly at Sunny.

"Because there was nothing you could do." Sunny shared his frustration. "Armenta was the only one who could deal with the situation."

"I still don't understand what happened." Ash shook his head. "Why did an old dress form turn into something malevolent?"

"That's what I wondered. But even more, I wondered why I'd never noticed it in the storeroom. Or the tablecloths hiding it, either. Those questions nagged at me when we finally got to bed. I got very little sleep. Armenta's snoring didn't help, either."

"It's my fault."

"No, it's not. I'd like to make whoever put the enchanted dress form in the storeroom very, very sorry."

"Did Armenta recommend burning it or drowning it in the bathtub?"

"Nothing so dramatic."

Sunny had to smile at the thought of Armenta ordering her to make a bonfire in the dumpster, no doubt drawing out firefighters from the nearby fire station, or holding the witch down in her bathtub. She'd never have been able to use that tub again.

"Armenta left it in the dumpster. I think she used a binding spell. I didn't ask. I've found it's better not to have to much information where her spells are concerned. The ingredients…" she shuddered at the memory of some concoctions she'd had boiling on her stove in the recent past.

"There's a lot going on in your world, lately." Ash drove into the parking lot of the Taricani Winery. "And I added to it by asking you to partner with me in your business and expand it."

"That part of my world isn't as stressful or confusing as some of the others, Ash." She rubbed her fingers over a tense spot between her eyebrows.

"Well, at least you don't have to worry about me," Ash said. "I'm an open book. I don't have any hidden weird stuff." He parked the Range Rover in front of the winery's entrance.

He'd finally given Sunny the opening she'd been waiting for. Maybe it wasn't the time or the place to broach the subject of his past, but then, when or where would be more appropriate?

"Are you *really* an open book?" she asked. "You've told me so little about those first two marriages of yours, and when you talk about your arguments with Caroline, I wonder how you ever got together, much less had children."

Ash frowned. "I don't ask you what you do with Mark after you have dinner with him."

"Ouch. Now you're really being personal." She got out of the SUV and turned to look at him across the hood.

"Takes two," he said, cryptically.

"Two what?" she asked.

"Whatever." He locked the Rover and walked over to the front door, which opened when he pulled on the handle. "After you." He ushered Sunny forward.

Sunny placed her hand on the doorframe. It didn't vibrate. She stepped inside.

"Good morning." Hixton got up from the couch and came forward, offering his right hand. "Mr. Valderos asked me to leave the premises after you arrive." He hesitated, like he wanted to protest. "I suppose that's all right."

"Since you're dealing directly with Mr. Valderos and not using a realtor, we won't have a chaperone," Ash said. "If it makes you feel more comfortable, I'm a retired Portland Police Bureau Robbery Division detective who's now a private investigator. Sunny's my partner."

"Mr. Valderos told me that." Hixton dropped his hand and shoved it awkwardly into a pants pocket. "He's a little difficult to communicate with. He issues orders and expects me to comply. I did cancel a morning meeting with the owners of the cidery. They're interested in making another counter-offer. They'd like to expand, and said plowing the grapevines under, treating the soil and planting fruit trees would be a better solution to replanting vines." He glanced first at Ash, then at Sunny. "Do either of you have experience in viniculture?"

"Only a preference for a good vintage," Ash said.

"Same here." Sunny gave Hixton a vague smile, like she was completely clueless about just about anything.

She remembered the vision she'd had of an orchard replacing the grapevines, which jogged her memory of the brochure Watcher had brought. The witch incident had caused the brochure to slip her mind. She thought she must have been channeling the conversation between Hixton and the cidery owners. She edged over to the reception desk and leaned against it, hoping she looked casual but sufficiently interested in Hixton's revelations. The desk wasn't vibrating, either.

"Do you have any trouble with your heating system?" she asked.

Hixton looked surprised. "Not that I know of. Why would you ask?"

"Oh, I thought there were some signs of the boiler malfunctioning when we were here last time." She gave him another vague smile. She hoped he wouldn't want details. How would he react to her telling him the entire building had vibrated like there was a large generator running in the wine cellar?

"I haven't experienced anything." Hixton looked genuinely perplexed. "It always feels like the same temperature in here. I keep the heat on so the pipes won't freeze if there's one of those sudden temperature dips this area's famous for this time of year."

"Oh, yes." Sunny moved on to the archway and leaned against it. No vibrations. She wished Hixton would leave, already.

"The cidery is willing to make a very good offer." Hixton turned his attention to Ash. "I told Mr. Valderos. He didn't say he'd counter."

"We're only here to inspect the premises," Ash told him. "Our job has nothing to do with negotiating the sale. But I'm interested...do you know why the direct heirs were passed over in Lorenzo. Taricani's will? From what I've heard, you don't have any prior knowledge of viniculture, which wouldn't make you an obvious choice to operate a winery."

"You're right." Hixton nodded, his little moustache waving overtime as his mouth moved. "I *was* surprised. Very surprised. Sofia and Arturo were really upset. They both came to see me. Their visit was...well...unpleasant."

Sunny was torn. She wanted to hear more from Hixton, but she needed to check for vibrations, buzzing noises, unexpected caretaker appearances, or other disturbances in what should be a quiet building. She sidled under the arch and left the men behind, their voices fading.

The furniture in the tasting room was stacked against the far wall, but a man stood behind the bar. Her heart took a dizzying leap. Was he real, or an apparition?

He nodded to her. "Hi. Sorry if I startled you. I guess Mr. Hixton didn't tell you I was coming to inventory the bar this morning. Count the liquor and glasses. He wants them boxed up ready to sell."

Sunny's anxiety subsided. "There's liquor here as well as wine?" She walked over to the bar. He was definitely packing. Several boxes were stacked next to him, one open and half-filled with wine glasses.

"After the vines stopped producing anything but corked wine, the tasting room became a real bar, stocked with every kind of spirit," the man said. "I was the bartender, so I was the obvious choice to inventory everything." He placed two shot glasses on top of the bar, joining a large selection of various shapes and sizes. "We'd started selling charcuterie plates and desserts. Mr. Lorenzo was looking at pizza delivery. Keeping this place open must have been really expensive. Even after it closed, it still needed temperature control." He looked around. "Otherwise, with the climate in the Valley, dampness sets in and mold follows."

"I suppose it does." Sunny tapped her fingers on the bar. Now there wasn't just Hixton or a caretaker getting in the way. What was next...a housekeeper? "I'm Sunny Weston," she told the man. "My partner, Ash Haines is with Mr. Hixton. We were told we'd have uninterrupted access to the premises today. Apparently, we were misinformed."

"I had no other availability," the man said.

"I wonder why Mr. Hixton didn't tell us you were here?" Sunny watched the man's hands. They looked solid enough. The backs of them were covered with fine golden hairs, his nails neatly trimmed. When she looked up, she found him staring at her with frank interest.

"I suppose he'll get around to it, eventually," the man said. "He talks non-stop. Me, I liked it best when it was just me, before the rest of the staff and the customers arrived."

"It's been quiet here for a while," Sunny commented. She felt she needed to move away from him. He had no visible phone, iPad or even paper. What was he inventorying? Just the number of cardboard boxes he filled?

She went over to the row of windows. Outside, the empty patio and bare branches of the vines looked dismal. A vista she thought only Valderos would appreciate.

The clinking of glasses stopped.

When Sunny looked back, the man was gone.

CHAPTER TWENTY-SIX

"Is the wine cellar open?" Ash asked Hixton.

Sunny found herself leaning on the reception desk. Her arm felt uncomfortable on the hard surface. She wondered what had happened? Had she been transported to the tasting room by a vision?

The man behind the bar had seemed so real. She took a quick glance at her watch. It showed she'd either been in a trance for 5 minutes or she'd actually left and returned. Each scenario was equally unsettling. As though she needed any reminders of the strange happenings at the winery, the counter vibrated.

"I unlocked the door before you arrived." Hixton's forehead looked shiny. Damp. Was he sweating, despite the reception area feeling like it needed a space heater? "You're not going to try sampling wine from any of the barrels down there, are you?" he asked. "I told Mr. Valderos the wine's not ready."

"From what we've heard, it'll never be ready." Ash's tone was dry and humorless.

Drier than a glass of the driest Cabernet Sauvignon, Sunny thought. She liked her analogy, although the thought of returning to that wine cellar was enough to make her go in search of a shot of whisky from the bar.

"I think I heard the word 'corked' being thrown around," Ash said. "Or worse. What I smelled down there wasn't anything as mild as corked wine."

"I did some reading," Sunny said, although neither man had solicited her advice. "There's Brettanomyces…I think I got that right…a kind of yeast… known as Brett in the industry."

Ash nodded. "I've wondered whether that's the problem with the Taricani wine."

Hixton developed a flush to go with his sweaty forehead. "It's just not ready," he reiterated. "It hasn't fermented long enough." He paused, as though mulling over his statement. "Or maybe it hasn't aged enough. I get those two terms mixed up."

"Some things never ferment long enough." Sunny looked at Ash. "It doesn't matter how long you leave them hanging around."

Ash frowned. Sunny didn't know why she was baiting him. Maybe because she hadn't slept more than a couple of hours. Meanwhile, Armenta, snoring like a freight train chugging up a steep hill, slumbered right through the night and awoke to say she felt refreshed and ready for the day. Sunny felt ready to go back to bed with a pair of earplugs and an eye-mask.

"Will you text me when you're ready to leave?" Hixton was edging toward the front door.

"I'll leave you two to work that out," Sunny mumbled. Feeling cold as well as sleepy, she left the reception area for the tasting room. She needed uninterrupted time there and hoped Ash wouldn't delay Hixton's escape.

She walked under the archway. Chairs and tables had been set up in conversational groups. Barstools lined the bar. Behind it, full wine bottles occupied shelves. Sparkling long-stemmed glasses were suspended in racks above the counter. She heard voices, turned, and saw the room was crowded with people. Tables for two occupied one side, their occupants engrossed in private conversations. Groups spoke loudly at other tables, some pushed together to accommodate larger parties. Laughter, both quiet and raucous, echoed around the vaulted space. Three men engaged in a deep conversation stood close to a roaring blaze in the huge fireplace.

Sunny smelled woodsmoke, perfume, and aftershave. Stronger than all those odors, a heavy aroma of wine filled the air. Two bartenders poured wine for patrons, and two servers carried drinks on loaded trays to the customers. None of them resembled the bartender she'd met before.

She blinked, closed her eyes, counted to ten and opened them to find the tasting room completely empty except for the stacked furniture. The three broken barstools remained on the floor, lying where they had fallen two days before.

"Ash," she called.

No answer.

"Ash?" She called again, louder. "Ash, where are you?"

"Here." He strode into the tasting room. "I was debating whether I should go down to the wine cellar alone or wait for you to go with me. Hixton left. I locked the front door. He reminded me the doors would automatically lock behind us if we went outside. Is something wrong?"

"No, I suppose not." She blinked twice more, closed her eyes, and counted to ten. When she opened her eyes, nothing had moved. No staff had materialized. Ash strolled over to the empty fireplace.

"That wine cellar's creepy," he said. "When I stood at the top of the stairs, I swear I heard something breathing down there."

"Ugh." Sunny's stomach muscles rippled, then clenched. "That's horrible." Thankfully, the spasm passed before she doubled-over.

"I wish I'd asked Armenta to give us something to throw down there. A potion or something." Ash's smile was rueful, and not at all reassuring. "Maybe send a half-ton of burning sage."

Sunny tried to laugh, but her throat felt too dry. She swallowed with difficulty. "It's been pretty creepy up here, too," she said. "I keep having visions. In them, this tasting room's full of people. There are bartenders and servers. I even spoke to a bartender who said Hixton asked him to pack up the bar and take inventory before everything's sold. He told me that after the vines stopped producing, they had to serve spirits."

"I think there are enough spirits in here without serving them." Ash wiggled his eyebrows.

"Not even remotely funny," she said, but she found her smile and used it.

At the periphery of her vision, something moved.

Sunny turned to face the windows. "Ash!"

She grabbed his arm.

The caretaker walked past on the patio, a leaf rake over his shoulder.

CHAPTER TWENTY-SEVEN

"Valderos told me there's no caretaker. Hixton confirmed that." Ash strode over to the patio doors. "I'm going out to talk to the guy. He's trespassing."

"I'll check out the wine cellar," Sunny said. "Let's meet here in ten minutes."

"Better make it five. I'm not chasing that old guy all over the vineyard. He's so stooped over, I don't know how he moves so fast." Ash opened the door. "And I'm not leaving you alone down in that wine cellar for ten minutes."

"I'll be fine."

She hoped she sounded more certain than she felt. Ash didn't look like he believed her, but she reckoned he wasn't going to hang around to argue and risk losing the caretaker.

"You'll have to let me back in unless you block the door open." Ash lingered on the threshold.

"I'll prop it open," she promised. She hoped none of the spirits were able to move furniture.

Ash left, jogging after the caretaker.

Sunny wasn't sure whether any of the furniture was real, but she grabbed a chair, which appeared to be made of solid, heavy wood, and jammed it between the door and the frame.

A cold wind sent several dead grape leaves into the tasting room. Scurrying across the floor, they sounded like knives scraping burned toast. She took another look behind the bar. No bartenders. The furniture remained stacked against the walls.

Sunny wasn't sure who had drawn the shortest straw. Ash might be chasing a phantom while she descended into what he had described as a breathing wine cellar. She reminded herself this wasn't their first rodeo, they didn't always follow each other around, and they were both wearing protection against dark magic. She fingered the evil eye amulet around her neck, then rubbed her thumb over a blue topaz bracelet on her left arm, which Armenta had told her would ward off evil. A sachet filled with dried dill, rosemary and parsley was tucked into one raincoat pocket, lavender and bay leaves in the other.

Together, they protected her against witchcraft, malevolent spirits, and ghosts. That pretty much covered anything and everything except Vincente Valderos, who knew ways around most of Armenta's protective measures. He did seem affected by some of the newer, more potent spells she and the shaman had created to keep their less-than-human team leader from wielding his increasingly-augmented powers. Or perhaps he was toying with them by *appearing* to be affected by the spells, she thought, feeling more than a cold draft on her back. Icy cold air felt more like fingers.

Sunny fought a desire to run out the door and made for the wine cellar. Uppermost in her mind was Ash's recounting of almost being pushed down the stairs. Perhaps Hixton had experienced something similar. That would be enough to make anyone leery of venturing downstairs. It could also account for his jittery behavior.

The cellar door stood open. All lights were on, painting the steps white and bathing the concrete floor below in a pool of yellow. She noticed a hook at the edge of the door and secured it over a corresponding ring anchored to the wall. Perhaps Ash should have taken that precaution. The heavy door could have swung and struck him. He might also have tripped over his own feet. She couldn't see Ash panicking enough to fall, but his mind could have protectively erased the memory of what had actually happened at the top of those stairs.

She took one step at a time, her left hand gripping the banister. Dampness mingled with a distinctly foul-smelling odor that increased with each step. Sadness surrounded her, not anger. That emotion appeared to have been directed toward Hixton. Standing on the cellar floor, she closed her eyes and allowed herself to become a vessel for whatever inhabited the cellar.

Desolation moved through her. The heaviness of abandonment surrounded her, sending tears coursing down her cheeks. A profound emptiness invaded her core. The heart of the winery…the wine…grieved. She had learned how to pull away from negative energy, and she used those protective techniques to mitigate the sorrow.

She needed to combat the oppressiveness bearing down on her. She drew a couple deep breaths. Her lungs filled with a heavy, repugnant odor. The cellar smelled like a barnyard. A really dirty one. She coughed, fought back the urge to gag and wiped her face with a tissue she found in her coat pocket. She felt dizzy, as though she'd over-indulged at a wine tasting. Should she leave the cellar until Ash could return with her?

Taking shallower breaths, the odor subsided to a tolerable level and the dizziness subsided. Did vintners become affected working in wine cellars, or did they become immune to the unpleasant side-effects of wine-making, she asked herself? She wondered how much of the aging wine needed to be sampled before it was pronounced ready for bottling. A couple glasses? A snootful? She'd always wanted to find a sentence she could use that phrase in. *How much wine was too much? Why, a snootful, that's what.*

Trying not to stagger, she made her way past floor to ceiling racks, many of them empty. Crates of open bottles littered both sides of the walkway. Deeper in the cellar, oak barrels lined the walls. A utility cart held a variety of plastic bottles, stainless steel cups, a temperature gauge, several glasses, funnels, and other items she didn't recognize.

The wine cellar wasn't breathing, neither did it seem to resent her intrusion. By the time she reached the back wall, she felt better. Retracing her steps, she touched several of the barrels. The wood felt cold, damp, and slightly slimy. None of the barrels vibrated. Sunny stopped, closed her eyes, kept her hand on a barrel and again invited spirits to communicate.

At first, nothing happened. She fought off a desire to wipe the sliminess from her palm onto her raincoat and kept her hand on the barrel. A slight buzz rewarded her tenacity. She turned to face the barrel and placed both hands onto its glistening surface. The buzz turned into a strong vibration that rippled along the rows of barrels on both sides, like a wave. The wave crested into a hum that filled the space.

"What do you want to tell me?" she whispered.

The air thickened. It quivered.

"You should get out of here," said a raspy voice. "Now."

CHAPTER TWENTY-EIGHT

Sunny knew she wouldn't find out anything useful if she reacted to her initial response, which was to bolt for the stairs. How had the caretaken gotten into the cellar? Either there had to be a back way she'd been too drunk to notice, or the caretaker was yet another illusion. An illusion Ash had seen and interacted with, too, she reminded herself.

"I have permission to be here." She hoped Ash wasn't far away. "Who *are* you?" she demanded. "No more of this," she made air quotes, "I'm the caretaker."

His bushy eyebrows rose. His mud-coated, bushy eyebrows.

Sunny did her best to ignore the flight part of her immediate response, but she did take a step back, colliding with the barrel behind her. Dampness seeped through her waterproof coat.

"I want your name," she told him, in what she hoped was her most-authoritative tone. "We've been told there's no caretaker employed here." She drew in a deep breath and felt choked by the musty, loamy odor.

He smelled like someone who had been lying in a field of rotting vegetation for weeks. Maybe months. She inadvertently breathed deeper. His odor, coupled with that of the rancid wine, almost gagged her.

"I'm the caretaker," he said. "I've always been the caretaker for this land. Doesn't matter what that man told you."

"Which man? My partner? The man I'm always with?"

"No, the other man."

"Mr. Hixton?"

The caretaker nodded. Mud dripped from his hair. "He doesn't belong here. He doesn't care for the land...for the vines." He leaned toward her. Even the crags on his face were filled with mud, as though it had oozed from his pores.

A large gob of mud dropped from his chin and splatted onto the concrete floor. Sunny felt moisture on her face and hands. Her first impulse was to step back, but that would only put her in closer proximity to the barrel, which was vibrating as though it was about to pop its bung.

She decided to try placating him. Distracting him while she edged toward the stairs. She felt like Hixton, who crept around the winery like he expected something to happen any minute, which it probably did.

"You care very deeply," she told him. "I can see that. My partner sees it, too." She forced a smile, which wasn't returned.

She wanted to glance at her tracker. Surely enough time had passed for Ash to come looking for her. Sweat ran down the side of her face. She shouldn't be sweating. The wine cellar was cold as well as gloomy. While she'd been preoccupied, half the lights had gone out. Then she heard the breathing. The space around her expanded and contracted with a raspy, uneven sound. Barrels rocked gently side to side and moved forward. If they kept going, they'd fall to the floor.

"What does the wine want?" she asked, mesmerized by the army of advancing barrels. When they toppled, hundreds of gallons of Taricani wine would fill the basement.

"The wine wants to be returned to the earth. To become one with the vines again. To be healed." The caretaker's voice was moving away, even as the barrels came closer to a tipping point.

Sunny tore her gaze from the barrels to where the caretaker had been standing. He was gone.

The barrels stopped moving.

Slipping and sliding on the wet, slimy floor, she ran for the exit.

CHAPTER TWENTY-NINE

"Sunny?"

She heard Ash's voice at the top of the stairs. "Don't come down," she called. "I'm on my way up."

"Okay."

Sunny glanced back. Nothing moved. Nothing vibrated. Bottles and barrels remained in place. She almost pinched herself to make sure she hadn't dreamed the entire unsettling incident. Instead, she ran up to join Ash.

His eyes narrowed. "What happened down there?"

"Not much," she lied. "Did you have any success?" Trying to appear casual, she brushed dust off her coat.

"I couldn't find him." Ash rubbed a hand over his chin. "This place may or may not be haunted, but something really hinky's going on."

"I met up with him in the wine cellar a couple of minutes ago," she said. "One minute he was there, asking what I was doing, and then he was gone. He disappeared as soon as I asked questions and pressed him for answers."

Ash pursed his lips, but didn't give her one of his 'I'm the protector, and you shouldn't be asking weird questions when you're alone in the middle of a wine cellar' type of sermons. Instead, his lips barely moved and his voice sounded tight. "What sort of questions?" he asked. "And in what context are you using the word *disappearing?*"

"I asked his name and why he insists on saying he's the caretaker when we were told there wasn't one. As for his disappearing act…I'm not sure how he did it. Maybe there's a hidden entrance we haven't found, yet."

TAINTED LEGACY

"Oh, Sunny." Ash shook his head. He seemed to have tucked away most of his frustration. "You'd do better getting answers if your questions were less confrontational. You want to put people at ease when you're trying to get information."

"I was polite, but he had mud dripping off him. Yuk." She made a gagging motion with her finger. "He smelled really bad. So did the cellar."

Ash gently took her arm and pulled her away from the steps. He flipped off the lights and closed the door. "I did more research. I think the wine's definitely infected with Brettanomyces. It may also be enchanted." He rolled his eyes. "I can't believe I'm saying that."

"What, about the wine being undrinkable?"

"No smart-aleck, about the enchantment." He tugging her along. "Let's go back to the tasting room."

"There are spirits in there, too," she said. "I've already had a conversation with a phantom bartender and seen the room filled with ghostly patrons."

"Just what I want to hear." Ash stopped under the archway. "Do you feel any of them now?"

"No, and the wine, although smelly, wasn't angry. I felt such sadness down there, before the caretaker interrupted me."

"What are we dealing with this time?" Ash took off his hat and ran a hand through his hair. "We need a reference book on demons and spirits."

"I've been reading up, but haven't had much success finding any references to enchanted wines or crops. Enchanted woods, yes. We already encountered one of those on our last case. Armenta said the caretaker didn't sound like anything she'd encountered or read about."

"None of that's giving me any warm, fuzzy feelings about this winery." Ash gazed around the empty tasting room. "Armenta's probably encountered a lot in her long life. I bet she remembers when Bram Stoker's novel came out."

"You're changing the subject in an effort to make us both less creeped out. I appreciate the effort, but you shouldn't pick on Armenta. She's not *that* old, Ash. Dracula was published in what year?"

"1897, not that I looked it up, or anything." His grin was sheepish. "No, I guess she's not over a hundred years old."

"She's a woman of indeterminate age, Ash, and neither of us is going to ask to see her driver's license."

"I know *I'm* not digging around in that big bag of hers." Ash evaded Sunny's good-natured swat. "Who knows what's in there?"

"I've only taken tins of cookies out of it when she asks me. Armenta likes her secrets, and I have no problem helping her maintain them."

"We should have her come out here and meet the caretaker. Maybe she'd recognize him as a senior when she was a freshman in high school." That time, he didn't move fast enough to escape Sunny's punch. "Ow!" He rubbed his upper arm. "That hurt."

"You deserved it." She walked quickly across the tasting room and pulled the door open. "That was a horrible remark. I hope we're not still working cases when *I* get older. You'll probably make some crack about my appearance, too."

Ash was right behind her. He blocked the door open with his back and ushered her outside. "I'm sure that if we still know each other when you're anywhere close to Armenta's age, I'll still be saying you're one of the most attractive women I've ever met." His smile was genuine. All traces of humor had left his voice. He closed the door behind them.

Sunny wasn't sure how to respond. "Er...thanks," she mumbled. For the first time since she'd met Ash, she felt really uncomfortable. It was like he'd poked the invisible barrier that stood between them as friends to see if it was penetrable.

The patio was not only wet but cold and windy. All those elements felt really good after the dank winery. The cold also tempered the warmth on Sunny's cheeks. When she looked up at Ash, she saw a new softness in his eyes.

"Of course, I probably won't be able to see very well, by then," he said, and the softness turned into a twinkle of amusement.

The awkward moment passed, borne off by a stronger gust of wind that gathered up Sunny's hair and used it to slap her face. She grabbed the fluttering golden strands and jammed them under her hat. "I should punch you again for that comment." She gave him what she hoped he'd interpret only as a friendly smile. "We should stop joking around and get back to our investigation."

What a lame comment, she thought, cringing inwardly as the light fled

TAINTED LEGACY

from his eyes. In the space of a moment, he returned to being reliable, solid Ash; her partner in paranormal investigations. Sunny wasn't sure she liked what she had done, but told herself she didn't need another emotional complication. Rejecting Mark had been more than enough.

Ash cleared his throat. "You're right. Come on, let's get back to the car."

Sunny fell into step beside him. "I think maybe you should make fun of someone other than Armenta in future. Her powers might have grown sufficiently for her to eavesdrop on us."

"Like Vinnie?" Ash pushed his hat down as a gust of wind threated to carry it off. "Like we don't have enough walls with ears as is. You said spirits hovered around all the time we were working the case in Independence."

"They were, and there's a different set here, too." Sunny felt a draft across the back of her neck. She shivered.

Ash must have seen her reaction. "Right now, I suppose."

"Well, no, not especially, but you may be right about Hixton sensing them. Each time we've seen him, he's been uncomfortable. Last time he wanted to rush us out of the cellar. This time, he suddenly wanted to leave while we were standing in the tasting room."

"Maybe." Ash didn't sound convinced. "We did make it obvious we didn't want him here."

They took the trellised walkway to the parking lot. "Don't you think he's been withholding information about whatever paranormal experiences he's had because he has to sell the winery?" Sunny asked.

"I do." Ash unlocked the Rover. "He doesn't want us hanging out here for any length of time in case we see or experience whatever he's seen or felt. As for that caretaker, either we're both hallucinating, or he's human and knows other ways to get in and out of the main building."

"There has to be a concealed back entrance to the cellar." Sunny watched Ash open the passenger door. "If there isn't, then the caretaker's a ghost. A very large, smelly one."

"I'll ask the attorney to send over a schematic. Maybe even the original plans." Ash handed Sunny up into her seat. "I doubt Vinnie asked for either of them."

145

She waited until Ash was seated behind the wheel before responding. "I agree," she said. "For someone who probably *is* older than Dracula, Valderos doesn't always display good business sense."

Ash started the engine. "It'll take a couple of minutes for the heater to warm up. Damn, it's cold in here."

Sunny wished he had a blanket in the back seat. He always carried water in the summer. Why not something warm for the winter? "The caretaker told me he's dedicated to the vineyard and land," she said. "He not only smells like he's been rolling around in a vat of moldy grapes, he's covered with mud. More today than before. I found it hard to concentrate on anything but the odor when he was standing right in front of me."

"I haven't gotten that close, but I'll take your word for it." Ash drummed his fingers on the steering wheel. "He must be living in one of the outbuildings, although I didn't see any evidence of that." He frowned. "I should find out who was taking care of the winery between the family leaving and Hixton taking over. The Taricani kids could have hired the guy without telling Hixton. Or maybe they did tell him, but Hixton wasn't listening. He's only interested in selling the property, not maintaining it."

"Why don't we tell Valderos he should look for another vineyard?" Sunny suggested.

"Because he could give us a worse case to solve." Ash's hands gripped the wheel so tightly, his knuckles whitened. "I'd rather be dealing with dead grapevines and a smelly caretaker than some of the other options that immediately popped into my head when you suggested that. Remember, I almost had Katie taking riding lessons from a witch during our last case."

"But, you didn't, and we solved it." She patted his arm.

Ash relaxed his grip and held one hand in front of a vent. "Heater's warming up. Haven't you sensed anything about those two deaths? All we've been doing is talking ad nauseum to Hixton and chasing a caretaker who may turn out to be a vagrant."

"I've got more from the wine than the dead Taricanis." Sunny shoved her cold hands into her pockets, where they found Armenta's sachets. She rubbed her fingers across them, feeling dry herbs through the linen. "I should try to contact the owner who was killed by the tree."

"That's Lorenzo," Ash said. "Giuseppe may be hovering around the creek."

"The spirit who won't communicate with me directly." Sunny thought about the caretaker suddenly distracting her with a flimsy excuse about repairing a fence with a roll of barbed wire. "Turn off the engine. I'm going back to the patio."

"Why did I know you were going to say that?" Ash killed the engine.

"If you see the caretaker while I'm working, keep him away from me," she said as they rapidly retraced their steps.

Ash sniffed the air. "I think he must have been here again, recently."

The wind slapped Sunny's face again. A frigid wind, pungent with odors of loam and mold. Her eyes watered. "Ugh. You're on guard duty. Keep your eyes peeled."

"And my nose downwind," Ash promised.

CHAPTER THIRTY

The next gust of wind brought fresh, cold air filled with the crisp accents of fall, not the odors of decay. Sunny turned to face the Coast Range. She swore the air, heavy with moisture, held a hint of the ocean. Her research had revealed the Van Duzer corridor funneled oceanic winds into the Willamette Valley, creating a cooling effect that occurred around 2:00 PM. The breeze dried out the vine canopy and decreased the need for fungus sprays. She thought she should bring some of that spray for her next visit, so she could unobtrusively mist the air around the caretaker. Maybe that would also reveal whether he was flesh and blood or a smelly phantom.

Silently, she chastised herself for having such unkind thoughts about a man who was probably not only human but completely harmless. So devoted to the Taricani family that he continued to work without pay. The caretaker labeled Hixton an outsider, giving him good reason to literally ghost chatty Bill.

"Are you getting anything?" Ash was seated on the wall a few feet away.

"Sorry, I wasn't trying." She gave him an abbreviated version of her inner monologue.

"You've done far too much research. You're becoming a walking travelogue on wines and wineries in this area of the Willamette Valley." Ash got up and surveyed the sloping vineyard. "The old guy's not down there. Do you feel comfortable enough staying here while I check to see if he's in one of the sheds?"

"Go ahead; I'll be fine. You can look for another entrance to the cellar, too."

"Will do. Call me if anything doesn't look or feel right." He started down an overgrown path leading toward the sheds, but a short distance away, he turned to look back at her. "If I don't pick up right away, call 911."

"I will," she promised. "And I'll stay right here. I won't wander off, like I did at the farm."

"You'd better not." He gave her one of those stern looks that always made her feel guilty.

"I learned my lesson working that case." Probably not enough of a lesson, but she wasn't about to tell him that.

"I hope so." He strode off.

The wind had picked up. It flapped the hood of her raincoat. Sunny tried to relax. She'd never had good experiences after tensing up before visions.

At least she wasn't smelling anything funky. She opened her arms wide, closed her eyes and lifted her face to the sky. Her hood flew back and her hair streamed behind her, but the cares of the day and worries about Valderos not getting the answers he wanted all fell away.

"What do you want here?" asked a faint voice. Definitely male, but without the grating quality of the caretaker.

Sunny slowly opened her eyes, lowered her arms, and turned toward the wall. A shadow hovered behind it.

"To make sure every spirit is where it wants to be," she said. "At peace; serene."

"I was." The shadow's outline danced around in an agitated manner.

"Until when?" Sunny asked.

The wind blew harder.

She thought she heard, "Before my son."

The voice faded as the shadow fragmented into gossamer threads that were carried away on the wind.

CHAPTER THIRTY-ONE

"No signs of anyone sleeping in any of the outbuildings," Ash said. "But they were all unlocked. Garages as well as sheds. I didn't find any other entrance to the cellar."

Sunny blinked. They were sitting in the Range Rover, engine running, heat blasting. "How did I get here?"

Ash frowned. "You met me on the patio." His eyes narrowed. "You don't remember?"

Sunny shook her head. It felt muzzy, heavy. "Did I say anything to you?"

"Just that you were done." He turned to face her. "You sounded drained, so I didn't push you for any other information." He reached into the back seat and brought two bottles of water from the pack he always kept there. "Is this enough, or do you need something stronger? The cider house may be open."

"Let me start with this." She took the bottle he offered and drank deeply. Licking her lips, she tried to reorganize her thoughts. "The shadow came," she told him. "It said it had been peaceful until…" She tried to remember, but her mind wouldn't cooperate. "I think there was something about a son." She rubbed an index finger down the frown line that ached between her brows. "I'm so muddled."

"You think the shadow's Giuseppe?" Ash prompted.

"I suppose that's the obvious answer." Sunny couldn't commit to a definite identification of that unstable outline. "But Lorenzo has a son, too… Arturo."

"That's true." Ash removed the cap from his own water bottle and drank.

"I think the heavy air allowed it to materialize, but the effort must have weakened it. I should go to the creek and see if the water makes a difference. I didn't get a sense that Lorenzo was anywhere nearby, even though he died on the patio." She stared at the windshield, covered by droplets from a fine, misting rain. "There must be spirits everywhere. I don't know why so few want to communicate with me. My gift is really strange."

Ash looked at the half-empty bottle in his hand. "I don't know about you, but I need something stronger." He, too, stared through the windshield. "To think the air could be filled with spirits…"

"I'm sorry. I voiced something I'm always wondering about in the middle of the night. Ignore me."

"Hard to do." He gave her a half-smile. "Do you want to go down to the creek right now?"

"No, but if I don't, do you really think we have enough information for Valderos? He wants an answer to his question about whether those deaths were accidental."

"Okay." Ash opened his door. "But you're not going alone this time."

"Fine." She reluctantly followed him out of the Range Rover. "Let's get this over with."

CHAPTER THIRTY-TWO

"Every time we get near this creek, it rains." Ash rocked back and forth on his heels as he stood several feet away from Sunny and the rushing water.

She squatted down and placed a hand on the rock Giuseppe had reportedly struck his head on. "I can't concentrate with you muttering away over there. Go look at the vines or something."

"Staring at dead vines won't help solve this investigation." He sounded frustrated. "Instead, I'll hop across the creek and see what part of the fence the caretaker repaired."

"You'll probably get wet feet," she warned. "The ground's so mushy, you'll even slip right in."

"I can still jump. I'm not *that* out of shape."

Sunny wished she'd kept her mouth shut. She watched him back up several feet, turn and run flat out for the water. Although she braced herself for a splash, he cleared the creek by a slim margin. Giving her a triumphant whoop, he went around the back of the bushes.

"Men," Sunny said to herself.

She tried putting herself in Ash's shoes. Of course he'd be frustrated over being at a loose end while she tried to communicate with any spirits who happened to be receptive to chatting. His feet were always firmly planted on terra firma, while hers were prone to floating off between earth and sky.

At least she could still *feel* the ground most of the time, she told herself, as the unsettling memory of Valderos's glide across the vineyard popped into her head. She shook off an even more unsettling thought of him gliding

TAINTED LEGACY

around wherever and whenever he wanted and turned her attention to the rock. It felt warm, as though someone had been sitting on it only moments before. She almost raised her hand, but told herself they hadn't traipsed down that steep, muddy slope for her to get spooked from taking a rock's temperature.

"Are you here?" she asked.

The water gushed by, only inches from her hand. It had been at least a foot away only moments before. "I want to talk with you." She closed her eyes. "You've been trying to contact me. Here I am."

Frigid water gushed over her fingers. Sunny opened her eyes in time to see a flood barreling toward her. She jumped up and sprinted out of its way.

Where could all that water have come from? She shouted Ash's name above the roar.

He ran around the bushes and stopped, staring at the racing torrent. "What the hell?" he shouted.

The torrent grew in volume, bounding over boulders that had appeared from nowhere.

"I'll have to wade." Ash sounded as doubtful as he looked.

"You can't wade through that." Sunny backed up again as the creek became a river of mud and debris. Sticks, branches, even small trees passed by at lightning speed. The tempo grew into a deafening roar.

Ash pointed toward the Coast Range and mouthed, "Flash flood." He took out his phone.

Shortly afterward, Sunny's vibrated in her pocket.

"I'll go through the orchard," he shouted when she answered. "There's still a hole in the fence."

"It's a long way from there to the road," she shouted back. "I can't pick you up. You have the fob."

He slapped a hand against his thigh. "This can't be a coincidence. Someone wants you isolated."

"I'll be okay." She hoped she sounded far less worried than she felt. "I've got all sorts of charms to protect me." She dug the pouches out of her pocket and held them up.

153

"I should never have crossed the creek." Ash shook his head. "Damn, damn, damn."

"You had no idea anything like this would happen." Water surged toward the vines. Sunny had to jump back. Hurry," she told Ash before hanging up.

Ash raised his hand. Sunny lost sight of him when he ran back behind the bushes. Shortly afterward, she spotted him walking on the other side of the fence line, before he found a way down into the orchard.

Despite telling Ash she was protected by Armenta's charms and spells, Sunny had to fight off the urge to panic. Running up the steep slope would soon fatigue her. She needed to pace herself. Clutching Armenta's sachets in one hand and her reassuring cell phone in the other, she repeatedly told herself she was going to be okay.

Dark clouds billowed in from the Coast Range. The rain started up again, icy pellets striking her. A gust of wind snapped her hood back and tugged her hair. Tangled vines surrounded her. Their unpruned canes reached toward her, waving like tentacles.

"Please don't let me see the caretaker," she whispered as she wrestled her hood back onto her head. "Please, keep me safe."

CHAPTER THIRTY-THREE

Someone or something didn't want Sunny communicating with spirits at the vineyard, Ash thought. He ran along the perimeter of the orchard, keeping the fence line in view to his right. As the sound of rushing water receded, he heard the distant roar of an engine.

He paused to catch his breath and tried to determine how much farther he had to run before he had to scale the barbed wire fence to get into the winery's parking lot. The engine roar grew closer. It sounded like an ATV.

Ash peered down a row of apple trees. It was definitely an ATV and heading his way. He hoped the rider was friendly toward off-season visitors. He refused to call himself a trespasser. After all, there were no apples to steal. He raised his arm and waved, then stood waiting, arms lowered, as a quad bike grew closer.

"Hello," he called, when its engine cut to a heavy purr. "I got trapped over here after the creek swelled."

The ATV cruised to a stop several feet away. The rider removed her helmet. Definitely a her, Ash thought, admiring shoulder-length red-gold hair. She took off her goggles. She was around Sunny's age and very attractive.

"What were you doing by the creek?" Her voice was clear, direct, and authoritative, but to Ash's trained eye, she looked a little jumpy. Her right hand stole to a bulging pocket in her pants.

Wary, he turned so his chest wouldn't make a prime target. She could very well be reaching for a firearm. "I was with my partner." He did his best to sound calm. "We have permission to be at the vineyard. We're working for a client interested in purchasing it. I never expected a flash flood to trap me on the wrong side of the creek."

"Flash flood?" Her eyebrows arched. Red-gold, like her hair. With her hand in her pocket, she no longer looked even slightly anxious about confronting a man who shouldn't be on the property.

"Completely unexpected." He wanted to tell her he didn't have time for a lengthy discussion, but opted to keep a lid on his agitation until he knew what she was keeping hidden.

"It's a long walk to the road," she said. To Ash's relief, she pulled out a walkie-talkie. "My dad's a few rows away. He's on a tractor."

Ash wanted to tell her to get off the ATV and let him have it, but without a badge and the authority it gave him, he had to wait. Otherwise, he could open himself up to charges, or risk getting shot. Meanwhile, his brain continued to send urgent messages about the need for haste. He ran through a short-list of calls he could make. Brad Schilling wasn't going to drop everything and drive out to Dallas because Sunny Weston was in an abandoned vineyard. Armenta was at least thirty minutes away. Should he call Valderos and tell him to use his powers to travel at lightspeed from wherever he was lurking?

Ash heard a tractor start up.

"My dad's on his way," the young woman said.

"Thank you." Ash gave her a smile he hoped was reassuring. He kept his arms at his sides. She watched him intently, like she expected him to take off running. "I'm worried about my partner," he told her. "I've got to call and make sure she's okay."

Although the woman looked wary again, he carefully and slowly got out his phone. Sunny didn't pick up. He decided to risk turning his back on the ATV rider to scan the vineyard. He didn't see Sunny anywhere. He called Valderos.

"I will assist," Valderos said, then hung up.

Ash hoped Valderos would send Serrano instead of coming himself. He had no idea what kind of demon Serrano was, but he'd helped them before.

The tractor arrived while his back was still turned. The engine cut.

"I need a good explanation for why you're trespassing," said the woman's father. "Otherwise, I'm calling the sheriff."

CHAPTER THIRTY-FOUR

Sunny trudged up the hill. Afraid she'd get pulled into the trellised vines by canes that reached for her, she kept her distance. Mounds and divots multiplied as she stumbled up a steeper and steeper slope. Long, wet grass entangled her feet, threatening to trip her. The ground shifted, like she was walking on a sand dune.

Even though a deep sense of self-preservation urged her to keep moving, lack of oxygen and pain in her chest made her stop to catch her breath. She gulped in air so heavy with loam and rotting vegetation, she started coughing. Her eyes teared up, blurring her vision. She pulled a tissue out of her pocket, wiped her eyes, and blew her nose. Overhead, the clouds parted. A shaft of light hit the tasting room. Sunny took that as a good omen. One more push, and she'd be on the patio.

But with each step, her feet sank deeper into mud at first syrupy, then of a thicker consistency, like molasses. A chill ran through her when she realized the ground really *was* moving beneath her feet. Ahead, it rippled like waves on an inland sea. Lazy but uniform, those waves moved back and forth as though preparing a rush to shore.

The soil couldn't be that wet, she told herself. Even if it was, she was standing still while the earth continued to move. Undulating waves moved faster and gained height. She considered retreating, but even if she got past the vines, she'd be trapped by the swollen creek. Waves of sod continued to grow in height, then merged. Sunny watched, horrified, as the giant upsurge towered over her.

"Ms. Kingston, my master sent me to assist you."

Relief flooded her. Serrano stood at her side.

The towering peak of soil sank back to ground level.

Sunny threw her arms around her rescuer and wondered what she was clutching. Everything about him felt strange. Solidity ebbed and flowed. Gradually, his form gained substance, and she felt bones and sinew beneath her hands as they clutched his narrow back.

"Ms. Kingston, you are well," Serrano's sepulchral voice informed her. "There is no need to hold onto me."

"Of course." Embarrassed, she let go. "I'm sorry. I'm so glad to see you. Something weird was happening with the…" She stumbled over a description of what she'd seen. Any explanation sounded preposterous. But she reminded herself Serrano belonged in the preposterous category. He'd probably understand. After all, he'd materialized out of thin air.

"I know." Serrano nodded. "My master feared this was a case of enchantment. Perhaps witchcraft, again, or worse."

"Your master shouldn't have sent us out here. I communicate with the dead. That's all. I don't have any additional skills to ward off the results of spells or incantations or hexes." She wasn't sure whether she felt inadequate or angry. "Armenta's the one to deal with those."

"Spirits are here. My master sensed them. He wants you to contact them and find out how to free them." Serrano shook his head. "But from what I have just observed, there is more to deal with here than spirits of the dead."

"You bet there is." Sunny wanted him to tell that to his master. "It's much stronger than any spirits of the Taricani family, and I don't know what it wants or whether it's a danger to me, Ash or any other human being."

"You must find out," Serrano said. "Now, I hear Mr. Haines coming. We must go to meet him."

Sunny had a lot more questions for Serrano, but she wanted Ash to know she was okay, so he wouldn't come looking for her in the vineyard. He might get trapped by the vines before he realized they were very much alive. She fell into step with Serrano as he began to walk up the hill. "Did you teleport?" she asked.

"Of course not. I came in a rental vehicle." A slightly amused expression animated his usually stoic face. "The limo will not be repaired for another week. I am driving something called a Leaf. Such a curious name. Easy for me to recharge, but no tinted windows. My master is housebound during the daytime. His allergy to sunlight, you understand."

"Oh, I understand, all right." Serrano was already striding away his long, thin legs. A discomforting distance built up between them. Sunny hurried to catch up. The ground beneath her feet felt flat and solid. She wondered if silently blessing him for protecting her would go against the rules for thanking demons or their minions.

Arriving in the parking lot, she saw Serrano hadn't spoken out of turn. Ash was riding up to the winery on the back of an ATV being driven by a slender person with long hair. They parked beside the other two vehicles in the parking lot and got off. Sunny watched a young woman remove her helmet and shake out an abundance of blonde hair accented by touches of reddish gold that shone even on an overcast late afternoon.

Ash spoke animatedly with the woman, extended his hand, and shook hers for what Sunny considered an overly-long period of time, his eyes locked with hers. Sunny bristled. He never looked at *her* that long. She must have become relegated to the position of the familiar and mundane. She turned to thank Serrano for his help, but the Leaf was already pulling out of the parking lot. She blinked, and it was no longer in sight.

"There you are." Ash's voice held relief. "Come meet one of the Taricanis' neighbors."

Sunny suspected the woman must be a witch, enchanting Ash and distracting him while Serrano pulled a vanishing act. She hoped Ash had remembered to wear the new amulet Armenta had given him. The seer believed in ensuring her magic remained fresh and potent. Sunny thought it wasn't potent enough to ensure Ash didn't succumb to the ATV-riding woman's charms.

"This is Andrea Fortuna," Ash said as Sunny joined them. "She and her father own the orchard and cidery on the other side of the creek."

"Nice to meet you," Sunny said.

Andrea Fortuna was pretty stunning up close, she admitted with a pang of what had to be jealousy. Andrea looked like the quintessential fresh-faced farm girl, but with a sophisticated edge. She emitted a confidence that convinced Sunny the woman was secure in her own skin. Her face, devoid of makeup, held a warm glow that mirrored her hair. Her eyes were a deep shade of almost violet, her nose long and straight, her mouth just wide enough to be called generous. So were her lips. Sunny could well imagine how Ash had become captivated by her.

In contrast, wearing a pair of muddy boots, her limp hair filled with tangles, and her makeup probably several points south of north, Sunny knew she must look as bedraggled as she felt. Andrea didn't even have a spot of rain on her jacket.

"Thanks again." Ash smiled at Andrea. "We'll definitely accept your dad's kind offer to drop by the cider house before we leave."

Andrea gave him an exclusive smile that didn't include Sunny. "I hope you do." Her gaze lingered on him for a long moment before briefly resting on his partner. "Nice to meet you, Ms. Kingston." She gave Ash another once-over before starting the ATV's engine and driving away.

"It looks like you had a much better time than I did after the creek swelled," Sunny remarked. "I had to be rescued from a sea of mud by Serrano."

Ash tore his attention away from a contemplation of Andrea Fortuna's departing figure. "You look like you fell into it," he said. "Good thing I called Valderos."

CHAPTER THIRTY-FIVE

Ash told Sunny that the Polk County Sheriff's deputy had recognized him and verified his identity, calling him 'a paranormal investigator.' Much to Ash's chagrin, the deputy even assured Andrea the trespasser was "a harmless half of a team." To Sunny's relief, he'd decided not to argue the point.

"Andrea's father invited us over," Ash said. "He laughed while extending the invitation, but it'll be a good intro for us to ask about their feud with the Taricanis. We'll see if it's fixable now Giuseppe and Lorenzo both passed away, whether their disagreement is limited to who owns rights to the creek, or if there's more to resolve. When I told the Fortunas I came through a hole in the fence, Andrea's father got really angry but refused to tell me why. Said it was none of my business. I wondered if someone's trying to move the fence section by section, either toward the orchard or back to the creek. Maybe deer aren't doing the damage. I'd really like to know whether the Fortunas can give us more information about the caretaker, too."

"I hope they can." Sunny wrapped her arms around herself. "Can we talk in the Rover?"

"Of course."

As soon as they were seated, he ran the engine and turned on the heater. Sunny told him about the trembling ground and the towering mud tsunami.

"Thank goodness I made that call to Valderos." The lines around Ash's mouth deepened. "I had a feeling you were in trouble. I wouldn't be surprised if that Leaf grew wings and flew Serrano over here."

"Me, neither. He must look like a creature out of a Tim Burton movie, folding himself into that little hatchback." She managed a brief smile. It took a lot of effort.

"I'm going to set up another appointment with Hixton," Ash said. "Away from here, so I can see if he really never shuts up, or it's his way of coping with the vibes he's getting." He took off his hat and ran a hand through his hair. "He's got to know something strange is going on out here."

"I bet he does, either from his own experiences or what he's heard from others." Sunny stared through the windshield at the reception area, dimly lit by a green glow from the exit sign over the front door. She swore she saw a shadow come from behind the counter, drift across the reception area, and disappear on the other side of the archway.

"I'd really prefer you take me home before you go to the cidery," she said. "It's totally out of your way, but my hair and my pants are wet. I'm a complete mess." She pulled down the visor. "Ugh!"

"You've got lipstick and a brush in your purse," Ash said. "Use them, and you look fine. Women are always so worried about appearances. How did you get so wet? Andrea told me she was out in the orchard all day, yet she managed to keep dry."

Something in the way he mentioned Andrea Fortuna's name didn't sit well with the bedraggled Sunny. "Maybe it only rained on the vineyard," she snapped. "Were you too preoccupied to notice?"

"I guess I was too busy trying not to get arrested, so I could get back to you." He put the Rover into gear and, after glancing in the rearview mirror, eased up on the brake. The vehicle slowly reversed. "I'll take you home and come back to the cider house later." He sounded really ticked-off. "I can talk to Andrea and her father without feeling guilty because I'm keeping you from a warm bath, leftovers, and an early night."

Sunny was taken-aback. "Thanks for making me sound like I complain all the time for no reason. You really think I've got nothing better to do evenings than sit at home watching reruns with the phantom cat on my lap and a TV dinner? You're wrong…I've got a date, so yes, you should drop me home so I can get ready."

She didn't have a date, but she could always take herself out to dinner.

TAINTED LEGACY

After the events at the winery, she deserved a 5-course gourmet meal.

"Well, excuse me." Ash gunned the motor. Gravel and mud flew. "I wouldn't want to make you late for your date."

"And I wouldn't want to keep you from hanging out with Andrea," Sunny shouted as the Range Rover made a fast turn, wheels screeching.

Suddenly, Ash stomped on the brake and pointed. "There he goes!"

Sunny stopped hanging onto her seatbelt. She saw the caretaker walking into the vineyard.

"Come on!" Ash had already turned off the engine and jumped out. "Get a move on, before we lose him again." He motioned wildly for Sunny to follow before sprinting away.

She reluctantly got out. The SUV's doors locked. Ash soon widened the distance between himself and Sunny, already tired from her long trek.

The earth trembled. Water in potholes rippled. She tried her best to ignore her aching thighs and cramping calves. Ash turned the corner of the building and she lost sight of him. Pausing at the gate to see if he'd run down the hill or toward the patio, she inhaled a highly unpleasant odor.

"Is there something I can help you with?" asked the caretaker. Cold breath fanned her cheek. Her heartrate surged. She turned to face him.

He leaned forward at an angle that should have toppled him.

Sunny looked down. His feet weren't just attached to the ground, they were part of it.

CHAPTER THIRTY-SIX

"What are you doing?' Ash's voice came from far away.

The caretaker had transformed into a pile of mud that seeped back into the earth. She turned to ask Ash if he'd seen what had happened and found herself poised at the brink of a deep and rapidly-widening chasm. Ash, standing on the other side, appeared to be on solid ground while she felt quaking and saw cracks appear all around her. She watched, horrified, as row after row of trellised vines fell into the pit. The sky darkened. Clouds brought rain that poured down, turning the soil into a quagmire.

Remaining where she was guaranteed she'd join those hapless grapevines. Her boots slipped in the goop as soon as she tried to retreat. She scrabbled for traction, found none, and slid toward the gaping hole. She gave herself a pep talk: the longer she resisted jumping across the pit, less chance she had of clearing it. With a strange feeling of detachment, she launched herself.

Beneath her, the chasm widened faster than she was traveling. She flapped her arms and thrashed her legs in an attempt to keep moving, but her pace slowed. The dreadful scenario reminded her of awful dreams from her childhood, where she fell and fell until she woke up, heart racing and gasping for breath. She'd heard that if she ever hit bottom before she awakened, she'd die.

"I'm here," said a deep voice that was definitely not Serrano's.

Strong arms wrapped around Sunny. Her fingers closed over damp wool. She smelled mothballs. Her rescuer was none other than Vincente Valderos. Her first instinct was to let go of him. To squirm away. But self-preservation conquered revulsion. She'd fall if she rejected her rescuer.

"You are safe, Sulis Minerva," he said.

Sunny stiffened. She had to be dreaming. She gazed up into putty-colored eyes with narrow black slits for pupils. Her stomach churned. He'd called her by her childhood nickname.

As a child, her parents had told her she became a twinkle in her mother's eye while they were traveling through Somerset, England on vacation. Sulis Minerva was a goddess with Celtic and Roman origins. Sunny had thought herself lucky they hadn't put that name of her birth certificate. She'd made her parents swear they'd stop calling her anything but Sunny when she reached the ripe old age of eight. How could Valderos possibly know?

Avoiding eye contact with him, she ducked her head. They were suspended above a chasm so deep, it stretched into infinity. A hot breeze gently raked the tangles from her wet hair. Steam rose from their clothing. Sunny wasn't sure whether heavy air was caressing the back of her neck or Valderos had another set of hands.

She opened her mouth to protest. Hot air flowed in, along with the odor of woodsmoke. She coughed. Inhaled again. Her eyes teared up. The odor was more acrid than any woodsmoke. Tinged with the smell of rotten eggs. It had to be sulphur.

Valderos held her closer. The mothball smell drifted up her nose. Sunny held her breath, even as his arms cradled her strongly, yet gently. Afraid of being dropped, she didn't dare pull away. Her face came into full contact with the woolen coat, leaving her with a couple of unpleasant choices…look down and draw in air that warmed her but smelled less pleasant with every breath, or look up and risk being mesmerized by his penetrating gaze. Instead, she closed her eyes.

Unable to hold her breath any longer, she gave in to the need for air. Surprisingly, she no longer smelled anything malodorous. Opening her eyes again, she realized he'd raised her so her nose was only inches from his white shirt and a thin, black tie. She turned her head, and her cheek came into contact with the shirt, which felt as soft as silk. Up close, Vincente Valderos smelled pleasantly of aftershave. He wore the same brand as Mark. She had an urge to burrow her head against his chest. Clinging to him began to feel natural, soothing. He felt far more real than she could ever have imagined.

The amulet hanging around her neck dug into her skin. Her topaz bracelet tightened until it turned into a painful vice. Sunny gasped. The spell broke. She knew what drew people to demons: They made their victims feel safe.

She wanted to look over Valderos's shoulder to see if he had grown wings, but how could he have concealed them under a coat? And how could he still be wearing that coat? When he gave a hollow chuckle, she realized he was invading her thoughts.

How long was he planning to hold her there, suspended above the pit? He didn't seem to be in any hurry to carry her over to solid ground. If she successfully pulled herself away from him, she'd fall. If she told him she hated him, would he drop her? But she didn't hate him, even for taking advantage of their present situation. He'd come to save her when her human protector couldn't. She didn't want to say that she owed him her life, but they both knew she did.

She tried to think of a good reason for him to fly them both over to join Ash. Every question in her head sounded provocative or banal. Finally, she decided simpler was better. "Why did this chasm appear?"

"Call it a dent in the atmosphere," Valderos said. "An anomaly."

His voice reverberated against her cheek. It lulled her. Her eyes drifted shut. She forced them open. "I don't like this," she told him. "Am I dreaming, or are we in an alternate reality?"

"For you," he said, "it must seem to be a dream. For now, I must keep it that way."

Her brain began sending out major flashing red danger signals. "Is this *your* reality?"

"Frequently." He sounded profoundly sad. His arms held her closer. "I wish it could be a dream that turned into a very different reality for me. One filled with hope for *my* future as well as yours."

Sunny felt his sorrow. It weighed down her heart, which beat slower, weaker. She became dizzy.

Sunny struggled to separate herself from him. He must be draining her essence. That was why she felt sorry for him. Why she was weakening. She had to get away from him, but she didn't dare let go. She didn't want to look at him, but she couldn't stop herself. His coat had become the cape he wore during the summer months. Floating back from his shoulders, it rippled behind him. There were no wings.

Sunny refused to be drawn into his illusion. She fought to keep him out of her mind. With all the remaining strength she possessed, she turned her eyes away from his and fought to bring lucid thought back into her befuddled brain.

What was a chasm doing in the middle of a Dallas vineyard? How had Valderos known she would need his help?

If he'd been unable to come when he sent Serrano, how had he come to save her from falling into the pit?

Was 'chasm' even the right word to use? It was a pit. Surely not a collapsed mining pit, although she seemed to remember mining had been a part of the region's past. Was it *the* Pit? Ash's 'Toasty Zone?'

"Your thoughts shouldn't stray in that direction," Valderos said. "Your destiny does not lie there, unless you choose it for yourself. You should complete your journey. It will free you. Free all of us."

All of us. The phrase lingered in the oppressive air. "Including you?" She needed to hear him say it. To own it.

"Yes, including me." He didn't elaborate.

Sunny was afraid to ask what freeing him would do, but she had to know. "And when that happens?"

"Then perhaps I will be waiting for you. And perhaps that will be good for us both."

Not a reassuring answer for Sunny. She had even more questions.

"That is enough information for you now." Valderos's voice sounded like velvet. It tried to wrap itself around her.

Sunny resisted. She didn't like velvet anymore. She wasn't going to allow Valderos and his snake-charming ways to lead her to another void; this time of forgetfulness.

"I have given you more information than I should." He sounded profoundly sad.

Sunny refused to feel sorry for him, again. For all she knew, he was behind everything that had happened at the Taricani Winery.

Valderos gave her a little shake. "I'm not responsible for any of this," he said. "Concentrate. You want to reach the other side. To rejoin Ash. You do not wish to remain here with me. Not at this time."

"I don't want to remain anywhere with you at any time." She hoped he believed her.

"Perhaps, in the future you will come to change your mind. Once you get to know me better." Both sides of his mouth curved up. His face lightened. His pupils rounded. The reptilian look faded, and he almost became human.

He released her, turned her around and gave her a less-than-gentle push. More like an outright shove, she thought as she barreled away at dizzying speed. She cast one final glance over her shoulder before doing what he'd told her to do…concentrate on reaching safety.

Valderos hovered above the chasm, cape billowing. His long, thin form swirled and twisted. He tipped his hat to her before a whirlwind surged up, trapping him, spinning him at a dizzying speed, and finally, pulling him down. A thin stream of black smoke curled up from the pit and became one with the clouds. A strong wind blew through the vineyard, dispersing the smoke. The chasm rapidly closed, and the vineyard returned to its dismal self.

CHAPTER THIRTY-SEVEN

Sunny landed on hard-packed soil. She sprawled, face down, her chin striking the ground with such jarring force, she wondered how she'd avoided cracking her front teeth.

Ash pulled her to her feet. "I'd better hold your arm if you're going to trip and fall that easily."

Her head spinning, Sunny felt him brusquely dust off her coat.

"Let's keep moving." He took her arm and tugged her into a stumbling run.

He seemed more concerned about hurrying than finding out if she'd been hurt. She wondered whether she'd had a vision. The entire episode with Valderos felt like an out-of-body experience.

"Come on, Sunny," Ash urged. "We should be on the patio before dark. I don't like the idea of you connecting with spirits when I can't see what's going on around us."

Sunny didn't want to try connecting with Lorenzo, but she kept moving, her jaw aching and her knees burning. Her bottom lip throbbed. She ran her tongue over it and tasted blood.

She *had* to have had a strange vision. She needed to remember it, so she could tell Armenta, but already, her memory of it was fading. The thing she remembered most…the *things* she remembered most …were sensations she *didn't* want to remember.

When Valderos had smiled before sending her back to Ash, she'd seen him as a man, not a demon. And she'd felt attracted to him in a way that was so immediate and visceral, it was beyond anything she'd ever experienced. That scared her more than anything else that had happened since he'd walked into The House of Serenity and bought the medicine buddha.

And he'd called her Sulis Minerva.

Why?

CHAPTER THIRTY-EIGHT

Sunny shook off Ash's hand and checked her tracker. An hour had passed. Her step-count was far greater than it should have been.

They left the trellised vines to walk across the lawn that separated the vineyard from the patio and tasting room. By that time, Sunny had decided her episode with Valderos and the pit hadn't been any kind of vision. Her memories might only be clouding because she felt so uncomfortable with her reactions.

She was supposed to share everything with Ash when they were working a case, but she wasn't about to tell him she'd had fuzzy feelings about their demon leader when, for a brief moment, he'd seemed more like a man. She didn't even know if she could confess that weirdness to Armenta. Maybe she'd try confiding in Watcher to see how *he* reacted.

Once they reached the back patio, Ash hung back, giving her the space she usually needed. She wasn't sure whether she wanted any space at that moment, but she walked on alone. Random thoughts flowed into her mind when she tried to clear it. Had the Taricanis, their architect or the contractor thought to consult an arborist about the health of that huge tree after its roots were disturbed for the new construction? Could Hixton have known about his inheritance and poisoned the tree, knowing Lorenzo frequently liked to sit under its shade? Would he care if guests as well as Lorenzo were killed when it toppled?

She circled the patio a couple of times at a slow pace before being able to concentrate enough to focus on the area where Lorenzo Taricani had been crushed. Echoes filtered through, coming from a distance: the cawing of a crow; water from the swollen creek skittering across rocks. Sounds sharpened by the raw, chill afternoon.

A fresh breeze added a snap to the air, mitigating heavy accents of loam and decay drifting up from the vineyard. Everything seemed remarkably tranquil. Maybe Valderos had staged everything so he could play mind games. She stopped guarding the gate to the most sensitive part of her psyche and opened her mind.

She sensed Lorenzo before she saw him. He was taller than she had expected. Lean. Tanned. A wave of silver hair skimmed his forehead.

He smiled as he approached. "You summoned me."

"Lorenzo Taricani?" She wanted verification.

He inclined his head and Sunny spotted a huge fissure in his scalp. She swallowed bile and forced herself not only to stay where she was, but to paste on a pleasant smile.

"What do you want to know?" he asked.

"Why you gave Bill Hixton the winery."

"That's the way it has to be." Lorenzo gestured toward the barren vineyard. "I made mistakes. I didn't listen to the land. To save my children, I have remained here as a penance. I want my father to move on, but he won't leave without me."

"I want to help all of you," Sunny told him. "I want to help you and your father leave here and to bring the winery back to life. It needs the Taricani family. The wine doesn't like Bill Hixton. Neither does the land. I've been visited by the caretaker."

"He makes it unsafe for my children," Lorenzo insisted. "My mistakes angered the land, and the caretaker materialized."

"I *know*."

Everything began to drop into place. The sense of foreboding she'd experienced in the wine cellar, when she'd told Ash the wine didn't like Bill Hixton. The vibrations. The caretaker, whose role she now understood.

Lorenzo Taricani's spirit became less substantial. A sense of urgency filled Sunny. "How do I remove the curse?"

"I don't know." He faded into a mist that drifted over to the vines.

Sunny knew she wasn't going to see him again. He had told her all he could, but it wasn't enough. Frustrated, she looked for the shadow she knew must be Giuseppe. He should have been able to manifest more readily in the fine, misting rain falling around her, but after Lorenzo left, her mind remained empty of anything but her own thoughts.

The misting rain stopped. A white fog replaced it, seeping between grapevines and trellises; surrounding the retaining wall; billowing across the patio. It became so dense it blanketed everything, even the sky. Sunny still had a flashlight in her pocket. She snapped it on. Its beam struck the fog and bounced back. Momentarily blinded, she hurriedly turned it off.

Time to call it a day. More than time. "Ash, stay where you are. I'm done, and I'm coming to you," she called.

He didn't answer.

Knowing the wall was on her left, she walked forward and bumped right into it. Confused, she turned her back and struck out for the tasting room.

Again, she bumped into the retaining wall. She refused to give in to panic. Either the spirits were playing around with her orientation or Valderos had a hand in it. She tried again. That time, her steps took her into a swirling vortex of white. Reaching out, her hands touched nothing but air, even after she knew she should have reached the glass doors.

"Ash," she called. "Where are you?"

The mist swirled, blanketing sounds. Her voice came back to her…dull, empty, and devoid of all feeling.

"Ash!" she shouted.

Had she managed to step through the gap in the wall? She looked down. No grass. Flagstones disappeared into the fog. If only Ash would answer her, she felt sure she'd be able to find him.

She turned around. If she couldn't find the building, at least she could go back to the wall. She bumped into it three steps later. One hand on top, she inched her way to the opening that led to the lawn. An odor of woodsmoke drifted up her nose. She almost wished she smelled mothballs.

She took a mental leap away from that thought and used the line where the flagstones ended and the grass began to continue moving forward. It seemed far too long before she reached the other side. The heavy, loamy odor persisted, but she couldn't detect mothballs or woodsmoke.

"Ash!" she shouted again.

"Sunny!"

"I'm here," she called, relief almost making her dizzy. "I'm coming toward you. Don't move."

"I won't," he promised. "I'm standing right next to the building."

"I'm using the retaining wall for guidance," she said. "Keep talking, so I can find you."

"Okay."

Silence.

"Ash, I asked you to keep talking."

"Sorry. I was trying to figure out what to say. Maybe I should ask your opinion why, as soon as the rain left, a thick fog set in?"

"I don't think the fog has anything to do with the weather." She inched forward again, trying to pinpoint the direction of his voice.

"I suppose it has everything to do with what appears to be this cursed vineyard," he said. "I'm using the word cursed very loosely, for whoever else is listening," he added, his voice louder. "We come in peace, here. We only want to find out if supernatural forces are trying to stop this property being sold, and if so, why. We'd really appreciate it if whoever's spooking around here leaves, crosses over, goes into the light or whatever it takes to vacate the winery and vineyard. Sunny's a psychic, and Armenta, her assistant, is a seer. They can help you leave, so we can, too."

She found he was close-by. She reached out her right hand and waved it around. It connected with something.

"Ouch," Ash said. "That was my cheek."

She peered into the fog and saw the outline of his coat. "There you are. Thank goodness."

"You need to cut your nails." Ash put his hand to his cheek. "You could put an eye out with those things."

"Well, hello to you, too." Sunny wasn't as happy to see him as she'd been only moments before. "I don't have long nails, and my hand was nowhere near your cheek."

"Well, someone scratched the holy...the dickens...out of me," he grumbled.

Sunny took his hand away. "Oh," she said.

Something really *had* scraped him. Ash had a livid welt on his right cheek.

CHAPTER THIRTY-NINE

Despite Ash downplaying the welt, Armenta insisted on tending to his injury. She pressed a cotton ball to his cheek. Searing pain shot through his face. He bit back a curse, shoved her hand away, and held his hand over the injury to protect it from any further well-intentioned torture.

. "What did you soak that cotton ball with?" he asked her. "Rubbing alcohol or iodine?"

"Witch hazel." She turned the bottle around so he could see the label. "It's not supposed to be painful." Her mouth pursed into a moue of concentration as she pondered the reddened area. "I'll prepare a potion. If I don't, that welt may fester."

"Great." Ash picked up a hand mirror Sunny had brought to the table and examined his war wound. "What scratched me...a witch's fingernail?"

"More likely, a cane from one of those diseased grapevines." Armenta dropped the cotton ball into the garbage can. "You've both told me how unpleasant the vineyard is. I'm sure it's filled with bacteria as well as dirt." She shook one long, bony finger at Ash, rings glinting. "Not everything you encounter is bewitched, you know."

"Maybe not this time," he allowed, "but you and I both know there are plenty of other examples I can give you. Don't mix up a potion. I've got triple antibiotic at home."

Armenta snorted her disapproval of modern medicine and began selecting herbs from a spice rack. He took the opportunity to study Sunny, pouring over a large book she'd taken from the coffee table. She appeared engrossed in her reading, scanning page after page, a full cup of mint tea cooling beside another hefty tome entitled *Green Witch Spells and Incantations.*

He thought Sunny's demeanor had been off all afternoon. He should ask Armenta if she'd observed the change, but he'd have to wait until they left the shop. Standing outside The House of Serenity in the dark, discussing his misgivings about Sunny's behavior with Armenta was the last thing he wanted to do. He never felt entirely comfortable with her, even in well-lit places. Besides, she'd probably tell him he was imagining things. Instead, he should go home, shower and order pizza. If he still felt the same misgivings in the morning, then he'd deal with them by talking directly with his partner.

"Sunny, what are you looking for?" he asked.

"A spell to do something about that caretaker." She put the book aside. "Would you like some coffee, or are you sticking with tea?"

"Coffee sounds good." He downed the mint tea, even though he didn't like it. Armenta had probably brewed it for what she deemed a very good reason. She'd also driven over to deal with yet another scrape the shop's team of private investigators had gotten themselves into, he reminded himself. His cheek smarted, and he tried to find humor in his use of the word 'scrape,' but he couldn't.

Ash longed to be done with Valderos and his demands. He'd caught the demon giving Sunny what he thought were speculative, even predatory looks. When she brought the carafe to the table and filled two mugs, she kept her attention on the task. She placed a mug in front of him before taking the carafe back to its base to keep the coffee heated. He thanked her, but she avoided eye contact.

"I need a couple more ingredients." Armenta bustled toward the shop door. "Don't discuss anything about the case while I'm gone."

"Wouldn't think of it." Ash felt drained. He hoped the coffee would perk him up.

"When did Valderos say he wanted another report?" Sunny asked. She sat down and picked up her mug.

The lights flickered.

"I think Valderos is here," Armenta said from the doorway. "I see a vehicle in the parking lot, but it isn't the limo. Must be the rental car."

"If it's a Nissan Leaf, then he's here." Ash felt even more drained at the thought of having to report to Valderos. "Serrano said it doesn't have tinted windows, so Valderos can only ride in it after the sun goes down. Ride or hide. Take your pick."

"I don't know what a Leaf looks like, but I expect that's them. Vincente doesn't need me to open the front door, so I'll get my herbs." Armenta went into the shop.

The front door crashed. A draft blew back the apartment door.

"He's definitely here." Sunny put her head in her hands. "I wish he'd waited until tomorrow."

Watcher screeched and flapped his wings. Valderos told Watcher to be quiet and leave him alone. The usual pantomime enacted between the gryphon and the demon. Ash had noticed Watcher sleeping in the gargoyle corner when they returned from the vineyard, his granite head tucked under his granite wing. He always became agitated when Vincente Valderos arrived, but he had stopped flying circles over the demon's head.

As long as Valderos behaved, Watcher stayed in the background. Ash felt bad about initially comparing Watcher to a garden gnome. He had no doubt the gryphon would attack anyone who tried to harm Sunny, Armenta, or Katie. His daughter and Watcher shared a special bond. Ash wasn't sure he liked that, but Katie loved her gargoyle friend, and Watcher fully reciprocated her affection.

Ash heard Armenta cordially greeting Valderos. She was a little too comfortable around the demon for his liking. He'd thought the seer, of all people, would stay vigilant. Inviting Valderos into her apartment definitely wasn't an example of Armenta keeping her distance. But why were vampires the only creatures that could be kept out of homes unless they were invited inside? Couldn't crosses or hexes keep Valderos out? With his background as an altar boy, Ash thought he should know more about vanquishing demons than he did. He'd left religion behind a long time ago, but it might be time to check in with a parish priest at the closest Catholic church.

The thought of entering a church again brought Ash back to the present.

He should help Sunny clear the remains of their snack from the table for the meeting. He leaned across to take her dishes and caught her in an unguarded moment. Her face looked flushed. Both her hands were shaking. The teapot rattled on the tray when she picked it up. Although he tried to dismiss it, he couldn't stop thinking that Sunny's reaction to Valderos's arrival was closer to what he had observed when she saw Mark Kingston walk into the shop.

A ripple of disquiet flowed through him. If Sunny was falling under Valderos's spell, he would never be able to trust her again. With both their souls on the line, how could he know she wouldn't put her own needs first? If she struck a side-bargain with Valderos, he'd lose his soul while she kept hers.

He told himself Valderos was manipulating reality again, but the doubts lingered, even as he took the tray from Sunny before it crashed to the floor.

CHAPTER FORTY

Valderos filled the kettle, which was his only contribution to making the tea that always accompanied their meetings. After setting the kettle on the stove, he pointed a finger at the burner. It promptly lit.

"What kind of cookies do you have today, Ms. Kaslov?" he asked.

"More of your favorites, Vincente." Armenta smiled, all benevolence.

Ash had seen her bring a sachet out of her pocket and dump the contents into one of the pots she had taken down from a cabinet. She uncorked a vial and scattered its contents into a small pot bubbling away next to the kettle. After stirring the frothing brew, she emptied it into a china bowl, carried the bowl to the table and placed it in front of Ash.

"I want you to dab the salve onto your finger, then wipe it on the welt," she instructed.

The scent of camphor drifted up his nose. He swore the thick yellow gel moved. He pushed the bowl aside. "No thanks."

"I'll do it for you," Sunny offered.

"Something's moving in there." Ash beckoned her over. "See for yourself."

The gel circled clockwise, then counter-clockwise. It reminded Ash of the swirling green tea Armenta had brewed several times in the past. Tea that made people forget what they'd seen.

Through the rising steam, Ash saw Valderos intently staring at Sunny. The pupils of his putty-colored eyes were rounder that day. Ash couldn't remember them ever being anything but disturbingly reptilian. The demon's mouth had lost its one-sided droop.

Sunny plunged the tip of one index finger into the salve. "There's nothing wrong with it," she said, rubbing the gel over her hand. "It's warm and soothing. I'm sure it'll make your cheek feel better."

"What is wrong with Mr. Haines?" Valderos peered at Ash. "Ah, I see." He raised his hand and waved it in Ash's general direction. "Easily taken care of."

A flash of blue light from the tips of Valderos's fingers, a sizzling sound and a puff of smoke brought Ash to his feet and his right hand to his face. "Are you crazy? You burned me!"

Sunny forced Ash's hand away. Her eyes widened. "That's *amazing*. You'd better look." She offered him the hand mirror.

Ash needed better lighting. He went into the bathroom and turned on the light over the sink. The blemish on his cheek had vanished. He returned to the table. "What the hell?" he asked Valderos.

"You do like to throw that 'h' word around, Mr. Haines." Valderos sat. He looked smug.

"You healed me." Ash warily sat down opposite Valderos. "How did you do that? It felt like an electrical charge."

"One of my parlor tricks." Valderos waved his hand again, that time without blue sparks flowing from his fingers. "An insignificant gift from me to you."

"With strings, no doubt," Ash said. "What do you want? Or did you already take it?"

CHAPTER FORTY-ONE

Valderos sighed heavily. He definitely did breathe, Sunny thought. She tried to remember if that was only a human characteristic. Her only guidelines were from a few childhood visits to Sunday school. She'd hated it, and her parents, who were more into museum visits or picnics in parks, didn't insist she continue going.

The kettle whistled loudly, startling her. She saw Ash jump, too. Armenta, completely unaffected, continued studying her cell phone, perhaps scrolling through messages, texts or reading a recipe. Sunny felt like shaking the seer, although she wasn't sure why Armenta's insouciance was annoying her. Armenta must have sensed Sunny's agitation. She placed her phone in her pocket and went, skirts rustling, to take the kettle off the stove.

"Do not forget to warm the pot first," Valderos instructed. "The British are correct. It does bring a stronger and more vibrant flavor to the tea."

Armenta, her back turned, poured water, added scoops of tea from three canisters, covered the pots with cozies, and brought two tins of cookies to the table. Sunny still didn't understand where all those cookies came from. She'd sneaked several peeks into Armenta's big bag since they started working together, never seeing tins inside. Yet any time tea was mentioned, Armenta would dig into her purse, pronounce she had baked, and bring out at least one tin of cookies. Sometimes more.

The first tin she opened contained thumbprint cookies, favored not only by Valderos but Katie. Sunny didn't mention Katie's name or her preference in cookies. Ash didn't like his daughter mentioned in front of Valderos.

TAINTED LEGACY

"I believe there was more than the incident of Mr. Haines' injury," Valderos said, opening the discussion about their trip to the vineyard.

"If you know so much, already," Ash responded, his tone dry, "why do you need a blow by blow from us?"

"I am not all-knowing, Mr. Haines, as much as you would like to believe it." Valderos took two of the cookies Armenta offered him. "I suspected there might be incidents when I heard you two were returning to the vineyard today. Mr. Hixton called me. He asked the reason for another visit. Was I really interested in purchasing, or was I sending spies to steal the winery's fermentation secrets?" He rolled his eyes, another new phenomenon for him. "I have enough problems with my own fermentation practices. I do not need further complications from another failing winery."

"That leads me to the obvious question," Ash interrupted. "Why do you want to buy the Taricani winery? Their vines aren't producing, and I suspect whatever's in all those barrels is completely undrinkable. The cellar smells like Brettanomyces is probably responsible for the problems with the winemaking process. Hixton's lying to you when he says is the wine isn't ready. I doubt it ever will be."

Sunny noticed a full cup of tea in front of her. She didn't remember the pots or the cups being brought to the table. She definitely had no idea what flavor tea had been served to her, and she wondered which pot her tea had come from.

"I agree with you, Mr. Haines. Despite his protestations to the contrary, I believe Mr. Hixton knows the true condition of the vineyard and the contents of those barrels. Why, otherwise, would he sell all the bottles?" Valderos turned his attention to Sunny. "You have been served the Oolong, Ms. Kinston. What have you discovered from your contact with the property?"

Sunny turned her attention from her cup to their leader. "For one thing, the wine hates Hixton. It's turned to vinegar to spite him. As for the vineyard, we may have gathered enough information to figure out why it stopped producing. I made contact with Lorenzo Taricani this afternoon. He said he cut his children out of the will because they'd be in danger if they inherited the winery. He said the land didn't like his farming methods." She paused, trying to remember Lorenzo's exact words. "He told me the caretaker was the land. I think he meant the land is responsible for everything, and the caretaker represents it."

Ash frowned. Armenta, lips pursed, nodded once, very definitively, as though that statement made perfect sense.

"Another cursed vineyard." Valderos gave another deep sigh. "It must be put to rights."

"And you're going to make us do the deed for you." Ash sounded resigned.

"Yes, indeed, Mr. Haines." Valderos tapped his index finger with the onyx ring against the table. A tiny blue spark shot out. "It must be done to complete the terms of your contract."

"So how are we supposed to deal with the caretaker?" Sunny asked. "He comes and goes whenever he wants, he's made of mud, and he almost smothered me before Serrano arrived." She didn't add anything about the pit opening up and Valderos saving her from falling into it.

A strange light flowed across Valderos's face before he asked Armenta: "What other tricks do you have up your sleeve, Ms. Kaslov?" He sounded slightly amused.

Sunny bit back a gasp. His features had softened. She wondered whether Armenta or Ash had noticed. Ash seemed preoccupied with his tea. He stared into the depths of it while toying with the handle. She wondered whether he was trying to find out if it would start swirling.

Armenta set down her own cup, which was empty. "I must consult with the shaman," she said as Valderos refilled it. "We're talking about an entire vineyard, plus the Taricani family and Mr. Hixton. That's a lot of cleansing, even for my strongest spells and potions."

"You had all better get moving on this," Valderos said. "You only have another week."

"Another short deadline." Ash didn't even sound angry.

Sunny couldn't say she was surprised, either. It was like she had been waiting for the other shoe to drop from the moment Valderos gave them the case.

"I must leave you." Valderos stood. "Thank you for the report, the tea, and the excellent cookies." He inclined his head toward Armenta before zeroing in on Ash, who had leaned back in his chair and folded his arms across his chest. "Mr. Haines, you will still benefit from using Ms. Kaslov's salve to avoid scarring to your cheek. I can heal infections, but my method does not restore a human's skin to its normal texture." He strode toward the door leading into the shop, the hem of his long woolen coat undulating in soft waves.

Before leaving, he doffed the hat that had suddenly appeared on his head, and his gaze focused on Sunny. Both sides of his mouth curved into a slight smile. A pleasurable warmth stole over her. An unnerving warmth. She remembered how chilled he used to make her feel.

It couldn't be her imagination…Vincente Valderos was becoming more human.

CHAPTER FORTY-TWO

Ash noticed Valderos wasn't as pale or waxy after exchanging glances with Sunny. Even the air in the apartment didn't feel as charged as it usually did during one of the demon's visits. As their self-declared leader swirled out the door, the hem of his black coat flapping, Ash wondered what might have happened to Sunny while he was talking his way out of a trespassing charge at the cidery.

She hadn't said much on their trip back to Salem, except Valderos had come to help her instead of sending Serrano. More than likely, Ash thought, anger bubbling inside him, the demon had taken the opportunity to put a spell on her, which Armenta was going to have to neutralize. He wished Valderos was susceptible to a silver bullet. He'd have melted down a bunch of silver tableware and jewelry, poured them into a mold, and made his own projectiles if he knew that shooting Valderos would have any effect. Armenta had assured him it wouldn't, and that so far, nothing else she or the shaman had researched would have any effect. Ash thought Armenta wasn't trying hard enough.

What he wanted most was to make sure Valderos understood that messing with Sunny and the trusted partnership they'd built was off-limits. The big problem was, Ash knew he had no bargaining power. No way to threaten Valderos. The fiend held all the cards.

Sunny laid a hand on his arm. "Go home, Ash. You look tired, another shipment comes tomorrow. Do you still want to be here to receive it?"

She sounded like she was eager to get rid of him. And why would she suddenly question whether he'd want to help her out with the shipment? Was she giving out subtle signals that she was going to refuse his partnership offer after all? Would she really be willing to stay in cramped quarters while he rented out the other part of the building to another business? He gave her one of the sharp looks he'd used on suspects. It had worked well for him on previous occasions.

Sunny evaded his tactic by quickly turning to Armenta. "Can you stay a few minutes after Ash leaves?" she asked the seer.

That wasn't even a subtle hint, Ash thought, his uneasiness growing. "I guess that's my cue to get out of here." He took his coat from a peg and shrugged into it.

"Get some rest." Sunny gave him what he knew was a fake smile. She wasn't very good at masking emotions.

"See you tomorrow." He jammed his hat on his head and opened the back door. "I'll be in the storeroom if you need me for any reason."

"I'll bring you a mug of coffee and a pastry," Armenta promised, when Sunny didn't answer.

Ash stepped outside. The door closed and locked behind him.

Something was definitely hinky, he told himself as he walked to the Rover. More than hinky. Thoroughly disturbing. He felt jittery and out of sorts. Not surprising, after being given the bum's rush from Sunny's apartment. She'd obviously needed to discuss something privately with Armenta. He wanted to think it was about whatever Armenta had put into the tea she'd served Valderos, but he sensed it was something else entirely. She had to have noticed the change in Valderos between coming into the apartment and leaving it.

Maybe he'd call her after taking Jake for a long walk and eating dinner. He needed to give her time to share her secrets with Armenta, even though he felt shut out and, if he was completely honest with himself, envious. He wanted Sunny to bond closer with him, not her tarot-card wielding, crystal ball-gazing assistant.

The House of Serenity crouched in the darkness. Ash hoped Armenta had put strong spells around not only the shop but the apartment. Then he told himself no spells would ever be strong enough while Vincente Valderos had free rein to come and go as he wished.

CHAPTER FORTY-THREE

Armenta had insisted on helping Sunny clean up while listening to an unedited account of the events at the winery. She closed the lids on the empty cookie tins. "This is very disturbing," she said.

"I believe Ash and I were deliberately isolated from each other." Sunny emptied the washbowl and rinsed out the sink. "The creek swelled before the clouds rolled in. I suppose it could have been a flash flood, but that's pretty unusual around here, isn't it?"

"Not my area of expertise." Seated at the table, Armenta tapped her gold tooth with one black-lacquered fingernail. "But I do remember hearing hundreds of homes in North Salem flooded back in the 1960's."

Sunny nodded. "I read about the Willamette and Mill Creek flooding several times, but nothing big has happened since, I think, 2012. Today's weather forecast was for only patchy showers."

Armenta planted her elbows on the table and tented her fingers. "I suppose flash floods could occur after heavy rains in the Coast Range, but you said the creek comes from a spring on the property."

"Ash told me it didn't rain in the orchard while he was there. I suppose it's possible a neighboring farm's irrigation system could have been damaged. Maybe water from that drained into the creek."

"Perhaps. You could check the Polk County website for information, or local news sources. A reporter might have gone out to wherever the flood started." Armenta didn't sound like she believed the event was anything other than the result of supernatural meddling, but she was giving lip-service to other possibilities.

"You and I both know that's highly improbable," Sunny said.

She agonized. If she withheld information from Armenta, how could the seer help her?

"You can trust me," Armenta said. "Unless I feel it's vital to your safety, I won't tell Ash anything you don't want him to hear. Is Mark the problem?"

"Not anymore, he's not." At least Sunny felt sure of that.

She told Armenta about Mark trying to take control of her day and how she'd left his car to walk back to the shop. Armenta told her she'd made the right decision. Encouraged by the seer's support, Sunny then told her about the pit and her reaction to Valderos's version of the cavalry arriving to save the damsel in distress. She tried to downplay the emotional component, but Armenta's wrinkles deepened to such a degree, many of them linked up with their neighbors. Her brow hung over her eyes, the corners of her mouth drooped close to her jawline, and her eyes became pinpricks of glittering light. Alarmed as well as humiliated, Sunny plowed on.

"Valderos knew my childhood nickname. I didn't like it, so my parents stopped using it when I was eight years old." Her mouth felt dry. "How could he know so much about me? Could he get into my medical records? The divorce proceedings? If he can alter a contract that's locked in my safe, then he could change anything he liked to give him leverage. Make me do things I don't want to. Unethical things. Dangerous things…"

Armenta waved away Sunny's misgivings. "Let's avoid wild speculation," she recommended. "Vincente's main interest is in you fulfilling the terms of the contract you signed, not whether you got antibiotics when you were a teenager or some other relatively useless piece of information."

Sunny could still see Valderos storing up every little scrap of information he could use to his advantage later, if and when it became necessary to force her to do something that conflicted with her personal code of ethics.

"I don't at all like you feeling such a strong connection with him, however." Armenta had moved on from an invasion of Sunny's privacy to that awful moment when she had discovered she was holding onto Valderos for more than safety.

Sunny wasn't even sure whether falling into a pit of undetermined origin had factored into keeping her arms wrapped around him. Under Armenta's intense scrutiny, she felt like she'd subjected herself to the seer's personal version of the Spanish Inquisition.

Searching for a way to avoid wringing her hands, she chose to grab the napkin holder and tidy up the paper napkins she had pushed haphazardly into it when Valderos arrived. "Holding onto him wasn't at all unpleasant," she confessed. It didn't sound so dreadful when she watered down the experience.

"An understatement is another form of lying," Armenta admonished.

Sunny's cheeks reddened before she had time to deny she was doing anything of the sort. Being cross-examined by Armenta was worse than being interrogated by Ash. "Fine…I'll give you the unvarnished truth. I think I liked the experience a whole lot more than I should have, and I think he really enjoyed it, too. But what if he appears in my apartment in the middle of the night? What am I supposed to do then? Light a smudge stick? Toss holy water at him? Would holy water even work on him?"

Armenta's eyebrows drew toward each other. "I don't see Vincente forcing his attentions on you." Although she definitely sounded reproachful, one corner of her mouth twitched. "We would have to investigate the effectiveness of holy water on a being of unknown species," she added.

Sunny refused to treat the situation lightly. "He could use the velvet quality in his voice or some other trick he's kept hidden up his sleeve to convince me to come willingly to the slaughter."

"I don't think he's planning on murdering you, either." Armenta shook her head and tsk, tsk'd, The second tsk came out as a snort. She grabbed one of the napkins and covered her nose and mouth. Her shoulders shook.

"It's not funny, Armenta." Sunny tried her best to be indignant, but when Armenta stopped trying to hide her laughter and guffawed, Sunny threw up her hands in surrender. "All right; I was exaggerating."

Armenta controlled herself with a visible effort and wiped her eyes. "I'm sorry, but that bit about the smudge stick and holy water…I couldn't help myself."

"I agree it sounds ludicrous, but I'm scared, Armenta. What if he *did* convince me to get closer to him? I don't know what I'd do when the spell broke, either because you managed to save me or he tired of me. He's pure evil."

"I've never believed him to be completely evil." Armenta slowly shook her head, like she had tried to fit the evil title onto Valderos, but decided it wouldn't fit. "I think he's here on a mission. Possibly to atone for a great sin."

"Wouldn't that make him human? Demons don't atone for sins. Valderos definitely *isn't* human." She remembered his thin form turning to smoke as he hung above the pit.

"No, I agree, he's not. But neither is he completely demonic. He has moments of humanity. More so than when he first came to the shop. Over the months, he's exhibited vulnerability, he's fallen in love..."

"Surely, you're not classing his preoccupation with that mega-demon Valentine a romance, Armenta? Thinking about what I saw them doing when I crashed into his study still gives me chills."

"He needed to feel wanted," Armenta's smile was sad, like she knew what being lonely really meant. "He was bewitched by her. All of us were to some degree, even the children."

"She had major spell-power," Sunny acknowledged. "Even more than Valderos."

"She did. I can only hope Vincente was truthful when he said she's gone for good." Armenta pulled her shawl tighter around her shoulders. "Valentine is one demon I really don't think I could have vanquished, even with help from the shaman."

"Don't say that aloud." Sunny put a finger to her lips and shushed her assistant. "She could still hear you."

"I've been taking precautions." Armenta took a black candle from beneath her shawl, inserted it in an empty holder Sunny didn't remember being on the table only moments before, and lit it with a match from a box she pulled out of a pocket in her skirt. "Training Stella. Working with the shaman. I want to be ready for whatever spirits materialize during the course of your investigations. Protecting both you and Ash." A deep furrow creased her brow again. "I sensed tension between you two. Have you been arguing?"

"No. Nothing beyond occasional bickering. Minor disagreements. He's seemed unusually tense since we began this investigation." Sunny abandoned her napkin tidying. She'd actually shredded more than she'd straightened. "I think he senses something, Armenta, but I don't want to tell him about me hugging Valderos while being suspended over a pit. He'd immediately think it was the entrance to…well…you know where." She worried her bottom lip, like that would help. "Do I mention it casually over one of his bagel breakfasts? Oh, by the way, Ash, I put my arms around Valderos and liked it while we were hanging over…"

"No, I see your point." Armenta traced the subtle pattern in the damask tablecloth with her fingers. "Let's give our brains a chance to work overnight on the right way for you to tell Ash tomorrow. The longer you wait, the harder it's going to be, and the greater risk his indignation will be justified. He still has the mindset of a detective. He'll believe you've withheld extremely sensitive information that you should have divulged immediately. You'll also give Valderos the leverage you fear. There might even be other ramifications we haven't yet considered."

"What you're suggesting sounds like pushing the problem onto a back burner, Scarlet O'Hara style, and I've already been there and done that since it happened."

"Sleeping on a problem allows your brain to work without those superfluous thoughts that crowd our minds during the day. You may discover a way to diplomatically tell him about the incident, rather than blurting out something spontaneously." Armenta sounded defensive. She stood and shook out her long taffeta skirt. "Do you need me to make you a sleeping potion?"

Sunny thought she might not notice Valderos coming to visit in the middle of the night if she took any kind of sedative. "No, but thanks for the offer."

"Ask Watcher to sleep in here," Armenta suggested. "He would never let anything happen to you."

"That's a much better idea." Sunny brought Armenta's coat while the seer was packing the empty cookie tins into her bag. "Thank you," she said. "I don't say that often enough. You always give me wise counsel."

Armenta patted Sunny's shoulder. "My most important job here, I think."

"Definitely." Tears welled in Sunny's eyes. "We all benefit from your knowledge and your fearlessness where Valderos is concerned."

For a moment, she had almost called him Vincente. A ripple of uneasiness passed through her. She was having one of those disturbing tipped-sideways moments when she wasn't sure what was real and what was imagined.

She made sure Armenta safely reached her car before closing and locking the back door. The shop was in darkness except for the usual low-level emergency lighting in the center aisle. She wondered whether she really wanted to go in search of Watcher. If he was needed, he'd easily find his way into the apartment. He'd already turned up in Ash's apartment one morning, and he'd flown in and destroyed an entire stand of trees before being brought back to the shop in Armenta's car.

Far from sleepy, she decided to watch TV. Propped up in bed with three pillows, she tried to concentrate on a 20/20 episode, but it involved a winery and a twisted family. Too close to the Taricani clan. She tried a Hallmark movie, but it, too, was about a winery, and too sugary for her taste. She turned off the TV and stared up at the covered skylight above the bed. That night, she thought she would have welcomed a view of the stars.

She closed her eyes. She'd left Tina's ugly lamp glowing in the living room. Its gentle light penetrated her lids in a comforting manner. She hoped she'd be able to sleep without any spirits interrupting. Second only to finding Vincente Valderos sitting at the end of her bed, Tina's apparition was the most disturbing. Over the months, the phantom cat's presence had become a welcome nightly occurrence.

After tossing and turning interminably for two hours, Sunny found a tolerable position on her left side, one pillow beneath her head and another clutched in her arms. She drifted off.

When she awoke, gray dawn penetrated the apartment through the only window, mounted high above the sink. At the end of the bed was an indentation. Sunny hoped it had been made by the cat. She sat up and stretched.

Something glinted on the nightstand. She found it was the amulet she always wore around her neck. She knew she hadn't taken it off before going to bed. Taking a closer look at the imprint on the end of her bed., she decided it was larger than those made by the cat.

CHAPTER FORTY-FOUR

Ash called at 7:30 AM. Sunny had made coffee and was about to take a shower. She picked up immediately.

"I thought I'd better speak to you instead of texting," he said. "The shipment's arriving early. I'll take it in before I go to the cider house, but I won't have time to unpack it. I'm hoping to catch the owner and his daughter at lunch. I'd like to get more information from them about the feud over the water rights to the creek."

"Do you think it's wise to go over there alone?" Sunny didn't.

She didn't like the thought of Ash going anywhere near the Fortunas or their cider house without her. What if the place was enchanted? What if the caretaker didn't keep to the Taricanis' side of the property line? She wasn't sure Ash would see supernatural trouble coming before he got into trouble.

"I've developed a heebie-jeebie meter of my own, working with you and Armenta," Ash said, as though he'd channeled her misgivings. "I didn't get any weird vibes from them or their property, but I definitely feel spooked whenever we're at the winery or in the vineyard." He sounded curt and detached.

"Will you call me when you leave there?" She didn't think that was an unreasonable request, but she heard his exasperated sigh. "Is there something you're not telling me?" she asked.

"Is there something you're not telling *me?*"

"No, I don't think so." *Liar,* she scolded herself.

"If you must know, I thought I had a connection with the daughter, Andrea," he said. "I should capitalize on that."

Sunny had some unkind thoughts about Ash and Andrea. Then she chastised herself for being possessive. The only friend Ash had outside their little dysfunctional band was Detective Brad Schilling. Katie and Brad's eldest daughter played on the same little league team.

Ash deserved a woman-friend. Andrea Fortuna was very attractive, and she'd definitely sent out signals to Ash that she was available and receptive.

"You should go. Ask her out on a date."

It took a lot of effort for Sunny to tell him that. Her mouth felt dry. She wondered what was wrong with her mouthwash.

"I'm glad I have your permission." His sarcasm was as dry as the inside of her mouth.

"I'd better let you go," she said. "Thank you for taking in the shipment this morning."

"I'll let you know I made it out of the cider house." He hung up.

CHAPTER FORTY-FIVE

Sunny's phone pinged, announcing a text. She hoped it was from Belinda or Stella, letting her know they were available to work. She had removed the 'closed for inventory' sign from the window. With all the new merchandise, much of it seasonal, she needed to have the shop open. But without more help than Armenta could give, she really didn't want to have to work the register, unpack the shipment and work the floor solo.

She wasn't feeling her best…she had a slight headache to go with her dry mouth. She started a pot of coffee before checking to see if she'd received bad news or just notification of a killer sale at one of the local department stores.

The text was from Mark. He hoped she'd liked the flowers and was willing to forgive him for being an idiot.

What flowers?

Sunny tightly girded her bathrobe before unlocking the apartment door. A soft caw from the front of the shop told her Watcher was awake. She had to weave her way around multiple displays to reach the counter. When she did, she saw a delivery van in the parking lot and a woman walking toward the front door, a huge bouquet held with both hands.

Sunny unlocked the door. The woman smiled at her. "Special delivery," she said, handing over the bouquet, which had a white envelope sticking out between sunflowers, lilies, daisies, and pink roses. The vase was so heavy, Sunny almost dropped it. She watched the woman climb back into the van before placing the bouquet on the counter and locking the door. When she turned around, Watcher had the card in his beak and was about to take off.

"Oh, no you don't." She had to play tug of war to get the envelope. "None of your business," she told him. He gave her what sounded remarkably like a bad word instead of a caw before allowing her to take the envelope. He eyed it. "Private," she said.

Watcher selected a pink rose from the bouquet, pulled it out and dropped it onto the floor.

"Watcher!" Sunny bent down to pick it up. A sunflower landed on her head. "Stop it." She stood up and wagged her finger at him. "Bad bird. Go to the gargoyle corner."

Watcher ignored her command. He ate a lily.

"All right." She opened the envelope and took out a card that told her Mark was very sorry for ruining what could have been an enjoyable lunch, and for acting like a fool. He said he loved her and asked her to reconsider shutting him out of her life. Could he take her out to dinner?"

Sunny found Watcher leaning over her shoulder. "Did you finish reading, big guy?" she asked.

The feathers on the back of his neck rose. He shook himself off energetically before using his whiplike lion's tail to knock the bouquet and its vase onto the floor at the back of the counter. While Sunny was still deciding how to respond, he took off, wheeling into the gargoyle corner.

"So, first you make a big mess, and then you take off?" Sunny wasn't sure what to do. If she cleaned up, she wouldn't have time to shower and make herself presentable. And she still hadn't taken even a sip of her coffee.

"I'd appreciate it if you'd clean up here," she said, peering into the darkened corner on her way back to the apartment. "I get it. You don't like Mark, and you don't want me to see him anymore. I don't have time to work through your grievances right now. We'll discuss them later."

While washing her hair, she wondered what she could possibly do to punish Watcher when he misbehaved. She hoped his concrete stomach would let him know he shouldn't eat lilies.

But as she scrambled to put the flowers and the broken vase into a garbage bag and mop up the water, she thought Watcher was probably right...Mark's gift wasn't enough to make up for his behavior. She returned his text, thanking him for the flowers, but told him she didn't want to go out to dinner, and she didn't want him sending any more gifts.

CHAPTER FORTY-SIX

Armenta and Stella both arrived at 8:50 AM. Stella checked to make sure all popular merchandise was well-stocked, while Armenta ducked under the fringed awning covering her arbor and turned on both the lamp illuminating the shelves at the back and the string of lights hanging at the front. She brought her tarot deck and crystal ball to the table and seated herself in the old highbacked chair with burgundy velvet upholstery that she refused to replace. At 8:58 AM, Stella took up her post near the door, ready to greet a small clump of customers already gathering outside.

Sunny went behind the counter. Watcher had flown in from the gargoyle corner and taken up residence beside the register. "I'm not going to see him again," she whispered. The gryphon's concrete feathers stirred beneath her hand as it traveled down his neck to caress his folded wings. "Did you see or hear anything unusual last night?"

The gryphon's talons gripped the edge of the counter.

Sunny was about to ask him more questions when Stella unlocked the door. Customers surged into the shop. They cheerfully greeted Stella, waved at Sunny and Belinda, then called hello to Armenta. All regulars, they picked up baskets before plunging into the crowded aisles. While Sunny waited for them to bring their purchases to the register, she mulled over her short conversation with Ash that morning. For the first time in their relationship, she felt they were both keeping secrets from each other, and those secrets were undermining the mutual trust they had built up over the past months.

Wilma and Betty, two of her favorite customers, came up to the register first.

They both lightly petted Watcher. "We do so love him," Wilma said, smiling at the gryphon's stony stare. "I swear, sometimes I almost believe he moves."

"He's so lifelike," Betty chimed in. "Do you have any idea where he came from?"

At least, Sunny thought, she could truthfully answer *that* question. "I don't. Neither does Armenta. She said he's been here since Tina opened the shop. I originally brought him to the counter from the gargoyle corner because I thought he was being overlooked. Now, he's such a part of the shop I would never sell him."

"I'm so glad to hear that. I'd really miss him." Wilma placed her wire basket on the counter. "Are you expecting anything new? I know another shipment's expected."

"We wanted to come tomorrow, but your sale ends today," Betty said.

"A new shipment arrives this morning, but we may not have time to put anything out until after the shop closes this evening." Sunny rang up the purchases and began wrapping the few items, all marked down. She added several incense sticks to Wilma's bag at no charge. Betty was the only other customer at the register. "You two can share these," she told them in an undertone.

"Oh, thank you so much." Betty beamed.

They were retired schoolteachers, and Sunny knew both were feeling the economic crunch. But they came in every week to browse, and they always bought a few cheap items.

After they left, Sunny looked for Stella. Although she had proved herself to be an excellent addition to the staff, Sunny still wasn't completely convinced her three-quarter timer wasn't working at The House of Serenity primarily so she could learn from Armenta, who had reluctantly taken on the self-professed witch as an apprentice.

Stella was nowhere to be seen, but several customers were clustering around the entrance to the gargoyle corner. Watcher turned his head in that direction. The feathers at the back of his neck rippled. Something was definitely up, Sunny thought. Since she had no one standing in line, she went to see what was so interesting.

After she worked her way through the onlookers, she spotted Stella the top of a rickety ladder they seldom used. The same one Sunny remembered falling from the first time Ash walked into the shop. Stella was attempting to reach a gargoyle on the top shelf, but she couldn't get her fingers around it. She leaned farther away from the ladder and rested her hand on the shelf.

As Sunny was about to tell Stella to come down and move the ladder, a number of things happened in rapid succession. A loud crack preceded the shelf detaching on one side. All the gargoyles slid to the opposite end. The ladder wobbled. Stella made a grab for the shelf, missed, and caught the one below it instead. That shelf completely detached. As gargoyles rained down, the ladder began to topple.

Sunny rushed forward, accompanied by an older man. Between them, they managed to stabilize the ladder. Stella clung to it, her face white, her chest heaving.

"Come down," Sunny told her. "Quickly. Before something else happens."

Despite her hands shaking badly and her feet missing a couple of rungs on the way down, Stella reached floor level without falling.

"Come away, everyone." Armenta's clear, authoritative voice rang out. Apart from the man who had helped stabilize the ladder, other customers rapidly dispersed.

"Are you all right, miss?" the man asked Stella.

"I…I think so." She pushed hair out of her eyes with a shaky hand.

"This was all my fault," he told Sunny. "I asked her to get a gargoyle down so I could take a better look at it. I had no idea it was going to be so difficult."

"It shouldn't have been." Sunny looked up at the shelving. She had never put anything up so close to the top of the unit. The only gargoyle ever occupying that shelf was Watcher, who always flew up there. The shelf that had collapsed was his usual perch. A strong misgiving came into her mind. Had something been done to that shelf deliberately, so Watcher would fall and possibly break? But who would have tampered with it, and when?

"Let me make this up to you," the man told Stella. "I'll take you to lunch after I help clean all this up."

"That's way too kind of you." Stella was smiling up at him. "But I don't get off until noon."

"Why don't you take an early lunch?" Sunny suggested. "It'll give you a chance to calm down. You almost had a nasty accident."

"I did." Stella nodded, still watching her benefactor. "Perhaps we could get a sandwich and a cup of coffee?"

"How about a proper lunch?" He was watching her, too, and smiling. "I'll take you to a restaurant downtown. Will that be okay with you?" he asked Sunny. "We might be gone an hour and a half."

"Fine," she said. "Take your time, Stella." The gargoyle corner was a complete mess, but at least she wasn't facing a workman's comp claim.

"We're closing early for lunch," Armenta shouted. "Bring your purchases to the counter. This way, everyone." She shepherded the customers toward the front of the shop.

As the man escorted Stella out of the gargoyle corner, he turned back to Sunny.

"My name is Nigel Whiting," he said. "I work with Mark. He recommended I come over here after I had a couple of clients cancel their appointments. He assured me you'd have something to mitigate more cancellations in future. I'll take any of the gargoyles that were damaged, plus whatever you think will give me good mojo."

"It's not necessary for you to pay for broken merchandise," she protested.

"I insist. Don't think another thing about it." He took out a business card. "Have it all bagged for me when we get back, and I'll give you the plastic." He grinned. "If you sweep up the pieces and put them into the bag, I'll have something to do on those long winter nights, trying to repair all of them."

"Thank you." Sunny felt overwhelmed by his generosity.

"I'll take good care of her," he said, looking down at Stella, who seemed to be enraptured by him. "We'll beat the noon crowd," he told her.

"I'll get my purse and coat." Stella rushed to the back of the shop, retrieved her belongings and ran to join him at the front door.

He had to be 20 years her senior, but at least Sunny knew where to find him if he wasn't a gentleman, she thought, tucking his business card into her pocket. She took a roll of yellow and black crime scene tape from the Halloween display and used it to block off the gargoyle corner and checked her watch. It was 11:00 AM. Ash should have already left for the cider house.

She looked around the crowded little shop with a critical eye and saw more potential hazards in all the shelving that required one of the staff to get onto a ladder. If there was a fire, she didn't know if everyone would be able to easily find their way out of the labyrinth of shelves and merchandise to either use the front entrance or the emergency exit. The fire marshal would probably make them reorganize or even remove some stock. All of which was selling. As of that morning, even more was in the storeroom.

The time had come to expand. She'd *have* to take Ash up on his offer, despite her reservations.

The fact that he had bought the insurance office and the warehouse without notifying her was a situation that still nagged at her.

What other secrets might he have?

CHAPTER FORTY-SEVEN

Ash arrived at the Clear Creek Cider House at 11:30 AM. He found it very underwhelming. Certainly, it wasn't a venue for a destination wedding or any other large event, he thought, parking in the empty lot. The roof wore a heavy coating of green moss. Several shingles were missing around the central chimney, which needed repointing before bricks began falling. If the Fortunas were aiming for a rustic look, they'd succeeded. He got out and locked the Range Rover.

Before taking three bowed wooden steps up to a small porch, he looked back at the orchard. Bare branches reached toward a leaden sky. Beyond the trees, trellises in the Taricani vineyard rose up the hill to the tasting room, a showy, silent sentinel above overgrown, bare grapevines.

The porch's overhang would barely cover two people huddled together. The front door, like the rest of the building, was built from unpainted dark wood. A small sign warned that it opened outward. Ash supposed that was to give a heads-up to those huddled on the porch. A glass insert dimly reflected lights inside.

Sunny's recounting of the earth trembling beneath her feet and then rising up in the vineyard came into his mind. He doubted the wooden slats beneath his feet would hold his weight in even the most minor earthquake, and the Willamette Valley did have those infrequently. He made a mental note to check whether any seismic activity had been recorded since they first started their investigation.

He opened the door. Without even seeing the inside of the cider house, he could understand why the Fortunas were so anxious to outbid Valderos to take over that enormous tasting room and turn it into an event space. The interior of the cider house was as underwhelming as its exterior.

"Well, hello," said a pleasantly modulated female voice. "Welcome back. I knew you wouldn't be able to resist tasting our cider." Andrea Fortuna pushed strands of red gold hair behind one ear. Her full lips gave him a broad smile. Her violet eyes sparkled.

Ash sincerely hoped their mutual attraction wasn't an illusion. He needed someone he could laugh with and hopefully like a lot. He returned her smile. "It wasn't only the cider that brought me here."

"Oh, really?" A little dimple appeared on Andrea's right cheek. Her hair had escaped from behind her ear again. As her hand came up to push it back, Ash gently curled the strands around his fingers. She placed her hand over his. "You're here for some other reason, then?"

Her hair felt like silk. Her hand was soft and warm. He inhaled her subtle perfume and liked that a lot. He was out of practice flirting. He hoped he wasn't being clumsy. She was at least 10 years younger; around Sunny's age. He'd always thought Sunny was too young to be anything more than his professional partner. Yet there he was, enjoying a fairly intimate moment with Andrea and wanting it to continue.

"I came to see *you*," he said.

"I hoped you would." She drew her hair away from his fingers, but kept holding his hand. "Shall we go inside? Are you hungry? We serve a light lunch."

He nodded. "I *am* hungry. Do you have time to eat with me?"

"I do." She kept holding his hand as they walked through a small vestibule into a room with a bar on one side, tables and chairs on the other. The cider house was empty apart from an elderly man behind the bar and a middle-aged woman holding an empty tray in one hand.

"Mom and Gramps, I'd like you to meet my friend, Ash Haines. He's joining me for lunch."

Andrea's mother stepped forward and extended her hand. Her smile was a smaller version of her daughter's; her eyes a washed-out shade of blue-violet.

"Nice to meet you, Ash." Her handshake was firm, her hand rough and callused. "I'm Pearl. The man behind the bar is my father-in-law, Norman."

Ash greeted Norman with a nod, which was returned. "Andrea, this is my treat. Order for us both. I'll take a glass of cider with my meal."

"We have marionberry, pear and apple right now," Andrea told him.

"Tuna on rye and chicken noodle soup okay, Ash?" Andrea's mother asked.

"Pear sounds good." He told Andrea and Norman. He really wanted plain apple cider, but he didn't want to look like he wasn't into trying something more exotic. "The soup and sandwich are both favorites of mine."

"Coming right up." Pearl went past the bar and through a pair of saloon doors. They creaked as they swung back and forth a couple of times.

"Why don't we sit in the small dining-room?" Andrea suggested. "It's more private." She actually winked at him with her head turned away from Norman. "Come on." She took Ash's hand again and led him through another set of creaking saloon doors into a wood-paneled room with matching overhead beams. Booths replaced the barrel chairs and small round tables occupying the larger dining area.

Andrea slid into a booth and patted the seat beside her. Ash wasn't sure her mother would approve, but he took the offered seat. Andrea took utensils from a plastic holder next to the wall and set both their places. She added paper napkins from a generous pile next to an impressive selection of condiments that included ketchup, barbecue sauce, three types of mustard, hot sauce, salt, pepper, and small containers of chopped onions, pickles and relish.

Norman brought two glasses of cider, a jug of water and two frosted glasses. He didn't seem taken-aback by the couple sitting side by side. "When's your dad coming in?" he asked.

"I'm not sure." Andrea's smooth forehead wrinkled for a moment. "He was busy in the cidery."

"I'll give him a call if he's not here in an hour," Norman said. "He gets so involved with what he's doing, he forgets to eat." With a quick sideways glance at Ash, but no change in his neutral expression, he left.

"So what have you been up to since I dropped you off at the winery?" Andrea's voice held a note of mirth. "I thought I might lose you off the back of the ATV before you put your arms around my waist."

"I wasn't expecting a fast ride over such uneven ground." Ash wasn't sure whether she was teasing him or pointing out his inexperience as a passenger.

"I'm joking with you." She leaned toward him. "You're out of practice flirting, aren't you?" She smiled. "We'll have to change that." Without further ado, she kissed him.

Ash was completely taken-aback. He heard the saloon doors creak again right after Andrea sat back with a broad grin on her face.

He decided she must have either heard or seen her mother coming. Pearl brought a loaded tray to their table. He wondered if she'd seen what was going on. He wasn't at all sure *he* knew what was going on.

Andrea was definitely coming on to him, and he felt like a freshman in high school, inexperienced and unable to figure out how to act after being kissed by a girl he was interested in. He was used to being the one who made the first move, and that wasn't usually at the start of an impromptu lunch date. Much less a lunch date in the back dining room of the family cider house, with her mom and her grandfather going in and out.

He felt Andrea's hand on his arm. "Too fast for you?" she asked. "Am I reading you wrong? I thought you liked me. I thought we had an instant connection?"

The little frown returned between her violet eyes. Her hair slid off her slender shoulders. He took her in his arms and kissed her thoroughly for so long, their soup was only tepid by the time they ate

CHAPTER FORTY-EIGHT

Armenta looked up from her tarot card reading when Sunny brought her a cup of coffee. It was a slow Wednesday morning. Stella had managed two cash transactions without jamming the register and was giving their only customer a tutorial in smudging. She was doing such a good job, Sunny decided to give her the monthly smudging class on a regular basis.

Sunny avoided looking at the cards. "Don't tell me we're going to have a lot more shoplifting this week," she said. "Watcher won't like it, and he could decide pecking offenders isn't enough of a deterrent. If he flies around the ceiling and dive-bombs the offenders, there could be mass hysteria."

"I don't think Watcher would create a situation like that. He's more subtle. A peck. A slight ruffle of feathers. The occasional prod of a talon." Armenta looked into the depths of her cup like she was expecting something other than coffee with a splash of milk.

"Did you sleep badly?" Sunny asked when Armenta set the cup down without taking a sip.

"No." Armenta gestured toward the chair on the other side of the table, usually reserved for clients.

Sunny sat and waited.

"I don't want to sound like a creature out of the Star Wars franchise." Armenta pursed her lips. "I almost said there was a disturbance in the force. What I will say is that there's definitely something brewing on the horizon." She shook her head from side to side, long golden earrings swaying. "I was already sensing discord before Vincente stopped by my apartment for tea yesterday evening.""

"You know you shouldn't let that demon into your home," Sunny admonished. "I'm afraid he's like a vampire…you can't uninvite him once you've set out the welcome mat."

"Hush, child. Vincente has redeeming qualities. Vampires do not."

"Redeeming…what a word. Not one I'd associate with Valderos," Sunny grumbled.

She wasn't feeling on top of her game that morning. She'd slept fitfully the previous night, disturbed by repetitive and frightening dreams of a sea of mud flowing down the creek-bed at the Taricani vineyard and rising up to engulf her. Ash was standing on the other side of the fence separating the vineyard from the orchard and completely ignoring her cries for help. She'd awakened at 5:00 AM, covered in sweat and with her heart hammering.

Armenta snorted. "Nonsense. Like Ash, you always blame Vincente when there's a crisis. He's a complex man with hard choices to make, and they depend heavily on whether you and Ash can fulfill the contract."

"I get that," Sunny admitted. "That's why he's giving us impossibly short deadlines to solve these cases. He has a deadline, too. But has he given you any hints about what could happen if he fails?"

Armenta pointed toward the first card in the array: The Tower. "Drawing information from him is a difficult process. When he feels I want to know more about him than he's willing to share, he completely shuts down. He did let his guard down when he told us that Hell to him was being on earth and having to manage a winery with a bad vintage."

"I remember that." Sunny also remembered almost feeling sorry for the demon.

"The other time he let us see his humanity was when he said the false Valentine was gone for good. I sensed he felt incredibly lonely. Almost hopeless. When you and Ash solve the crimes, haven't you noticed that although he appears momentarily relieved, his dark side seems disappointed?"

Sunny wasn't about to feel sympathy for Valderos at that moment. "He's an illusionist, flapping that black cloak to distract us or doing some other sleight of hand. He could have a big future in Vegas if his current gig as a winery owner continues to fall flat."

Armenta's eyes narrowed, and the corners of her mouth turned down.

Sunny was past caring whether Armenta approved or disapproved of what she thought of Valderos. "If he's such a big, bad demon, why does he waste his time hanging around the Willamette Valley and buying up wineries that won't turn a profit?"

"I don't know." Armenta drank down her coffee in a couple of quick gulps and put her cup aside. She scooped up the cards and shuffled. "I'm giving you a reading."

"I don't want one."

If there were strange forces around, Sunny would rather not know what was ahead. She felt better able to tackle things coming out of the blue than trying to anticipate the future, even if Armenta was the best fortune-teller in the Pacific Northwest.

"You're getting one whether you want it or not." The cards snapped. "I already did one reading for you and another for Ash. I didn't like either of them. I'll try one for both of you."

"You can do that?" Sunny wasn't sure she liked the idea of linking her fortunes with Ash's.

"Of course. I can do anything."

Armenta's speed shuffling stirred up a breeze. A cool draft caressed Sunny's face and whispered through her hair before leaving the arbor. The striped awning swayed, and the fringe rippled.

Snap, snap, snap. The cards met the table. Sunny refused to look at them. Instead, she focused on Armenta's bony hand as it hovered first over one card, then another. With difficulty, Sunny dragged her gaze from the cards to Armenta's face. Her eyes were closed, and her features elongated as Sunny stared, unable to look away. A shaft of light appeared from nowhere to shine down on one card in particular: the Devil.

Armenta's eyes snapped open. Without looking down at the cards, she scooped them up and took the deck to its shelf at the back of the arbor.

"Well?" Sunny croaked. Her throat felt so dry, she had trouble swallowing.

"Forces are attempting to weaken the bond between you and Ash," Armenta said. "They are succeeding. Doubt and suspicion have been driving you apart. It is unfounded." She grew taller, which had to be an optical illusion. Sunny had trouble standing upright beneath the canopy. Armenta was a couple of inches shorter, but she wasn't that short. Her head shouldn't be touching the top of the canopy, yet it was. As she grew, her face elongated further. Sunny stared at her in awe.

"Do you hear me?" Armenta roared. The table shook, the tarot cards cascaded from the shelf to the floor. The crystal ball glowed.

"I do," Sunny said, awe filling her. "I really, really do."

"Good." Armenta sat back down. Her features returned to normal.

The tarot cards flew back to the shelf. The glow inside the crystal ball faded, then disappeared completely with an audible *pop*.

CHAPTER FORTY-NINE

At 5:58 PM, The House of Serenity's front door opened and Ash strode into the shop. Sunny breathed a sigh of relief. She had thought for one horrible moment Valderos might be making an unscheduled visit.

Stella, busy pulling up the zipper on her coat, almost collided with Ash, who held out a bag. "I bought Thai for all of us. I hope you like it."

"Oh, I *love* Thai food." Stella beamed up at him and took the bag.

Sunny decided her part-timer was into older men. She'd already heard Stella's enthusiastic recounting of her luncheon with Nigel Whiting, with whom she had a dinner date Friday evening.

Ash held up a bigger bag. "For the rest of us. We've got a lot to discuss."

Sunny didn't feel like eating anything. All she wanted was to kick off her shoes and relax on the couch. But Armenta was pushing her toward Ash.

"Help him with the food while I close up the shop," the seer insisted.

Knowing from previous experience that arguing with Armenta was fruitless, Sunny led the way into her apartment. She brought plates and glasses to the table while Ash unpacked their meal. Her initial reluctance to eat fell by the wayside. Everything smelled and looked delicious. Her mouth watered. Her stomach rumbled. Even her fatigue ebbed away. He had brought salad rolls, Pad Thai and Sunny's own favorite, Tom Yum soup. A separate bag held chopsticks and napkins.

"Did I do okay?" He grinned.

"You did…it's absolutely perfect. I would have laid on the couch and eaten a bag of chips with a soda. I couldn't face cooking this evening."

"A sure sign you're really tired. Take off your shoes and have a seat." He brought a bottle of Riesling out of a separate bag. "It's chilled. I'll start tea, too. I've never seen Armenta drink anything alcoholic."

The tension in Sunny's shoulders eased. The tightness in her head subsided. She'd been anxious all day about how Ash was going to act after seeing Andrea Fortuna. Why had she felt that way? Were her feelings for him purely platonic or a little more complicated?

She followed his instructions, stowing her shoes in the closet, putting on her comfortable fake fur-lined slippers and rejoining him at the table, where he had a glass of wine waiting for her. She told herself she shouldn't begrudge Ash a relationship with any woman he liked. Although, she quantified, maybe not with a woman who might be involved in their latest investigation.

She took a sip of her wine. Ash was her friend and her partner in their paranormal investigations. No more, no less. But that statement wouldn't hold once she signed the promised papers that would make him a partner in her metaphysical shop. His life would be even more connected to hers, but in a professional way. Somehow, although her rationalization should have comforted her, it didn't.

"Tough day, huh?" He sat down opposite her and raised his glass. "Cheers. Here's to a better evening."

"Cheers, yourself." She clinked glasses with him, took another sip of the Riesling, then put down her glass. "We had an unusually slow day. Which is strange, even though the shop's usually quiet mid-week. I expected us to have constant foot traffic because Halloween's coming up fast. It didn't rain, it wasn't particularly cold, and I don't think any other store is having a big sale in competition to ours, so I'm a bit concerned for the shop's bottom line. I hope sales improve steadily from here on out." She took another sip of wine. "Mmm, this really does hit the spot."

"I've always found keeping busy makes a day go faster." Ash twirled his wineglass by the stem, his gaze lowered.

"Armenta only had three readings all day," Sunny continued, feeling suddenly uncomfortable. She wondered where his thoughts had drifted off to. "She said she's usually fully booked this time of year. I think even she's a bit concerned, although she'd never admit it."

The door between the shop and apartment opened. Armenta bustled in with the cash drawer, which she deposited in the safe. "The food smells wonderful, Ash."

"The water's nearly ready." He gestured toward the stove, where the kettle made chirping sounds that preceded outright whistling.

"Thank you, Ash. How did your lunch meeting go with that young woman at the cider house?" Armenta had a wicked little grin.

Sunny watched Ash return the grin, like they were co-conspirators. She frowned, which brought tightness back to her forehead. She took three bottles of water out the refrigerator and drank half of one while Armenta busied herself making the tea.

Ash really did look smug. "It went very well."

"As it should have." Armenta brought the teapot to the table, along with a cup and saucer.

Sunny noted lilacs on the china. The significance of the design wasn't lost on her: The fireworks of initial love. Armenta was fond of non-verbal communication. Sunny felt sure the seer's choice of china wasn't accidental. The goal was to underline the favorable impression Ash must have made on his lunch companion. Sunny controlled an impulse to roll her eyes.

"I want you both to know I took one for the team." Ash sipped his wine.

Sunny was very glad she had nothing in her hands, or she might have thrown it at him. *What?*

"Relax, Sunny." Ash chuckled. "I only used my considerable charms on Andrea while we were eating lunch. I still have some, you know. I got her to tell me her father and Giuseppe argued over the property line the same day Giuseppe was found dead in the creek."

"Did your considerable charms include kissing her?" Sunny reached for her wine and knocked it over.

Ash grabbed the dishtowel and used it to blot up the spill. "I had to. How else was I going to slip a potion into her drink?"

"You *drugged* her?" Sunny couldn't believe her ears, but she already knew the answer before she heard Armenta's dry leaf cackle.

"It was merely a little something to relax her. Ash did the rest." The seer's gold tooth glinted. Her eyes sparkled. "Sounds like it had more effect on Andrea than it did on Vincente."

"You tried to drug Valderos?" Sunny remembered the sachet she'd seen Armenta take out of her pocket when making tea the last time he came for a report. Her thoughts rocketed from Andrea Fortuna easily 'relaxing' to the danger of experimenting on a demon.

Armenta waved off the risks. "I only gave him a little dose, to see if anything happened, which it didn't. The shaman told me not to try anything stronger. He's concerned about adverse effects."

"As he should be. As we *all* should be." Sunny wondered again about that large indentation at the end of her bed. Had Valderos really sat watching her sleep? Her heart skipped a beat, and she felt a little lightheaded.

Something about Ash's smugness didn't sit right with her. The dishtowel he'd used on the spill had been permeated with something more potent than water. She sniffed. A scent stronger and more alluring than aftershave wafted up her nose and filled her head. A tingling warmth stole across her face, down her neck, and plunged straight into her chest. Her heart began pumping like she was 10 yards away from winning the final race in the Triple Crown.

She gasped. Drained her water bottle. Needed something stronger and picked up her empty wine glass. Ash refilled it for her. She drank it right down. Only then was she able to gain some control over her surging hormones.

"Pheromones," Armenta said. "I merely gave nature a little boost."

Between the pheromones and the wine, Sunny had a full-on buzz. "Just how far did you go to get all that information out of Andrea? She incriminated her father, for goodness' sake."

"None of your business how far." Ash folded his arms across his chest.

Sunny could only imagine how far Ash's investigation had gone. "Her place or yours?"

"Neither." Ash straightened his tie. "I'm a gentleman."

"You don't need any more information about that part of his investigation." Armenta's voice was sharp. "Now, why don't you tell us everything you learned from Andrea while we eat dinner, Ash?" Her mouth twitched when she looked at Sunny. "Don't worry. Food counteracts any lingering effects from the pheromones."

Ash deftly removed lids from all the containers and passed the salad rolls to Sunny.

She felt like she had fallen down yet another rabbit hole; this one far deeper than anything that had been quarried by a March Hare.

CHAPTER FIFTY

Ash loosened his tie before helping himself to a salad roll and a teaspoon of peanut sauce. "At first, Andrea was reluctant to talk about the feud between her father and Giuseppe. It took a lot of encouragement before she opened up."

Sunny restricted herself to commenting "I bet" before spooning Tom Yum soup into a bowl.

"Well, anyway," he chased the peanut sauce around the plate before corralling it with a fork Armenta handed him, "the creek formed a natural boundary between the two properties, and was shared equally by the Taricanis and the Fortunas until Andrea's father, Alex, added a cidery. About the same time, Giuseppe had the tasting room enlarged. The spring couldn't keep up with demands. The Taricanis put up a fence and built a makeshift dam."

"How long have the Taricanis and the Fortunas owned their properties?" Sunny asked. "Did they purchase around the same time?"

Ash opened his water bottle and drank deeply before answering. "Giuseppe and his partner initially bought their land in the early 1970s. Alex already had a smaller orchard. He found a regular buyer for his apples and planted more trees around the same time the Taricanis figured out the right grapevines for this area. Water usage increased and the spring had trouble keeping up with demands."

Armenta picked up the plate with the remaining salad rolls. "Either of you want another one?" After Sunny and Ash both shook their heads, she tipped both rolls onto her plate and spooned the remaining peanut sauce over them.

"Sounds to me like poor long-term planning," she said. "They should have discussed what to do before that happened."

"I don't think either of these families had good businessmen at the helm, and from what Andrea told me, neither side was willing to compromise." Ash grimaced. He stirred his Tom Yum soup but made no attempt to eat it. "Anyway, let me fill you in on what Andrea told me happened when Lorenzo joined Giuseppe in the business. She said she was friends with Arturo, and when he got frustrated with his father, she'd always listen to him unload. Lorenzo convinced Giuseppe they should take their wine to the next level. The wine industry in Oregon was growing in leaps and bounds. They entered competitions, but only had modest success."

"I'd never heard of the Taricanis and their wines until Valderos brought the case to us," Sunny said. "When Mark and I were together, we went winetasting with friends on a regular basis. Mark and his buddies always knew which wineries were award-winning."

Ash nodded. "I'd never heard about Taricani wines, either. Anyway, Lorenzo blamed Giuseppe's old ways for their low rankings. He brought in modern methods to increase grape production and solve ongoing issues with a strain of fungus. Strong pesticides, according to Arturo, who finally agreed to speak to me on the phone this morning. Neither he nor Sofia approved of their father tampering with what they said was working well. They both argued with their father. A rift developed. After Giuseppe passed away, Arturo and Sofia had no further contact with Lorenzo. Although the Fortunas' cider *has* won awards, they struggle financially because of the water situation. I was left wondering whether the squabble over the water rights wasn't worsened by the Fortunas earning those awards."

"Jealousy, greed and envy." Armenta put her chopsticks aside, pushed her bracelets up her forearms and dug a fork into a large serving of Pad Thai. "No wonder spirits linger at the winery."

Ash nodded. "My personal opinion is that Giuseppe got tired of his son's complaints and handed over the winery so he could enjoy a peaceful retirement. That man had worked hard all his life. After Lorenzo no longer had his father putting the brakes on all the changes he wanted to make, he worsened the fungal issue instead of curing it, and all the pesticides he used ultimately over-stressed the vines. Doesn't take a viticulturist or a viniculturist to figure that out. He wouldn't listen to his children, who were trying to give him good advice. Sofia had a degree in viniculture by that time, and Arturo was highly successful using organic farming. His wines have garnered international recognition. The conclusion I came to was that Lorenzo was too bull-headed for his own good, or for the good of the winery."

"Not unlike some others we know." Armenta didn't elaborate. She waved her fork at Ash. "This is so good, I've had two servings of everything."

Sunny chose to leave Armenta's designation of bull-headed behavior hanging in the air. "So, does it seem like there could be a solution, or is it too late?"

Ash laid his chopsticks down. He'd only eaten a small portion of the food. "Hard to say. I believe the products Lorenzo used led to run-off that polluted the water-source. Maybe even leeched into the orchard, since it's down the bottom of the hill from the vines. Over the past three years, the Fortunas trees became distressed. Apples fell before they ripened. Leaves turned yellow. That led to what Andrea said was a really ugly argument between Giuseppe and Alex."

Sunny leaned her elbows on the table. "There was definitely an argument." She was no longer speculating. "Alex…no, Giuseppe…became physical. He shoved Alex, who retaliated. Giuseppe lost his balance. He fell and hit his head on the rock beside the creek."

Ash nodded. "When questioned by the police, Alex told them he'd left Giuseppe angry but unharmed, but Andrea agonizes over how Giuseppe ended up face-down in the creek. Did her father leave Giuseppe unconsciousness? Did Giuseppe try to get up after Alex left but slipped into the creek, or was Alex so angry, he forced Giuseppe into the creek and held his head underwater?"

"What a terrible thing to live with…that uncertainty would make me ask him to tell me the truth." Sunny's appetite had left her. She knew why Ash had no stomach for food that evening.

"All the direct heirs would have inherited from Lorenzo was a tainted legacy." Armenta took the rest of the Pad Thai without asking if anyone else wanted to finish it.

"The Fortunas can't sell their dry orchard. They only way they can save their trees is to buy the Taricani property. Lorenzo left the property to his nephew to save his children from inheriting a financial disaster." Ash ran a hand over his chin. "What he had against Bill Hixton, I haven't figured out. Lorenzo must have really hated the guy."

"I wonder if Lorenzo knew his father's spirit was haunting the place before he died and became one, too?" Armenta's bracelets jangled as she dabbed her mouth with a paper napkin. Her dishes and all the take-out containers were empty.

"He must have." Sunny felt her consciousness shifting. She began to lose touch with reality. Voices whispered to her, human and supernatural, asking her to intervene. She refused to drift away with them, but she knew what they were telling her. "The land hates the entire family for what Lorenzo did, which is why the tree fell on him. If his children had contested the will, then they could have died, too."

"You're getting that look." Ash's voice sounded like a radio that had slipped from its signal. "What else can you tell us?"

Sunny snapped back to reality. "We have to tell Valderos and the police what we know. That's the only solution. The only way to quieten the spirits and heal the land."

"The investigation into Giuseppe's death certainly needs to be reopened," Ash said.

"Mr. Fortuna needs to suffer for his sin, but his daughter doesn't." Armenta's voice was uncharacteristically quiet. "The same goes for Arturo and Sofia. I wonder if there's a way to clean the land and restore the spring?"

"Much as I hate to say it, I have to speak with the caretaker," Sunny said. "It scares me to think of the force that could be unleashed when I give him the entire story. There's so much anger at the vineyard. But if the situation isn't resolved, Bill Hixton could be in danger, and who knows what might happen if he sold the winery to someone else?"

"Andrea said her father will have to file for bankruptcy if Hixton doesn't sell to them He swears he can get a loan."

Ash rubbed his chin again. "From who...a loan shark?"

"Did someone mention my name?"

Sunny turned to see Vincente Valderos standing in the living room.

CHAPTER FIFTY-ONE

Armenta made tea for Valderos while he listened intently to an update given by Ash, then to the threesome's deductions. He took a cookie from a tin Armenta produced from her big purse.

"Oatmeal with raisins," she told him. "Another of your favorites." She smiled at him, her gold tooth glinting.

Valderos returned her smile with a brief one of his own. Sunny swore the corners of his eyes crinkled before his mask-like expression returned. He was definitely becoming more animated. Less waxy. She remembered how he'd looked at her when they were suspended over the pit. Fond. No, more than fond, and something else…hopeful.

She caught Ash watching her. His focused attention made her uncomfortable. What was he searching for?

"Ms. Kingston, are you with us, or are you daydreaming?" Valderos asked.

"I'm listening," she said. "I've been trying to problem-solve a number of, well, *things.*" She didn't know how to express her jumbled thoughts or how much she wanted to share with the group. She certainly wasn't going to share her inner thoughts about Valderos with Ash, or her inner misgivings and doubts about Ash with Valderos.

With both men watching her, Sunny directed her attention to Armenta. The seer wore even larger earrings than usual. Big hoops with several strands of golden cords entwined within them. She also had stars and moons decorating the piercings that went up to the top of both ears. A cluster of long gold necklaces were decorated with spiritual symbols.

TAINTED LEGACY

Even her black shawl had golden threads woven into its pattern and mingling with the black fringe. Several golden cords encompassed her tiny waist, with amulets hanging from them. Armenta was weighed down by about 10 pounds of demon-repellent. Sunny wondered whether the seer had anticipated Valderos popping in unannounced.

"Mr. Haines, I would like you to arrange a meeting with Mr. Hixton," Valderos said. "You must also speak with the children of Lorenzo Taricani. Find out if they would be willing to manage the property after I purchase it. Return the methods used by Giuseppe. They will receive a generous salary. Once the vineyard regains health and produces grapes that can be turned into wine, we will renegotiate the terms of their employment, adding a percentage of the profits and an opportunity for them to repurchase the property."

"That's a generous offer" Ash sounded like he had reservations.

"What if Hixton refuses to sell?" Sunny asked. "Or what if his counter-offer is unrealistic? The entire property has to be replanted. Those vines are dead."

"Perhaps they are only dormant." Valderos turned his full attention to Sunny. "You are correct, Ms. Kingston. You must speak with the caretaker. You believe he represents the land, the vines and ultimately, the wine. I doubt the land and the vines wish to remain distressed. For them, a return to Giuseppe's ways will be acceptable. The wine may not be as easily placated."

"He really scares me." Goosebumps arose on Sunny's forearms at the thought of confronting that creature. "You have no idea what happened the last time."

"I *do.*" Valderos's voice was quiet, even kindly. "Ms. Kaslov will prepare you. I can send Serrano to you, or perhaps you would prefer the gryphon to accompany you?"

"I'll take Watcher, if he's amenable," she said. "I'll have to ask him."

Valderos inclined his head. "Do so. I will also give you something to summon me if needed."

Sunny felt an object in her palm. She looked down. An ancient coin. Gold. Heavy. Deathly cold. She almost dropped it.

"Keep that in your hand when you speak with him," Valderos said. "If you feel threatened and the gryphon cannot protect you, drop it. I will come immediately."

That was a lot of responsibility, Sunny thought. What if she dropped the coin accidentally?

"You will not," Valderos said inside her head.

Sunny flinched.

"Are you okay?" Ash looked suspicious. "Open your hand and show me what he gave you."

"It's just a coin," she said. A slight vibration came from the coin. It hummed its way up her arm. She carefully placed it on the table. "How am I supposed to summon the caretaker?" she asked Valderos.

"Ms. Kaslov will assist you by casting a spell. She must also accompany you. The caretaker will not appreciate my direct presence." Valderos wrapped two cookies into a paper napkin and stood. "I must leave. You have a plan to execute. If you perform it correctly, there will only be the matter of Mr. Fortuna admitting his guilt in Giuseppe's death and suffering the consequences of his action. Mr. Haines will attend to that."

"If I get the sheriff to arrest her father, that'll leave Andrea alone to take care of the bankruptcy proceedings," Ash protested. "Hasn't she lost enough, already?"

"She will have only lost a season of crops if she successfully convinces their creditors that the only problem hampering the business is restoring clean water to the spring. Then there will be no bankruptcy." Valderos straightened the collar of his wool coat and brushed cookie crumbs from the lapels. "Since I am now the main creditor, there will be no further talk of bankruptcy."

"But the orchard," Sunny protested. "One season without water will kill the trees."

Valderos put on his hat, which had materialized from thin air. "Speak with the caretaker. Negotiate the return of life to the land. Then contact the water district and have them do something about the polluted spring." He waved a hand. Blue sparks sizzled. "Do I really have to lead you humans up to the trough and force you to drink the water?"

"You'd really have to force me to drink the muck in that spring," Ash said. "It probably glows green in the moonlight."

"Undoubtedly, Mr. Haines." Valderos vanished.

CHAPTER FIFTY-TWO

"I don't want to do this," Sunny told Armenta as they stood at the edge of the Taricani Winery's patio the following day. "The last time I saw the earth move, a pit opened up, and…um…"

"Valderos saved you." Armenta's violet and deep blue shot silk skirts whirled and flapped below her black cloak A strong wind had developed as soon as they stepped out of Sunny's Forester.

Perched on the wall, Watcher let out such a piercing screech, Sunny's ears popped. He unfolded his enormous wings and took off, soaring into the sky to wheel on thermals strong enough to support his weight.

Sunny took a moment to watch the gryphon dive, climb and circle. What a motley group they were, she thought. The reluctant psychic, the seer, and the concrete gargoyle, all coming to communicate with a supernatural representative of the land. The punished land…mishandled by humans trying to force more return for their investments. More crops to create more wine. More cider. More money.

The land had revolted, and now she had been tasked, aided by Armenta and protected by Watcher, with restoring life and balance to what amounted to scorched earth.

"How did you know so much about that horrible incident before I told you?" Sunny asked.

The seer smiled. "The crystal ball, of course. I don't have visions like yours."

"What else did the crystal ball show you?" Sunny felt both curious and suspicious. Armenta had said very little since their meeting with Valderos.

225

"You don't want to know." Armenta held up her left hand and pointed her index finger toward Sunny. "Remember what I've told you before… predictions can be changed by the actions of those involved. Nothing is set in stone except the gryphon that flies over our heads."

"It wasn't *a* pit, Armenta. It was *the* pit. It smelled awful." Sunny's stomach muscles clenched at the memory. "It looked like there was no end to it," she added, when Armenta didn't comment.

She scanned the vineyard from one end to the other, convinced that despite what he'd said, Valderos had to be hiding somewhere on the property. "It's where he comes from," she said, keeping her voice low, although she doubted whispering would stop a demon from eavesdropping.

The landscape didn't make hiding an easy task. Bare-branched trees. The grapevines were also bare, but not dead, if Valderos was to be believed. She remembered the cane that had slapped her on their first visit. She doubted it had been accidental. She looked down at the creek. Bushes on the property line had been stripped bare by the raging flood. Broken sections of fencing were scattered over a wide area, including the orchard.

"Did we all make a mistake, agreeing that Ash shouldn't come with us?" Sunny felt the wind reach under her hair to touch her skin with those frozen fingers she'd felt before. She drew up her raincoat collar.

"He'd be of no help to us here. Besides, he had business of his own." She sounded frustrated. "Let's get on with this. I'm already cold, and I have to take off my coat to cast such a big spell." She laid her coat over the wall and walked to the center of the lawn. She had fastened her shawl with a large pin decorated with a thistle, its flower an amethyst. Strength and protection. The golden cords girding her waist streamed behind her.

Sunny backed up until she felt the wall behind her legs. "Do you want me to get any farther away?" she asked.

"No. I don't want you too far away from me." Armenta shielded her eyes and looked up.

Sunny's gaze followed Armenta's. Watcher stopped freewheeling. He swooped down to land on the repaired section of the wall, where the tree had fallen on Lorenzo.

Armenta's hair freed itself from her topknot and streamed behind her as she lifted her face to the leaden sky. She opened her arms wide. Sunny waited and watched as the seer recited her incantation.

After Armenta completed that part of the ritual, she brought a bag from her pocket, opened it, and shook out the contents. A thin stream of sparkling dust blew westward, toward the Van Duzer corridor, then reversed, traveling eastward, toward the Cascades. Finally, the dust swirled in an ever-increasing circle to encompass the entire vineyard. Awed by the sheer volume and power of Armenta's spell, Sunny watched the dust gather itself back together before shooting out across the creek, opening into a sunburst, and traveling at lightning speed through the bare branches of the orchard beyond. The sheer magnitude of the seer's spell and her ability to harness the wind to carry out her wishes left Sunny both stunned and awestruck.

Then it started...

The tremors, mild at first, grew in volume. Armenta returned to the patio. The ground cracked. Flagstones split. The retaining wall crumbled. Watcher whirling up into a vortex. Cracks widened and lengthened. Sunny thought the pit was about to reopen.

She clutched Armenta, who wrapped the cords at her waist around them both. Sounds intensified; became deafening. The building groaned. The earth split from the top of the hill to the bottom. With a dreadful tearing sound, a huge fissure appeared at their feet.

Sunny opened her mouth to scream, but couldn't make a sound. Armenta's cords frayed. Heat shot up from the fissure. Terrified, Sunny called out silently to Valderos, certain he was the only one who could save them. But was this the event he'd been waiting for? Had he tricked the two humans with the strongest powers into becoming the sacrifices he'd needed?

She clung to Armenta and silently told Valderos exactly what she thought of him. How she would curse him for all eternity for his betrayal.

Suddenly, the earthquake stopped.

The roaring wind abated.

Watcher circled down to land on the remains of the wall.

And the caretaker arrived...

CHAPTER FIFTY-THREE

He came from the earth, building into a human form as Sunny watched, so terrified that rational thought threatened to desert her. He was coming to speak with her. She wouldn't need to summon him.

Her mind told her to ignore rational thought and start running. Sunny told her mind to be quiet. It was time to listen to her instincts, and they were telling her to meet the caretaker literally on his own ground.

Armenta released her and stepped aside. Sunny trod slowly and carefully across the remains of the lawn and into the vineyard. She stood where the chasm had opened and hoped she would be able to communicate with the caretaker successfully enough that the pit wouldn't reappear and swallow her.

The old man studied her with eyes the color of loam. Mud dripped from his hair, his beard, and matted his eyelashes. His feet remained one with the soil.

"You summoned me." His voice was as dark, cold, and lifeless as the troubled land from which he came.

Sunny had spent the entire night thinking up the right speech. She wasn't about to mess it up by losing her mind to terror. "The seer did the summoning," she said. She hoped he wouldn't hear the tremor in her voice. "On my behalf," she added. "We…my team and I…want you to know we've heard you, and we're going to put everything to rights. Restore the land and the water. Use the old methods of cultivation that made the vines strong. Abandon the new ways that angered and damaged the earth and all that depend on it."

TAINTED LEGACY

"Why should we believe you?" asked the caretaker.

"Because we came today with no other motives. We only want to restore peace and harmony."

A heaviness in the air began to lighten. As Sunny took deeper breaths, her panic subsided.

She gave Valderos mental instructions to go into a holding pattern. Maybe he was right…. she *could* fix this with nothing more than the help Armenta had already supplied. She didn't dare take her attention from the caretaker, but she knew without doubt that Armenta and Watcher were right there for her, and that Ash was taking care of all those loose ends that humans scrambled into their messy existences.

"We believe you." The caretaker leaned forward. His smell brought tears to her eyes and almost gagged her.

She fought off the nausea. "My partner is negotiating…" She stopped, unsure how much a towering mound of earth could possibly understand about contracts, wills, inheritances, and the consequences of breaking laws. "There was an accident," she said, opting for an easier explanation. "Giuseppe died. He respected you. He nurtured you. His grandchildren will do the same; I promise."

"Human promises are empty words." The caretaker sounded angry.

"These won't be."

Armenta came to stand at Sunny's left side. Watcher hovered on her right.

"We come in *peace,*" Sunny said, endeavoring to emphasize the truthfulness in that overused phrase. "Giuseppe's grandchildren will bring back the old ways. The good ways. The nurturing ways that brought abundance to this land."

"The land accepts and understands these terms," the caretaker said. "But this must be a promise kept, or the consequences will be deadly to your species."

With that, he sank back into the earth, the tremors ceased, and the cracks disappeared.

Sunny took a deep breath. It brought sweet, clean air into her lungs.

"Good job." Armenta patted her back.

Watcher screeched before wheeling away over the tasting room.

229

Sunny had no doubt they'd find him sitting in the back of her Forester. It was a reassuring thought. She only hoped Ash's negotiations had been as successful.

"Let's go around the side of the tasting room instead of through it," she told Armenta.

She wanted the wine to have time to receive the good news from the land before she went anywhere near the cellar. Although she felt she was going to have to, her first reaction was never to return to the Taricani Winery again. She'd seen more than enough of that vineyard's underbelly already.

"We should close the shop so we can all come to the grand reopening." Armenta picked her coat off the ground and shook it before draping it around her shoulders.

"I was afraid you'd suggest something like that." Sunny shook her head. "I don't know if I'll ever be able to drink another glass of wine."

"That's your fatigue talking." Armenta linked arms and tugged her along. "Come on, let's go back to the car. I'm sure Watcher's already waiting there for us."

"I'm sure he is. With his seatbelt on." Sunny managed a brief chuckle. "I'm so glad he was with us. Even if he didn't have to do anything, I knew he would carry both of us away if he had to."

"Congratulations are in order." Armenta gave Sunny's arm a gentle squeeze. "You did a fine job of negotiating."

"Thanks. I was shaking in my waterproof boots the entire time."

"I'm hungry," Armenta announced. "Let's pick up burgers while we wait for Ash to join us."

"I may need more than a couple of days to recover from what we did here today, but I'll take what I can get. Halloween's getting closer and closer. The merchandise won't sell itself." Sunny wrinkled her nose. She still smelled the caretaker. "I'll pass on lunch. My stomach's still queasy from the overpowering smell of composting plant matter. I'll opt for putting my feet up and sipping mineral water."

"No need for that. I'll brew you a pot of my special tea." Armenta's gold tooth glinted.

TAINTED LEGACY

"Oh, joy. Green tea, Valderos, and an upset stomach." Sunny groaned. "Worse than a roller coaster ride after a chili dog and cheese fries at a carnival."

Armenta's dry leaf cackle reverberated in the crisp fall air.

CHAPTER FIFTY-FOUR

Vincente Valderos stood next to his limo when Sunny and Armenta walked into the parking lot. "You are not leaving without resolving the issues with the wine," he told Sunny. "Ms. Kaslov, you are free to go if you wish. I will bring Ms. Kingston home."

"What makes you think I still have more to do?" Sunny stopped before telling him she had balked about visiting the wine cellar, but since he was able to read minds, she figured he already knew she hadn't gone down there.

"Really, Ms. Kingston?" Valderos's right foot impatiently tapped the ground. "You have to ask that?"

"No, I suppose not." She avoided looking at his putty-colored eyes. "I don't need any help getting where I'm going," she added, afraid he'd transport her to the dank cellar.

"How was Ash's meeting with the Taricani heirs, Vincente?" Armenta asked.

"It has not yet taken place."

Valderos shifted his attention to Armenta. Sunny crossed her fingers behind her back. Maybe that wasn't a way to hex demons, but she figured it wouldn't hurt to try.

"The son and daughter are now coming to the winery," Valderos clarified. "Mr. Haines is at present meeting with the owners of the orchard. There are issues to resolve; then we will all meet with the Taricanis and Mr. Hixton."

"I see." Armenta drew her shawl over her head as the wind whipped around her. "I'll stay," she said. "Sunny, do you need me to go down to the cellar with you?"

Sunny wanted to say yes. She wanted to recruit an army of seers before she went down the stairs to communicate with the angry and rancid wine, but she sensed Valderos was testing her, yet again. "No, thank you," she told Armenta. "But I would like you to stay within shouting distance, in case something goes wrong."

"I will be your second." Valderos stepped forward. "Ms. Kaslov will drive your car back to Salem."

"I'm not leaving without Sunny." Armenta grew visibly taller as she confronted Valderos. "Vincente, you have enough to cope with, already. The room has to be prepared for the meeting."

"I do not move furniture." Valderos clapped his hands. "Serrano, see to it. And make sure that the caretaker keeps away."

Serrano appeared from the other side of the limo. "Yes, Master." He hurried past Armenta and Sunny. The front door opened for him before he reached it and closed by itself after he entered the winery.

"Go, then, Ms. Kingston." Valderos waved a dismissive hand in Sunny's direction.

Heat and strength from an unseen force pushed her toward the winery. The front door opened and she cruised through, a foot off the ground. Her flight continued, but when she saw the cellar door coming up, she resisted, flailing her arms. The cellar door opened. Already slightly dizzy and definitely nauseated, she had no intention of being spirited down the stairs.

"Put me down," she shouted. "If you don't, I'm going to throw up."

"Oh, very well."

Valderos appeared right beside her. A flick of his wrist, and Sunny felt the floor under her feet. A loamy, musty, moldy odor drifted up the stairs. She bolted for a nearby restroom.

"Ah, mortals," she heard Valderos complain.

She pulled open the door and ran into the first stall.

CHAPTER FIFTY-FIVE

"I'm giving you the chance to come clean," Ash told Alex Fortuna as they stood in front of the bar at the empty cider house. He'd laid out his theory of what had happened when Alex confronted Giuseppe at the creek.

Andrea had refused to leave them alone. She'd locked the front door and remained beside it. Her pale skin looked almost translucent, contrasting with the warm tone of her hair. Ash felt sure she'd never forgive him for what her father was about to confess.

"It was an accident." Alex's voice quavered. "We were arguing, and he wouldn't give an inch. He said he'd had the land surveyed, and the property line wasn't in the middle of the creek. He said it was where he had that damned fence installed. He shook his fist at me. Said he'd make sure my land wasn't irrigated by his water. He tried to hit me, but he missed. Old and slow, he stumbled. Slipped at the edge of the creek and fell backward.

"He laid there, staring up at the sky as though he couldn't believe he'd hit his head. I thought he was dead. I panicked. I wasn't going to confront his son. Lorenzo had an even worse temper than his father. I waded through the creek and went back into the orchard through a hole I'd cut in the fence. No one saw me. Andrea was at the other side of the orchard. She had the work crew with her. I started the cider press and worked there all afternoon. I heard Giuseppe had been found when a customer came in to pick up his order."

"You can tell that to the sheriff," Ash said. "I called and asked him to meet us here. You can either turn yourself in or have me do it for you."

"Dad," Andrea said, her voice quiet and brittle. "Do it yourself."

TAINTED LEGACY

"Andrea…" Alex lowered his head, "…I'm so sorry."

"I'm going to marry Arturo," she said. "What you say doesn't matter anymore."

"Arturo?" Ash thought he must have misheard. "Arturo Taricani? Lorenzo's son?"

Andrea nodded. "Yes." The color had returned to her cheeks. She strode over to her father. "The feud's over, Dad. You'll probably go to prison for what you did. I'm going to marry the man I've always loved." She turned toward Ash. "I'm sorry I led you on." She wrung her hands, as though attempting to wash away the guilt. "I was trying to get information out of you, but you're too good at what you do." She had the grace to blush.

"Thanks for the apology," Ash muttered.

So much for him being charming and irresistible to an attractive woman. She certainly knew how to deflate a man's ego.

CHAPTER FIFTY-SIX

Sunny slowly descended the cellar stairs. Armenta had made her chew mint and fennel the seer found growing in a patch of weeds close to the winery's front door. Sunny still felt pieces of fennel seeds between her teeth, but the nausea had abated.

She ran her tongue over her front teeth. They felt furry. She almost wished she hadn't refused the bottle of water offered by Serrano. But since she was never sure whose side he was on, the word hallucinogen had slipped into her mind when he produced the bottle from out of nowhere.

She'd counted 20 steps the last time she'd descended those stairs. That time, she counted 22. At least the handrail felt solid, and the lights stayed on. She knew Armenta was standing close to the door but out of sight, as though her presence might be more of a trigger to whatever lurked below. Sunny wondered what she should say to open the dialogue?

"I come in peace" sounded pretty silly, but she said it, anyway, as she stepped onto the uneven cellar floor. The lights flickered in response.

"I know things have been difficult since Giuseppe died," she continued. "But all the changes are about to be reversed." That was true as long as Ash bargained a resolution for the internal and external battles at the winery. "My partner has arranged to bring Arturo and Sofia here."

She waited. The lights flickered again.

"He wants Bill Hixton to strike a bargain with them." Sunny wasn't sure how much the wine would understand about contracts and inheritances. Probably as little as the caretaker.

The lights went out.

Her hand was still on the railing. Sunny backed up onto the lowest step.

The lights came back on, but at a lower wattage. Shadows lengthened. Somewhere deep in the cellar, something shifted. A barrel moving? Her heart beat so fast, she felt dizzy again. She tried to calm herself by silently repeating the mantra: "I can do this; I can do this."

With violent explosions, half the lights went out that time. The rancid smell intensified. The cellar smelled like a pile of dirty old gym socks. Sunny sucked on the pieces of fennel seeds and hoped they'd retained some of their potency.

"I realize you're angry," she said. "I know about the caretaker, and about the practices that poisoned the vines and tainted the wine. But you have to believe me...my partner can persuade Bill Hixton to make the necessary changes that bring the old farming methods back. He can persuade Arturo and Sofia to help him."

Violent popping noises came from deep inside the cellar. Sunny hoped barrels weren't popping their bungs and leaking spoiled wine onto the floor.

"Please give us the opportunity to convince Hixton," she said.

Despite her fear, she closed her eyes, took her hand off the rail and opened her mind. Blind rage flooded her. She fought the urge to recoil. Bottles rattled. Several cases of them fell to the floor. Wine ran along the floor to gather around her feet. A dark mist formed. It gathered into a towering figure that filled the available space in front of her. With a powerful surge that almost took her off her feet, the figure moved through her. Sunny almost fell. At the top of the stairs, the door flew off its hinges.

A moment later, Armenta's voice drifted down. "Are you okay?" She sounded calm. "That was quite a blast."

"I think so." Sunny looked up.

Armenta was standing at the top of the stairs. Her topknot was level with her left ear, and her shawl had lost most of its fringe. "Come upstairs, quickly," she said. "The Taricanis and Bill Hixton have arrived. They're following Ash inside."

Sunny ran up the stairs. "You'd better tidy yourself up," she recommended. "I suppose I'll need to do the same."

Her pants were covered with white powder. She dusted them off, then sniffed her denim jacket. It held a faint odor of what might be Merlot, but nothing unpleasant. Armenta had made a valiant attempt to reposition her topknot and draped her shawl around her neck instead of her shoulders, so the tattered fringe wasn't so noticeable. Sunny heard Ash's familiar and very welcome voice as he ushered a group of people into the tasting room.

She stepped away from the broken door, part of which was still lying close to the doorway. The rest of it had ended up halfway down the corridor that led to the offices.

"Come on," Armenta said. "We don't want to miss anything." She sounded far more excited over the meeting than she had when the door blew off.

Sunny allowed the seer to propel her into the tasting room, where Ash was encouraging three people to take seats at a large, round table.

CHAPTER FIFTY-SEVEN

"I can't stay." Bill Hixton wiped his brow. "I'm late for a meeting."

"This won't take long." Ash beckoned Sunny and Armenta over to the group. "You've met my partner, Sunny Weston. This is her assistant, Ms. Kaslov."

"Pleased to meet all of you." Armenta sailed forward and took the chair Ash pulled out for her. She beamed at the young man and woman seated on the other side of the table. She had a large smudge of what looked like grape juice on her left cheek.

Ash tapped his own cheek. Armenta took the hint and used her shawl to rub away the purple mark.

Sunny came up to the table at a slower pace. She felt the collective presence of the wine at her back. Serrano was behind the bar. He uncorked a bottle with a resounding pop and poured champagne into flutes.

"A little celebration is in order." In a haze of mothballs and black wool, Valderos passed Sunny.

Hixton took one look at Vincente Valderos and turned chalk-white. He immediately stopped complaining about being late and sat down hard, as though his legs refused to hold him up any longer.

"Mr. Hixton," Valderos said. "So nice to see you in the flesh." He took the seat next to the reluctant winery owner, pulled out a chair on the other side and patted the seat. "Come along, Ms. Kingston."

That phrase 'in the flesh' lingered in Sunny's brain. It sounded ominous. She wondered what Hixton would think or do if he knew he was about to have a meeting with not just an imposing figure, but a powerful demon. She also wondered whether the caretaker would suddenly come through the door, but when she looked outside, all remained quiet in the vineyard.

"Do hurry, Ms. Kingston. We're all waiting for you." Valderos smiled at her.

The smile felt like that of a close friend. It startled Sunny. Reluctantly, she sat next to him.

Arturo was seated at the other side of Sunny, Sofia to his left. Olive skinned, with dark, wavy hair and dark eyes, they definitely resembled each other, and their father. Sofia's hair tumbled around her shoulders as she perched at the front of her chair. She wore a crisp navy jacket over a cream turtleneck sweater. Arturo kept casting surreptitious glances toward Andrea Fortuna, seated across from him, between Ash and her father. He wore a brown, zippered jacket with a couple of dark stains, one on the front, another on his right elbow. Sunny wondered whether he'd come straight from working on his farm.

Armenta completed the circle, seated between Ash and Sofia. Hixton picked up a pen lying in front of him and tapped the table. His moustache wobbled.

Ash gave her a slight smile. She hoped that was a hopeful sign.

"I've invited all of you here today to save the vineyard and the orchard," he said. "My partner and I discovered the modern viticulture practices used by your father," he looked toward Arturo and Sofia, "damaged the vines and tainted the grapes. Bacteria rendered the wine undrinkable."

Arturo opened his mouth.

"You are here to listen." Valderos raised his index finger, the gesture well-known to Ash, Sunny, and Armenta.

Arturo's mouth sealed. At first, he looked surprised, but when he was unable to open his lips, fear came into his eyes.

"You will also listen." Valderos turned his gaze to Sofia, who was staring at him, eyes wide and lips tightly closed, as though she expected to suffer the same fate as her brother.

Valderos ignored Hixton, who was already sweating like he was in a sauna.

"Now we've established that I'll be conducting this meeting," Ash gave Valderos a warning glare, "I have a proposal to make. Mr. Serrano will bring each of you a glass of champagne while you think over the terms. The champagne is completely drinkable. It's from a popular winery in the area. Mr. Valderos insisted we stay local."

Serrano brought full flutes to the table. He served the champagne effortlessly, as though he regularly waited on patrons at a 5-star restaurant, before returning to the bar with an empty silver tray.

"You would like to partake of the champagne, would you not, Mr. Taricani?" Valderos looked at Arturo, who gave a curt nod. Valderos flicked his index finger, and Arturo's mouth dropped open.

Arturo hurriedly raised his glass, moistened his lips, and cleared his throat. "Will there be a toast?"

"I will give it." Valderos sounded pleased with himself. He half-turned toward Sunny and raised his glass. "Let us drink to success with our negotiations. You have already demonstrated success in your own part of the proceedings, Ms. Kingston."

"I hope so," she said. Whatever presence had passed through her and wrecked the cellar door was probably still lurking somewhere inside the building.

Armenta raised her champagne flute. "Of course she did."

"Here's to a successful resolution," Ash said, his voice clear and firm. "All parties will benefit from what Mr. Valderos proposes." He glanced over Sunny's left shoulder and nodded.

She wanted to see who else had come into the winery, but she didn't want to distract any of the people seated at the table, so she remained attentive to Ash while trying to ignore the energy radiating from Valderos. She wondered whether Ash had felt affected by it at their previous meetings, when he always placed himself between her and their leader.

"Mr. Valderos?" Ash prompted.

"Ah, yes." Valderos placed both hands on the table.

Serrano rushed over to pull back his master's chair. Valderos hadn't removed his coat, which undulated around his calves before widening its circular movements to include stroking Sunny's leg.

She wanted to smack the coat away, but instead, she edged closer to Arturo. That brought a distinct scowl to Andrea Fortuna's face. Alex gave his daughter a disapproving glance. The atmosphere thickened.

"Mr. Hixton, I have a proposal for you first," Valderos said. "I will purchase the Taricani Winery and Tasting room from you. I have a cashier's check." He motioned to Serrano.

Serrano brought an envelope to Bill Hixton, who opened it and partially slid out the check. His eyes widened and his mouth formed a perfect O.

"Is this satisfactory?" Valderos asked. "Speak now."

Hixton nodded rapidly. "Oh, yes. Definitely."

Sunny felt Arturo stiffen beside her. Waves of anger emanated from him.

"Then we shall sign the paperwork immediately." Valderos snapped his fingers.

A man came forward. Dressed in a black woolen coat that did not smell like mothballs.

"My attorney, Mr. Havrilak," Valderos said. "There is no need for you to have the contract reviewed by your own attorney, Mr. Hixton, I assure you." He waved his left hand nonchalantly.

"No need," Hixton echoed. He already held his pen. Havrilak placed a document on the table and Hixton signed it.

Sunny wanted to tell him he'd better not change his mind, and he should have gotten an attorney to review it, but kept her mouth shut. She didn't like Hixton. She sided with the wine in wanting him out of the vineyard ASAP.

"Now, leave," Valderos told the former winery owner. "Take your check to the bank. You will never contact the Taricani family again."

"Yes, sir." Hixton stood. "No, sir; I won't bother anyone ever again." He tucked the envelope into an inside pocket of his suit jacket. "I'll be very relieved to get away from this property for good. In fact, I may even leave the country."

"That would be a very good idea." Valderos sounded deceptively mild.

Sunny could well imagine what could happen to Hixton if he reneged on his promise. He might even turn into a bullfrog. They were considered an invasive species in Oregon. She remembered that little nugget of trivia from a visit to the Oregon Garden in Silverton, where bullfrogs were responsible for eating the native tree frogs. Armenta might compound him into her toad tea, she thought, catching the seer's smug smile.

Hixton almost ran out of the winery.

"Now." Valderos turned toward the Taricanis. "I have a proposal for you, Sofia. I already own a winery in Oak Grove. My interest in this vineyard is strictly financial. I want you to assume responsibility for managing the viticultural practices at this property. You must return to the methods used by your grandfather, Giuseppe. The land will heal and the vines will produce again next year."

Sofia stared at him, wide-eyed.

"Arturo, I want you to manage the wine production here, in addition to your own small winery. You will hire additional staff to ensure both wineries operate smoothly. Sofia, you will hire back the staff that made this a successful business. We will discuss their remunerations after this meeting."

He turned toward the Fortunas. "Mr. Fortuna, you will surrender yourself to the sheriff, who is waiting for you in the reception area. Andrea, you are fully capable of managing both the orchard and the cidery with some assistance from your new fiancé."

Andrea blushed. Arturo opened and then closed his mouth without saying anything.

"Those details will be worked out later," Valderos continued. "My time is too valuable to waste on reunions and vows that should have been taken many years ago." He rocked back and forth on his heels for a moment, as though he'd suddenly lost his train of thought.

Ash cleared his throat.

Valderos stopped weaving back and forth. The mothball smell was becoming overpowering. Sunny sneezed. Valderos gave her a sharp look.

"There is one more detail that must be resolved at this moment." Valderos returned his attention to both the Taricanis and the Fortunas. "The property line will revert back to the center of the creek. There will be no more fences between the orchard and the vineyard. There will be harmony and accord, not discord and tension. Both properties will be irrigated by the creek and its spring, supplemented as necessary by other sources. The feud that has existed between the Taricanis and the Fortunas must end at this table."

A long moment of silence followed his speech. Then movement erupted.

"Agreed." Arturo jumped to his feet. He and Andrea met halfway between their seats and embraced. Sofia stood, looking a mixture of confused and hopeful. Armenta grinned like a Cheshire cat and clapped Ash on the back so hard, he dropped his champagne flute, which should have fallen to the floor and shattered. Instead, it found its way back up to the table without losing a drop of champagne.

"Cheers." Valderos raised his glass. "Here's to a successful end of your third case, Mr. Haynes and Ms. Kingston."

"Cheers," Armenta echoed, standing up and drawing her tattered shawl around her.

Sunny watched Alex Fortuna leave the room in handcuffs with the Polk County Sheriff. She saw Serrano open two additional bottles of champagne and start pouring. She heard Sofia telling Valderos she was fully up to the task of bringing the Taricani Vineyard and Tasting Room back to a successful and profitable business.

Sunny felt overwhelmed. Overstimulated. She took her champagne out to the patio and drew in deep breaths laced with a familiar scent of loam.

"Are you here?" she asked.

The land undulated softly, like waves on a summer lake.

"I want you to give Sofia all the help she needs," Sunny said. "I want you to cooperate. I want the wine to turn from vinegar into one of the finest vintages in the Willamette Valley."

"I would like you to wish those things for *my* winery," Valderos said. He was so close, she felt his breath on her neck. Warm. Soft. Sunny trembled and turned to face him. "You have to do that for yourself. Your powers are far greater than mine."

"I agree my powers are stronger, but yours are used only for the good of the dead. To reconcile wrongs so the living can go forward with their lives." He touched her cheek with a gentle hand.

Sunny's first response was to pull away from him, but he wasn't hurting her. In fact, his touch was far from unpleasant. "That's true," she said, trying to keep his attention focused on their conversation. "I wonder why I haven't thought that before?" She felt better about her gift. Like it was more than a curse. "How could you come to that insightful conclusion?"

His eyes were strange pools of darkness. "Say my name."

"Valderos," she said. "Vincente Valderos."

"Say it again." He drew even closer.

"Vincente…"

She couldn't finish. His finger was against her lips. The index finger with the onyx ring.

His finger was warm. Alive. His mouth was smiling on both sides. "Sunny," he whispered. "My Sulis Minerva." He slowly removed his finger from her lips. The skull gleamed in late afternoon sunlight that had suddenly filtered through heavy clouds.

And then he was gone. Into thin air.

Sunny felt very cold and very alone.

"What are you doing out here?" Ash walked up behind her. "It looks like rain." He held two full champagne flutes.

"I was talking to Valderos," she said, taking the glass he offered. "But he left. You know, how one minute he's here and the next he's gone." She didn't tell Ash that when she'd been close to Valderos, she'd felt something she hadn't for a long time. Not since she and Mark had first become a couple. Instead, she took a sip of the champagne. Bubbles fizzed on her tongue before she swallowed.

"I wanted to talk to Vinnie." Ash gave her the look he usually reserved for those who weren't telling the entire truth. "We're getting requests to review unsolved cases. Mostly from other law enforcement agencies, but one's from a woman in Stayton. Her husband disappeared several years ago. She wants to know what happened."

"You like that one, don't you?" She drank down the champagne. Her cheeks flushed. It was definitely going straight to her head. "This is really good stuff." She held up her empty flute.

He nodded. "Krug. Very expensive. Classic. Only the best for Vinnie. As for this woman and her missing husband, she told me she hears someone or some*thing* moving around the house. Day as well as night. Doors and windows open and close for no reason. Her two dogs either cower or wag their tails at nothing. The three cats have mixed reactions, everything from raised fur, dilated pupils, hissing, or running off to hide under furniture. The woman thinks there's something evil living with her, but she also thinks her husband's ghost is fighting it off."

"Sounds like a case for the House of Serenity's team." Armenta had joined them on the patio. She held a glass of what looked like sparkling water. She looked pointedly at Sunny's empty flute and held out her hand. "No driving for you. I'll take us all back. Watcher's already in the back of the Forester."

Sunny dug her key fob out of her pocket and handed it over. "I don't usually feel the effects of one glass, but this champagne is really potent."

"Armenta, you don't have to drive us all," Ash said. "I've only had one glass, and I'm not feeling the effects like Sunny. I'll bring her back." He took Sunny's empty glass from her. "You do seem a bit out of it. This was a tough case. You should rest."

Sunny forced a smile. It took a lot of effort. "Must be the equivalent of jet lag from all the activity in the cellar. I hope that wine's decided to turn sweeter."

"You did an excellent job," Ash said. "I wasn't much help to you on this case."

"Nonsense." Sunny patted his shoulder. "You're always here for me. Here, there, and everywhere. The perfect partner."

"The perfect partner," he echoed, sounding wistful.

Sunny had a really strange thought, but dismissed it. Then she had an irreverent thought she wanted to dismiss but couldn't. Joining the thoughts together left her with a perplexing problem: two new rivals for her affections. One was her partner. The other was a demon. The first was older than she usually dated. The second was probably so ancient he was past being called old.

She would really have liked to climb onto Watcher's back and fly far away.

But nowhere was far enough to hide from Valderos, and Ash was such a good investigator, sooner or later, he'd find her, too.

"Let's go to The House of Serenity," she said. "We could all do with dinner. Something easy, like pizza."

"That sounds good. I'll have to stop off to take care of Jake. He really needs some TLC."

Armenta rubbed her hands together. "Bring him back to Sunny's apartment. After we eat, you and Ash can take Jake for a walk."

"That sounds really good. Especially the walk." Ash's rich voice held a low and intimate tone. It kind of made Sunny's toes want to curl. He held the door open. "Come on, ladies."

Armenta dry leaf cackled. "You two will enjoy your walk. Very much." She grinned up at Ash when she passed him.

"Is that a prediction?" He sounded hopeful.

"More like a certainty." Armenta ran her hands down her tattered shawl. Her fingers found several holes. "I don't think I can repair this."

"I'll buy you a new one," Ash said. "Get what you want and send me the bill. Come on, Sunny."

A familiar fatigue settled its mantle over Sunny. The aftermath of using her psychic energy. "I need a couple of minutes alone," she said. "Go ahead. I'll meet you in the parking lot, Ash."

"Make sure it's only a couple of minutes," Ash warned her. He went inside, and the door closed behind him.

Sunny walked over to the wall. She closed her eyes and held out her arms. A chill wind wafted over her, and the smell of loam intensified. Opening her eyes, she saw the caretaker standing on the other side of the wall. Without acknowledging her, he walked off down the hill. Sunny watched him until he reached the creek. A mist billowed up from the water. He raised an arm before vanishing into it.

"Goodbye," she whispered. "Be at peace."

She hoped the restless spirits of Giuseppe and Lorenzo would find a more fulfilling destination. She reentered the tasting room and heard the door lock behind her. After she walked out into the parking lot, she heard the winery's front door lock, too.

She never wanted to go near the Taricani Winery and Tasting Room ever again. Beneath her feet in the parking lot, the ground trembled slightly. She got into the Range Rover.

"Ready?" Ash asked.

"Very ready."

He lightly squeezed her hand, his grip as warm and comforting as ever.

Was he really too old for her? Was that moment she'd experienced only a flight of fancy, or a premonition?

Ash gripped the steering wheel with both hands as he drove out of the parking lot. "The papers are ready for you to sign." He sounded more than a little anxious. "If you still want to become partners."

"I do." Her reservations felt foolish now the winery and its complexities were literally behind them.

They lapsed into companionable silence, the Rover's engine purring gently as pastoral scenery flashed by. The clouds passed over. A warm amber glow stole across the landscape. A wide ribbon of water appeared on the right side. The Willamette River, sparkling brightly. As they approached the outskirts of Salem, Sunny reached over and took Ash's hand. It was her turn to return some of the comfort he'd given her during the past tumultuous months.

He gave her a surprised look, followed by a warm smile. A glow spread inside Sunny that she hadn't experienced after reconnecting with Mark. She hadn't been able to lower the wall she'd erected to protect her deepest emotions. She'd never fully trusted her heart to her ex-husband again.

But she trusted her life to Ash.

With all those thoughts roaming around in her head and her hand holding his, she felt strangely content. Even though she and Ash stood on a precipice, their futures dependent on fulfilling Vincente Valderos's contract, she had hope for the future.

Valderos wanted more from her than her soul. She'd realized it when he saved her from the pit. She'd *known* it when he'd asked her to say his name.

"Everything will work out," Armenta's voice whispered in her head. "The way it's supposed to."

Sunny could only hope the seer's prediction was more concrete than fanciful thinking. She sensed even more dangerous times ahead, but with pleasurable moments within the uncertainties, the heartbreak, and the fear.

She watched the river meander gently down toward Salem, secure in its path.

Her own future felt more like the creek flowing between the winery and the cidery. Sometimes erratic. Sometimes overflowing. Sometimes deviating from the path it had always taken.

But just as surely returning to its course after a downpour had passed.

THE END

ALSO BY HEATHER AMES

Ghost Shop Series
Tapped By Fate (Book 1)
Tread Softly (Book 2)

Brian Swift & Kaylen Roberts Mystery/Suspense Series
Indelible (Book 1)
A Swift Brand of Justice (Book 2)
Swift Retribution (Book 3)

Suspense
Night Shadows

Romantic Suspense
All That Glitters

Contemporary Romance
The Sweetest Song

Upcoming Books 2024/2025
Brian Swift & Kaylen Roberts series—Book 4
Ghost Shop series—Book 4

ABOUT THE AUTHOR

Heather Ames has enjoyed a nomadic life, living in 5 countries and 7 states. Currently, she lives in Salem, Oregon, where after a long career in the healthcare industry, she finally achieved her dream of writing full-time. She is a past finalist in Romance Writers of America's prestigious Golden Heart contest, and while living in Boston and Los Angeles, she took classes in TV production. She wrote, produced, directed, and edited two documentaries, one of which was nominated for an award.

She currently moderates a highly successful online critique group that has been exchanging manuscripts for over fifteen years. She can be found on Facebook, LinkedIn, Instagram, Goodreads and Pinterest, as well as her website heatherames.com and has been affiliated with Sisters in Crime, Mystery Writers, Willamette Writers, the Electronic Publishing Industry Coalition (EPIC,) Alameda Writers Group and Romance Writers of America. She served AWG twice as a board member as well as host and moderator for the Fiction Special Interest Group, and was a coordinator for several of RWA's local and national conferences. She is currently a board member of Portland Oregon's Harriett Vane Chapter of Sisters in Crime and an active member of both Northwest Independent Writers Association (NIWA) and the Salem chapter of Willamette Writers.

ACKNOWLEDGEMENTS

Thanks again to Pacific Online Writers Group (POWG) members Bonnie Schroeder and Miriam Johnston for their support as well as their insightful critiquing.

Thanks also to Nate Wilson, Cellar Master at Wetzel Estate Winery in Dallas, Oregon for answering my questions and assisting me in finding the best (or worst) way to taint the wine at my fictitious winery. Modern methods of viniculture and viticulture produce excellent wines. The angry wine and over-active yeast in this book are both figments of this writer's active imagination.

Last, but definitely not least, thanks to my readers, whose support is always much appreciated. Again, I hope you will all enjoy reading Tainted Legacy as much as I enjoyed writing it.

Made in United States
Troutdale, OR
11/02/2023